I0542268

ROUND ANVIL ROCK

A Romance

NANCY HUSTON BANKS

1st WORLD
LIBRARY
Literary Society

Round Anvil Rock

Nancy Huston Banks

© 1st World Library, 2006
PO Box 2211
Fairfield, IA 52556
www.1stworldlibrary.com
First Edition

LCCN: 2007920694

Softcover ISBN: 978-1-4218-3991-2
Hardcover ISBN: 978-1-4218-3891-5
eBook ISBN: 978-1-4218-4091-8

Purchase *"Round Anvil Rock"*
as a traditional bound book at:
www.1stWorldLibrary.com/purchase.asp?ISBN=978-1-4218-3991-2

1st World Library is a literary, educational organization
dedicated to:

- Creating a free internet library of downloadable ebooks

- Hosting writing competitions and offering book
publishing scholarships.

Interested in more 1st World Library books?
contact: literacy@1stworldlibrary.com
Check us out at: www.1stworldlibrary.com

1ˢᵗ World Library Literary Society

Giving Back to the World

"If you want to work on the core problem, it's early school literacy."

- James Barksdale, former CEO of Netscape

"No skill is more crucial to the future of a child, or to a democratic and prosperous society, than literacy."

- Los Angeles Times

Literacy... means far more than learning how to read and write... The aim is to transmit... knowledge and promote social participation."

- UNESCO

"Literacy is not a luxury, it is a right and a responsibility. If our world is to meet the challenges of the twenty-first century we must harness the energy and creativity of all our citizens."

- President Bill Clinton

"Parents should be encouraged to read to their children, and teachers should be equipped with all available techniques for teaching literacy, so the varying needs and capacities of individual kids can be taken into account."

- Hugh Mackay

TO MY FATHER

A PREFACE

In weaving a romance round a real rock and through actual events, this tale has taken no great liberty with fact. It has, indeed, claimed the freedom of fiction only in drawing certain localities and incidents somewhat closer together than they were in reality. And it has done this notably in but three instances: by allowing the Wilderness Road to seem nearer the Ohio River than it really was; by anticipating the establishment of the Sisters of Charity; and by disregarding the tradition that Philip Alston had gone from the region of Cedar House before the time of the story, and that he died elsewhere. These deviations are all rather slight, yet they are, nevertheless, essential to any faithful description of the country, the time, and the people, which this tale tries to describe. The Wilderness Road—everywhere—came so close to the life of the whole country that no true story of the time can ever be told apart from it. The Sisters of Charity were established so early and did so much in the making of Kentucky, that a few months earlier in coming to one locality or a few years later in reaching another, cannot make their noble work any less vitally a part of every tale of the wilderness. The influence of Philip Alston over the country in which he lived, lasted so much longer than his life, and the precise date and manner of his death are go uncertain, that his romantic career must always remain inseparably interwoven with all the romance of southern Kentucky. And it is for these reasons that this story of nearly a hundred years ago, has thus claimed a few of the many privileges of fiction.

CONTENTS

I

THE GIRL AND THE BOY

The Beautiful River grows very wide in making its great bend around western Kentucky. On the other side, its shores are low for many miles, but well guarded by giant cottonwoods. These spectral trees stand close to its brink and stretch their phantom arms far over its broad waters, as if perpetually warding off the vast floods that rush down from the North.

But the floods are to be feared only in the winter or spring, never in the summer or autumn. And nearly a hundred years ago, when the river's shores were bound throughout their great length by primeval forests, there was less reason to fear at any season. So that on a day of October in the year eighteen hundred and eleven, the mighty stream lay safely within its deep bounds flowing quietly on its way to join the Father of Waters.

So gently it went that there was scarcely a ripple to break its silvery surface. It seemed indeed hardly to move, reflecting the shadowy cottonwoods like a long, clear, curving mirror which was dimmed only by the breath of the approaching dusk. Out in the current beyond the shadows of the trees, there still lingered a faint glimmer of the afterglow's pale gold. But the red glory of the west was dying behind the whitening cotton-woods and beyond the dense dark forest—reaching on and on to the seeming end of the earth—a billowing sea of ever deepening green. The last bright gleam of golden light was passing away on the white sail of a little ship which was just turning the distant bend, where the darkening sky bent low to meet the darkened wilderness.

The night was creeping from the woods to the waters as softly as the wild creatures crept to the river's brim to drink before sleeping. The still air was lightly stirred now and then by rushing wings, as the myriad paroquets settled among the shadowy branches. The soft murmuring of the reeds that fringed the shores told where the waterfowl had already found resting-places. The swaying of the cane-brakes—near and far— signalled the secret movements of the wingless wild things which had only stealth to guard them against the cruelty of nature and against one another. The heaviest waves of cane near the great Shawnee Crossing might have followed a timid red deer. For the Shawnees had vanished from their town on the other side of the Ohio. Warriors and women and children—all were suddenly and strangely gone; there was not even a canoe left to rock among the rushes. The swifter, rougher waving of the cane farther off may have been in the wake of a bold gray wolf. The howling of wolves came from the distance with the occasional gusts of wind, and as often as the wolves howled, a mysterious, melancholy booming sounded from the deeper shadows along the shores. It was an uneasy response from the trumpeter swans, resting like some wonderful silver-white lilies on the quiet bosom of the dark river.

A great river has all the sea's charm and much of its mystery and sadness. The boy standing on the Kentucky shore was under this spell as he listened to these sounds of nature at nightfall on the Ohio, and watched the majestic sweep of its waters—unfettered and unsullied—through the boundless and unbroken forests. Yet he turned eagerly to listen to another sound that came from human-kind. It was the wild music of the boatman's horn winding its way back from the little ship, now far away and rounding the dusky bend. Partly flying and partly floating, it stole softly up the shadowed river. The melody echoed from the misty Kentucky hills, lingered under the overhanging trees, rambled through the sighing cane-brakes, loitered among the murmuring rushes—thus growing ever fainter, sweeter, wilder, sadder, as it came. He did not know why this sound of the boatman's horn always touched him so keenly and moved him so deeply. He could not have told why his eyes grew strangely dim as he heard it now, or why a strange tightening came around his heart. He was but an ignorant lad of the woods. It was not for him to know that these few notes—so few, so simple, so artlessly blown by a rude boatman—touched the deep fountain of the soul, loosing the mighty torrent pent up in every human breast. Pity, tenderness, yearning, the struggle and the triumph of life,—the boy felt everything and all unknowingly, but with quivering sensibility. For he was not merely an ignorant lad; he was also one of those who are set apart throughout their lives to feel many things which they are never permitted to comprehend.

When the last echo of the boatman's horn had melted among the darkling hills, he turned as instinctively as a sun-worshipper faces the east and drank in another musical refrain. The Angelus was pealing faintly from the bell of the little log chapel far up the river, hidden among the trees. The faith which it betokened was not his own faith, nor the faith of those with whom he lived, but the beauty and sweetness of the token appealed to him none the less. How beautiful, how sweet it was! As it thus came drifting down with the river's deepening shadows, he thought of the little band of Sisters—angels of charity—kneeling under that rough roof; those brave gentlewomen of high birth and delicate breeding who were come with the very first to take an heroic part in the making of Kentucky and, so doing, in the winning of the whole West. As the boy thought of them with a swelling heart,—for they had been kind to him,—it seemed that they were braver than the hunters, more courageous than the soldiers. Listening to the appeal of the Angelus stealing so tenderly through the twilight, with the strain of poetry that was in him thrilling in response, he felt that the prayers then going up must fill the cruel wilderness with holy incense; that the coming of these gentle Sisters must subdue the very wild beasts, as the presence of the lovely martyrs subdued the lions of old.

"Ah, David! David!" cried a gay young voice behind him. "Dreaming again—with your eyes wide open. And seeing visions, too, no doubt."

He turned with a guilty start and looked up at Ruth. She was standing near by but higher on the river bank, and her slender white form was half concealed by the drooping foliage of a young willow tree. There was something about Ruth herself that always made him think of a young willow with every graceful wand in bloom. And now—as nearly always—there was a flutter of soft whiteness about her, for the day was as warm as mid-summer. He could not have told what it was that she wore, but her fluttering white garments might have been woven of the mists training over the hills, so ethereal they looked, seen through the golden green of the delicate willow leaves that were still gilded by the afterglow which had vanished from the shadowed river. Her smiling face could not have been more radiant had the sunlight shone full upon it. The dusk of evening seemed always lingering under the long curling lashes that made her blue eyes so dark, and her hair was as black at midday as at midnight. So that now—when she shook her head at the boy—a wonderful long, thick, silky lock escaped its fastenings, and the wind caught it and spun it like silk into the finest blue-black floss.

"Yes, sir, you've been dreaming again! You needn't pretend you were thinking—you don't know how to think. Thinking is not romantic enough. I have been here watching you for a long time, and I know just how romantic the dreams are that you have been dreaming. I could tell by the way you turned,— this way and that,—looking up and down the river. It always bewitches you when the sun goes and the shadows come. I knew I should find you here, just like this; and I came on purpose to wake and scold you."

She pretended to draw her pretty brow into a frown, but she could not help smiling.

"Seriously, dear, you must stop dreaming. It is a dreadful thing to be a dreamer in a new country. State makers should all be wide-awake workers. You are out of place here; as Uncle Philip Alston says—"

"Then why did he put me here?" the boy burst out bitterly.

"David!" she cried in wounded reproach, "how can you? It hurts me to hear you say things like that. I can't bear to hear any one say anything against him—I love him so. And from you—who owe him almost as much as I do—"

The tears were very near. But she was a little angry, too, and her blue eyes flashed.

"No; no one owes him so much—as myself. He couldn't have been so good—no one ever could be so good to any one else as he has always been to me. Still"—softening suddenly, for she was fond of the boy, and something in his sensitive face went to her tender heart—"think, David, dear, we owe him everything we have,—our names, our home, our clothes, our education, our very lives. We must never for a moment forget that it was he who found us all alone—you in a cabin on the Wilderness Road and me in a boat at Duff's Fort—and brought us in his own arms to Cedar House. And you know as well as I do that he would have given us a home in his own house if it had not been so rough and bare a place, a mere camp. And then there was no woman in it to take care of us, and we were only little mites of babies—poor, crying, helpless morsels of humanity. Where do you think we came from, David? I wonder and wonder and wonder!" wistfully, with her gaze on the darkening river.

It was an old question, and one that they had been asking themselves and one another and every one, over and over, ever since they had been old enough to think. The short story which Philip Alston had told was all that he or any one knew or ever was to know. The boy silently shook his head. The girl went on:—

"Sometimes I am sorry that we couldn't live in his house. You would have understood him better and have loved him more—as he deserves. It is only that you don't really know each other," she said gently. "And then I should like to do something for him—something to cheer him—who does everything for me. It must be very sad to be alone and old. It grieves me to see him riding away to that desolate cabin, especially on stormy nights. But he never will let me come to his house, though I beg and beg. He says it is too rough, and that too many strange men are coming and going on business."

"Yes; too many strange men on very strange business."

She did not hear or notice what he said, because the sound of horses' feet echoing behind them just at that moment caused her to turn her head. Two horsemen were riding along the river bank, but they were a long way off and about turning into the forest path as her gaze fell upon them. She stood still, silently looking after them till they disappeared among the trees.

"Father Orin and Toby will get home before dark to-night. That is something uncommon," she said with a smile.

Toby was the priest's horse, but no one ever spoke of the one without thinking of the other; and then, Toby's was a distinct and widely recognized personality.

"But who is the stranger with them, David? Oh, I remember! It must be the new doctor,—the young doctor who has lately come and who is curing the Cold Plague. The Sisters told me. They said that he and Father Orin often visited the sick together and were already great friends. How tall he is—even taller than Father Orin, and broader shouldered. I should like to see his face. And how straight he sits in the saddle. You would expect a man who holds himself so to carry a lance and tilt fearlessly at everything that he thought was wrong."

She turned, quickly tossing the willow branches aside and

laughing gayly. "There now, that will set you off thinking of your knights again! But you must not. Truly, you must not. For it is quite true, dear; you are a dreamer, a poet. You do indeed belong to the Arcadian Hills. You should be there now, playing a gentle shepherd's pipe and herding his peaceful flocks. And instead—alas!"—she looked at him in perplexity which was partly real and partly assumed—"instead you are here in this awful wilderness, carrying a rifle longer and heavier than yourself, and trying to pretend that you like to kill wild beasts, or can endure to hurt any living thing."

David said nothing; there seemed to be no response for him to make. When a well-grown youth of eighteen or thereabouts is spoken to by a girl near his own age as he had just been spoken to by Ruth, he rarely finds anything to say. No words could do justice to what he feels. And there is nothing for him to do either, unless it be to take refuge in a dignified silence which disdains the slightest notice of the offence. This was what David resorted to, and, bending down, he calmly and quietly raised his forgotten rifle from the ground to his shoulder. He did it very slowly and impressively, however, in the hope that Ruth might realize the fact that he had killed the buck whose huge horns made the rifle's rest on his cabin walls. But she saw and realized only that he was wounded, and instantly darted toward him like a swallow. She caught his rigid rifle arm and clung to it, looking up in his set face. Her blue eyes were already filling with tears while the smile was still on her lips. That was Ruth's way; her smiles and tears were even closer together than most women's are; she was nearly always quiveringly poised between gayety and sadness; like a living sunbeam continually glancing across life's shadows.

"What is it, David, dear?" she pleaded, with her sweet lips close to his ear. "What foolish thing have I said? You must know—whatever it was—that it was all in fun. Why, I wouldn't have you different, dear, if I could! I couldn't love you so much if you were not just what you are. And yet," sighing, "it might be better for you."

She laid her head against his shoulder and drew closer to him in that soft little nestling way of hers. David looked straight over the lovely head, keeping his grim gaze as high as he could. He knew how it would be if his stern gray eyes were to meet Ruth's wet blue ones. He was still a boy, but trying to be a man—and beginning to understand. No man with his heart in the right place could hold out against her pretty coaxing. It was sweet enough to wile the very birds out of the trees. It made no difference that he had been used to her wiles from babyhood up. To be used to Ruth's ways only made them harder to resist. No stranger could possibly have foreseen his defeat as clearly as David foresaw his at the moment that she started toward him. But self-respect required him to stand firm as long as possible, although he felt the strength going out of his rifle arm under her clinging touch. She felt it going, too, and began to smile through her tears. And then, sure of her victory, she threw caution to the winds—as older and wiser women have done too openly in vanquishing stronger and more masterful men. She let him see that she knew she had conquered, which is always a fatal mistake on the part of a woman toward a man. Smiling and dimpling, she put up her hand and patted his cheek—precisely as if he had been a child.

The boy shrunk as if the caress had been a touch of fire. He broke away and strode off up the hillside with his longest, manliest stride. This humiliation was past bearing or forgiving. He could have forgiven being called a dreamer—a useless drone—among the men of clear heads and strong hands who had already wrested a great state from the wilderness, and who, through this conquest, were destined to become the immortal founders of the Empire of the West. He could have overlooked being spoken to like a child by a girl who might be younger than himself for all he or she knew to the contrary—though this would have been harder.

He might even have forgiven that pat on his cheek which was downy with beard, had he been either younger or older. But as it was—well, the matter may safely be left to the sympathy of the man who remembers the most sensitive time of his own youth; that trying period when he feels himself to be no longer a boy and nobody else considers him a man.

David did not know where he was going or what he meant to do. He was blindly striding up the river bank away from Ruth, fairly aflame with the determination to do something—anything—to prove his manhood. For nothing ever makes a boy resolve quite so suddenly and firmly to become a man instantly as to be treated by a girl as he had been by Ruth. Had the most desperate danger then come in David's way, he would have hailed and hazarded it with delight. But he could not think of anything to overwhelm her with just at that moment, and so he could only stride on in helpless, angry silence. Ruth flew after him as if her thin white skirts had been strong, swift wings. She overtook him before he had gone very far, and clung to him again more than ever like some beautiful white spirit of the woods wreathed in mist, with her soft blown garments and her softer blown hair. She merely wound herself around him at first, breathless and panting. But as soon as she caught her breath the coaxing, the laughing, and the crying came all together. David kept from looking down as long as he could, but his pace slackened and his arm again relaxed. Finally—taken off guard—he glanced at the face so near his breast. The dusk could not dim its beauty and only made it more lovely. No more resistance was possible for him—or for any man or boy—who saw Ruth as she looked then. David's big rough hand was now surrendered meekly enough to the quick clasp of her little fingers, and—forgetting all the daring deeds that he meant to do—he was led like any lamb up the hill to the open door of Cedar House.

II

THE HOUSE OF CEDAR

So far as they knew, there was no tie of blood or relationship binding them to the kind people of Cedar House. Yet it was the only home that they could remember and very dear to them both.

It was a great square of rough, dark logs, and seemed now, seen through the uncertain light, to stand in the centre of a shadowy hamlet, so many smaller cabins were clustered around it. The custom of the country was to add cabin after cabin as the family outgrew the original log house. The instinct of safety, the love of kindred, and the longing for society in the perilous loneliness of the wilderness held these first Kentuckians very close together. So that as their own villages thus grew around them and only their own dwelt near them, they naturally became as clannish as their descendants have been ever since.

The cabin nearest Cedar House contained two rooms, and was used by its master, Judge Knox, for his own bedroom and law office. There was a still larger cabin somewhat more distant from the main building, which was intended for the use of his nephew, William Pressley, on the marriage of that young lawyer to Ruth. But the wedding was some time off yet, having been set for Christmas Eve, and the cabin which was to welcome the bride from Cedar House was not quite complete. The smallest and the oldest cabin was David's. The long black line of cabins crouching under the hillside where the shadows were deepest, marked the quarters of the slaves,—a dark storm-cloud already settling heavily on the fair horizon of the new state.

Cedar House itself was the grandest of its time in all that country. Built entirely of huge red cedar logs it was two stories in height, the first house of more than one story standing on the shores of the southern Ohio. Its roof was the wonder and envy of the whole region for many years. The shingles were of black walnut, elegantly rounded at the butt-ends. They were fastened on with solid walnut pegs driven in holes bored through both the shingles and the laths with a brace and a bit. For there was not a nail in Cedar House from its firm foundation to its fine roof. Even the hinges and the latch of the wide front door were made of wood. The judge often mentioned this fact with much pride, and never failed to add that the leathern latch-string always hung outside. But he was still prouder of the massive, towering chimney of Cedar House, and with good reason. The other houses thinly scattered through the wilderness had humble chimneys of sticks covered with clay. The chimney of Cedar House was of rough stone—of one hundred wagon loads, as the judge boasted—which had been hauled with great difficulty over a long distance, because there was none near by.

On the wide hearth of this great chimney a fire was always burning. No matter what the season or the weather might be, there was always a solemn ceremony around the hearth when the fire was renewed, at the beginning and the close of every day all the year round. In winter it was a glorious bonfire consuming great logs. In summer it was the merest glimmer that could hold a flickering spark. Between winter and summer, as on this mild October evening, a bright flame sometimes danced gaily behind the big brass andirons, while all the windows and doors were wide open. But through cold and heat, and burning high or low, the fire was never entirely forgotten, never quite permitted to go out. Thus ever alight it burned like a sacred flame on the altar of home.

Streaming from the doors and windows that night, it gave the youth and the maiden a cheerful welcome as they came up the darkening hillside. Lamplight also began to glimmer, and candles flitted here and there before the windows and door, borne by the dark shapes of the servants who were laying the table for supper. The main room of Cedar House opened directly upon the river front; and when brightly lighted, it could be distinctly seen from without. Ruth and David paused on the threshold, still unconsciously holding one another's hands, and looked in.

There were five persons in the room, three men and two women, and they were all members of the household with the exception of Philip Alston, the white-haired gentleman, whose appearance bore no other mark of age. And he also might have been considered as one of the family, since he had been coming to the house daily for many years. He came usually to see Ruth, but of late he had found it necessary to see William Pressley more often; and they were talking eagerly and in a low tone, rather apart, when the boy and girl paused to see and hear what was taking place within the great room. William Pressley sat in the easiest chair in the warmest corner, close to the hearth. There are some men—and a few women—who always take the softest seat in the best place, and they do it so naturally that no one ever thinks of their doing anything else or expects them to sit elsewhere. William Pressley was one of these persons. In the next easiest chair, on the other side of the hearth, was his aunt, the widow Broadnax, whose short, broad, shapeless, inert figure was lying rather than sitting almost buried in a heap of cushions. This lady was the sister of the judge and the half-sister of the other lady, Miss Penelope Knox,—the thin, nervous, restless little old woman,—who was fidgeting back and forth between the hearth and the doorway leading to the distant kitchen. The relationship of these two ladies to one another, and the difference in their relationship to the head of Cedar House, caused much dissension in the household, and gave rise to certain domestic complications which always rose when least expected.

The fire had been freshly kindled with small twigs of the sugar maple, that priceless tree often standing fifty to an acre in the wilderness, and giving the pioneers their best fire-wood, their coolest shade, and their sweetest food. Vivid blue sparks were still flashing among the little white stars of the gray moss on the big backlog. From the blazing ends of the log there came the soft, airy music and the faint, sweet scent of bubbling sap. This main room of Cedar House was very large, almost vast, taking up the whole lower floor. It was the dining room as well as the sitting room; and when some grand occasion arose, it served even as a drawing-room, and did it handsomely, too. This great room of Cedar House always reminded David of the ancient halls in "The Famous History of Montilion," a romance of chivalry from which most of his ideas of life were taken, and upon which most of his ideals of living were formed. Surely, he thought, the castle of the "Knight of the Oracle" could not be grander than this great room of Cedar House.

The rich dark wood of its walls and floor—all rudely smoothed with the broadaxe and the whipsaw—hung overhead in massive beams. From these low, blackened timbers there swung many antique lamps, splendid enough for a palace and strangely out of place in a log house of the wilderness. On the rough walls there were also large sconces of burnished silver but poorly filled with tallow candles. In the bare spaces between these silver sconces were the heads of wild animals mingled with many rifles, both old and new, and other arms of the hunter. Over the tall mantelpiece there were crossed two untarnished swords which had been worn by the judge's father in the Revolution. On the red cedar of the floor, polished by wear and rubbing, there lay the skins of wild beasts, together with costly foreign rugs. The same strange mixture of rudeness and refinement was to be seen everywhere throughout the room. The table standing in the centre of the floor, ready for the evening meal, was made of unplaned boards, rudely put together by the unskilled hands of the backwoods. Yet it was set with the finest china, the rarest glass, and the richest silver that the greatest skill of the old world could supply. The chairs placed around the table were made of unpainted wood from the forest, with seats woven out of the coarse rushes from the river. And there, between the front windows, stood Ruth's piano, the first in that part of the wilderness, and as fine as the finest of its day anywhere.

It is true that something like the same confusion of luxury and wildness was becoming more or less common throughout the country. The wain trains which had lately followed the packhorse trains over the Alleghanies—with the widening of the Wilderness Road—were already bringing many comforts and even luxuries to the cabins of the well-to-do settlers. But nothing like those which were fetched constantly to Cedar House ever came to any other household; and it was not the family who caused them to be brought there. For while the judge was a man of wealth for his time and place, and able to give his family greater comfort than his poorer neighbors could afford, he was far from having the means, much less the taste and culture, to gather such costly, beautiful, and rare things as were gathered together in Cedar House. It was through Philip Alston that everything of this kind had come. It was he who had chosen everything and paid for it, and ordered it fetched over the mountains from Virginia or up the river from France or Spain—all as gifts from him to Ruth. It was natural enough that he should give her whatever he wished her to have, and there was no reason why she should not accept any and everything that he gave. She was held by him and by every one as his adopted daughter. He had no children of his own, no relations of any degree so far as any one knew, and he was known to be generous and believed to be very rich. Indeed no one thought much about his gifts to Ruth; they had long since become a matter of course, a part of the everyday life of Cedar House. They had begun with Ruth's coming more than seventeen years before. As a baby she had been rocked in a cradle such as never before had been seen in the wilderness,—a very gem of wonderful carving and inlaid work from Spain. As a little child she had been dressed—as no little one of the wild wood ever had been before—in the finest fabrics and the daintiest needlework from the looms and convents of France.

Very strange things may become familiar through use. The simple people of Cedar House and their rude neighbors were well used to all this. They had seen the beautiful blue-eyed baby grow to be a more beautiful child, and the child to a most beautiful maiden, and always surrounded by the greatest refinement and luxury that love and means could bring into the wilderness. Naturally enough they now found nothing to wonder at, in the daily presence of this radiant young figure among them.

It was only for an instant that the girl and boy stood thus unseen on the threshold of Cedar House, looking into the great room. Philip Alston saw them almost at once. He had been watching and waiting for Ruth, as he always was when she was out of his sight even for a moment. He sprang up, quickly and alertly, like a strong young man, and went to meet her with his gallant air. She held up her cheek smilingly; he bent and kissed it, and taking her hand with his grand bow, led her across the room. The judge and his nephew also arose, as they always did when she came in or went out. The judge did this unconsciously, without thinking, and scarcely knowing that he did do it; for he was a plain man, rather awkward and very absent-minded, and deeply absorbed in the study of his profession. William Pressley did it with deliberate intention and self-consciousness, as he did everything that he deemed fitting. It was his nature to give grave thought to the least thing that he said or did. It was his sincere conviction that the smallest matter affecting himself was of infinitely greater importance than the greatest that could possibly concern any one else. There are plenty of people who believe this as sincerely as he believed it, but there are few who show the belief with his candor. When he now stood up to place a chair for Ruth beside his own, he did the simple service as if the critical eyes of the world had been upon him. And his manner was so consciously correct that no one observed that the chair which he gave her was not so comfortable as his own. He was uncommonly good-looking, also, and tall and shapely, yet there was something about his full figure—that vague, indescribable something—which unmistakably marks the lack of virility in mind or body, no matter how large or handsome a man may be. He stood for a moment after Ruth was seated, and then, seeing that Philip Alston was about to lift a candle-stand which was heaped with parcels, he went to aid him, and the two men together set the little table before her. She looked at it with soft, excited cries of surprise and delight, instantly divining that the unopened parcels and sealed boxes contained more of the gifts which her foster-father was constantly lavishing upon her. He smiled down at her beaming face and dancing eyes, and then taking out his pocket-knife he cut the cords and removed the covers of the boxes. As the wrappings fell away, there was a shimmer of dazzling tissues, silver and gold.

"Oh! oh!" she cried.

"Just a few pretty trifles, my dear," he said. "You like them?"

"Like them!"

Repeating his words she sprang up, and running round the candle-stand, stood on the very tips of her toes so that she might throw her arms about his neck. He bent his head to meet her upturned face, and if ever tenderness shone in a man's pale, grave face, it shone then in his. If ever love—pure and unselfish—beamed from a man's eyes, it was beaming now from those looking down in the girl's face. His tender gaze followed her fondly as she went back to the candle-stand and began to examine each article again more than once and with lingering and growing delight. She found new beauties every moment, and pointed them out to the three men and the boy who were now gathered around her. She called the ladies also, over and over, but they did not come, although they cast many glances at the candle-stand.

Miss Penelope was engaged in making the coffee for supper; and while she did not consider the making of the coffee for supper quite so vital a matter as the making of the coffee for breakfast, she still could not think of leaving the hearth under

Nancy Huston Banks

any inducement so long as the coffee-pot sat on its trivet above the glowing coals. The widow Broadnax stirred among her cushions once or twice, as if almost on the point of trying to get out of her chair. She was fonder of finery than her half-sister was, and she would have liked very much to see these beautiful things nearer. But she was still fonder of her own ease than of finery, and it was really a great deal of trouble to get out of her deep, broad low chair. And then she never moved or took her eyes off her half-sister while that energetic lady was engaged in making the coffee.

Knowing the ladies' ways, Ruth did not expect them to come. She was quite satisfied to have the men share her pleasure in the presents. They were looking at her and not at the gifts lying heaped on the candle-stand, but she did not notice that. She gave the judge a priceless piece of lace to hold. He took it with the awkward, helpless embarrassment of a manly man handling a woman's delicate belongings,—the awkwardness that goes straight to a woman's heart, because she sees and feels its true reverence—a reverence just as plain and just as sweet to the simplest country girl as to the wisest woman of the world. The perception of it is a matter of intuition, not one of experience. The least experienced woman instantly distrusts the man who can touch her garments with ease or composure. Ruth's gay young voice broke into a sweet chime of delighted laughter when the judge seized the airy bit of lace as if it had been the heaviest and hottest of crowbars. She laughed again when she looked at his face. He had an odd trick of lifting one of his eyebrows very high and at an acute angle when perplexed or ill at ease. This eccentric left eyebrow—now quite wedge-shaped—had gone up almost to the edge of his tousled gray hair. Ruth patted his great clumsy hands with her little deft ones.

"Well, I'll have to take to the woods, if there's no other way of escape," said the judge, making his greatest threat.

"You dear!" she said, running her arm through his and giving it a little squeeze. "That's right. Hold it tight—be careful, or it will break. Here, William," piling the young man's arms full of delicately tinted gauze, "this is a sunset cloud. And these," casting lengths of exquisite tissue over the boy's shoulder, "these are the mists of the dawn, David,—all silvery white and golden rose and jewelled blue. But—oh! oh!—these are the loveliest of all! A pair of slippers in orange-blossom kid, spangled with silver! Look at them! Just look, everybody!"

Holding them in her hand she ran round the table again to throw her arms about Philip Alston's neck the second time, like a happy, excited child. The little white slippers went up with her arms and touched his cheek. And then he drew them down, and clasping her slender wrists, held her out before him and looked at her with fond, smiling eyes.

"I don't believe that the Empress Josephine has any prettier slippers than those," he said. "I ordered the prettiest and the finest in Paris."

"Who fetched all these things?" the judge broke in, with something like a sudden realization of the number and the value of the gifts.

"Oh, a friend of mine," responded Philip Alston, carelessly, and without turning his head,—"a friend who has many ships constantly going and coming between New Orleans and France. He orders anything I wish; and when it comes to him, he sends it on to me by the first flatboat cordelled up the river."

"What is his name?" asked the judge, with a persistence very uncommon in him.

Philip Alston turned now and glanced at him with an easy, almost bantering smile.

"I don't like to tell you his name, because you—with a good many other honestly mistaken people—are most unjustly prejudiced against him. And then you know well enough that I am speaking of my respected and trusted friend, Monsieur Jean Lafitte."

The judge dropped the lace as if it had burnt his hand. He went back to his seat by the window in silence. He sat down heavily and looked at Philip Alston in perplexity, rubbing his great shock of rough grizzled hair the wrong way as he always did when worried. His thoughts were plainly to be read on his open, rugged face. This liking of Philip Alston's for a man under a national ban was an old subject of worry and perplexity. Yet Alston was always as frank and as firm about it as he had been just now, and the judge's confidence in him was absolute. Robert Knox's own character must have changed greatly before he could have doubted the sincerity of any one whom he had known as long, as intimately, and as favorably as he had known Philip Alston. We all judge others by ourselves,—whether we do it consciously or not,—since we have no other way of judging. And the judge himself was so simple, so sincere, so essentially honest, that he could not doubt one who was in a way a member of his own family. And then he was absent-minded, unobservant, easy-going, indolent, and the slave of habit, as such a nature is apt to be. Moreover, he was not always master of the slight power of observation which had been given him. That very day, while on his way home from the court-house, he had stopped at a cabin where liquor was sold. As a consequence, this sudden touch of uneasiness which aroused him for an instant was forgotten nearly as suddenly as it came. So that after looking bewilderedly at Philip Alston once or twice, he now began to nod and doze.

III

"PHILIP ALSTON, GENTLEMAN"

Philip Alston still stood before the candle-stand. His gaze rested on the girl's radiant face with wistful tenderness. It was plain that he thought nothing of all these rich, rare gifts which he had given her, save only as they gave her pleasure and might win from her another loving look, another butterfly kiss on his cheek.

As he stood there that night in the great room of Cedar House, before the firelight and under the beams of the swinging lamps, he scarcely appeared to need the help of any gift in winning a woman's love. His was a presence to hold the gaze. He was very tall and straight and slender, yet most finely proportioned. The heavy hair, falling back from his handsome face and tied in a queue, must once have been as black as Ruth's own; surely, no paler shade could have become so silvery white. His eyes, also, were as blue as hers, and none could have been bluer. His skin was almost as fair and smooth as hers, his manner as gentle and kind, his voice as soft and his smile as sweet. He was elegantly dressed, as he always was, his fine long coat of forest green broadcloth had a wide velvet collar and large gold buttons. His velvet knee-breeches and the wide riband which tied his queue were of the same rich shade of dark green. The most delicate ruffles filled the front of his swan's-down vest and fell over his hands, which were remarkably white and small and taper-fingered, like a fine lady's. His white silk stockings and his low shoes were held by silver buckles. So looked Philip Alston, Gentleman,—and so he was called,—as he stood in the great room of Cedar House on that night of October, nearly a hundred years ago. And thus he is described in the few rare old histories which touch the romance of this region when he ruled it like a king, by the power of his intelligence and the might of his will.

He was foremost in the politics of the time as in everything else, and he and William Pressley had been discussing this subject at the moment of Ruth's appearance, which had interrupted their conversation. Philip Alston had forgotten the unfinished topic, but William Pressley had not. He, also, had been pleased to look on for a while at the girl's radiant delight; and he, also, had enjoyed the charming scene. But there was a lull now, and he at once turned back to the matter in which he was most deeply interested. Ambition for political preferment was the theme which most absorbed his mind, and ambition was the one thing which could always light a spark of fire in his cold, hard, shallow hazel eyes. This was not for the reason that he cared especially for politics in itself, which he did not. But he turned to it in preference to warfare, since the choice of the ambitious young men of the wilderness lay between the two. Politics seemed to him to open the surest and shortest road to the prominence which he craved above everything else. He was one of those unfortunates who can never be happy on a level—even with the highest—and who must look down in order to be at all content with life. Yet with this overweening and insatiable craving for distinction and prominence, he had been given no talent by which distinction may be won; had been granted no quality, mental, moral, or physical, by which he might rise above the mass of his fellows. It was a cruel trick for Nature to play, and one that she plays far too often. The sufferers from it are certainly far more to be pitied than blamed, and it is harmful only to the afflicted themselves, so long as it meets, or still expects, a measure of gratification. When they are permitted to reach any height from which to look down, the terrible craving appears to be temporarily appeased; and they become kind, and even generous, to all who look up with willing, unwandering gaze. It is only when the sufferers fail to reach any height, or when they lose what little they may have attained, r when the gaze of the world wanders, that they become hard, sour, bitter, and merciless toward all who have succeeded where they have failed. The only mercy that Nature has shown them in their affliction, is to make most of them slow to realize that they can never gain the one thing they crave. And this miserable awakening had not yet come to William Pressley. On that evening he had every reason to be content and well pleased with himself. The future promised all that he most earnestly wished for. He was already moderately successful in the practice of his profession. This was mainly owing to his uncle's influence, but he was far from suspecting the fact. His domestic life, also, was admirably settled; he was fond of Ruth and proud of her, as he was of everything belonging to himself. But the thing which made him happiest was a suggestion of Philip Alston's, first offered on the previous day; and it was to this that he now recurred at the first opportunity.

He spoke with an eagerness curiously apart from his words:

"There seems to be no doubt that the Shawnees are really gone. Men, women, and children, they have all disappeared from their town on the other side of the river. A hunter who has been over there told me so yesterday. It appears reasonably certain that the warriors are gathering under the Prophet at Tippecanoe."

"Yes, it is undoubtedly true that the Indians are rising," replied Philip Alston, still looking at Ruth. "Well, it was bound to come,—this last decisive struggle between the white and the red race,—and the sooner the better, perhaps. I hear, too, that the troops are already moving upon the Shawnee encampment."

"Have you heard anything more about the attorney-general's offering his services? Is it decided that he will go?" asked William Pressley.

He spoke more quickly and with more spirit than was common with him. And he sank back with an involuntary movement of disappointment when Philip Alston shook his head.

"However, there is little doubt that he will go. He is almost sure to," Philip Alston went on. "It is his way to put his own shoulder to the wheel. You remember, judge—"

"What's that!" cried the judge, starting up from his doze.

"We are talking about Joseph Hamilton Daviess," said Philip Alston.

"A great man. A great lawyer—the first lawyer west of the Alleghanies to go to Washington and plead a case before the Supreme Court," said the judge.

"He has certainly been untiring and fearless in the discharge of his duty as the United States Attorney," Philip Alston said warmly. "I was just going to remind you of the journey that he made across the wilderness from Kentucky to St. Louis to find out, if he could, at first hand, what treason Aaron Burr was plotting over there with the commandant of the military post as a tool. He didn't find out a great deal. That old fox knows how to cover his tracks. But the attorney-general did more than any one else could have done. He hauled Burr to trial, almost single-handed, and against the greatest public clamor. He leaves nothing undone in the pursuit of his duty. I understand that he is to be here soon. He thinks that something should be done to put down the lawlessness of this country as Andrew Jackson has subdued it in his territory."

"But he must, of course, resign the office, if he intends going to Tippecanoe," said William Pressley.

He was so intent upon this one point of interest to himself that he had scarcely heard what had been said. He now turned with dignified impatience when his aunt broke in, speaking from the hearth. Miss Penelope always spoke with a greater or less degree of suddenness and irrelevance. She commonly said what she had to say at the instant that the thought occurred to her, regardless of what others might be talking or thinking about. The tenor of nearly everything that she said was singularly gloomy. Her mind was full of superstition of a homely, domestic kind. She was a great believer in signs, and the signs with which she was most familiar were usually forewarnings of some great and mysterious public or private calamity. Her voice was remarkably soft, low, and sweet, so that to hear these alarming threats and these appalling prophecies uttered in the tones of a cooing dove, was very singular indeed.

"'Pon my word!" she now exclaimed, facing the room, but still keeping close to the coffee-pot. "How you all can expect anything but terrible troubles and awful misfortunes is more than I can understand. The warning of that comet sent a-flying wild across the heavens is enough for me."

No one noticed what she said—which certainly seemed to require no notice; but it never made any difference to Miss Penelope whether her remarks were warmly or coolly received. After stooping to turn the coffee-pot round on its trivet she faced the room again.

"Yes, the warning is plenty plain enough for me!" she cooed. "And just look at the dreadful things that have happened already! Just look at what came to pass between the time we first heard of that comet early in the summer, and the time we first saw it early in September. Didn't all the wasps and flies go blind and die sooner than common, right in the middle of the hottest weather? Who ever heard of such a thing before? And look at the fruit crop,—the apple trees, the peach trees, all kind of fruit trees—and the grape-vines a-bending and a-breaking clear down to the ground because they can't bear the weight."

"It is probable that the early dying of the wasps and flies may have had something to do with the fineness of the fruit," said

William Pressley, quite seriously, with formal politeness and a touch of impatience at the interruption.

Miss Penelope took him up tartly in her softest tone: "Then, William, may I ask why the people all over the country are calling this year's vintage 'comet wines'? For that's the way they are marking it, and everybody is putting it to itself—as something very uncommon. But never mind! I am used to having what I say mocked at in this house. It's nothing new to me to have my words passed over as if they hadn't been spoken. I can bear it and it don't alter my duty. I am bound to go on a-doing what I believe to be right just the same, however I am treated. I can't sit by and say nothing when I know that I ought to lift up my voice in warning. So I say again—you can mark my word or not as you think best—that we are all a-going to see some mighty wild sights before we see the last of that comet's tail."

"Pooh! Pooh! Pooh!" cried the widow Broadnax, roughly and hoarsely, as she nearly always spoke, and sitting up suddenly among her cushions. "Who's afraid of a comet with only one tail? I'll have you to know, sister Penelope, that my grand-mother—my own grandmother and Robert's own grand-mother, not yours—could remember the famous comet of seventeen hundred and forty-four, and that had six tails."

Miss Penelope was daunted and silenced for the moment. She did not mind the greater number of the rival comet's tails. It was not that which made her feel herself at a disadvantage. It was the slur at her lesser relationship to the master of the house. Any reference to that was a blow which never failed to make her flinch; and one which the widow never lost a chance to deal. But Miss Penelope had not yielded an inch through the ceaseless contention of years, and held her ground now; since there was nothing to say in reply, she ignored the taunt as she had done all that had gone before. She turned upon William Pressley, however, as we are prone to turn upon those whom we do not fear, when we dare not attack those with whom we are really offended.

"Well, William, maybe you think that the early dying and the going blind of the wasps and the flies caused the breaking out of the 'Jerks,' too. You and the rest all think you know better than I do. I don't complain—maybe you all do know better. But some day, when I am dead and gone, some day, and it mayn't be very long, when my hands are stone cold and crossed under the coffin-lid, you will think differently about a good many matters," she cooed, as if saying the mildest, pleasantest things in the world. "The Jerks have brought many a proud head low. Others besides myself will see a warning in the Jerks before they are gone. And now here are the Shawnees a-coming to welter us in our blood. And the Cold Plague already come to shake the life out of the few that are left. But it is their own fault. There's nobody but themselves to blame. It's easy enough to keep from having the plague," Miss Penelope added confidently. "Anybody can keep from having it, if they will only take the trouble to blow real hard three times on a blue yarn string before breakfast."

William Pressley turned gravely and was about to protest against such absurd superstition, but Philip Alston interfered tactfully, to assure the lady that she was quite right, that it could not fail to benefit almost any one to breathe on anything, especially if the breathing were very deep and very early in the morning.

"And then the new doctor knows how to cure the plague, aunt Penelope, dear," said Ruth, suddenly looking up from the things on the candle-stand. She was always the peacemaker of the family. "The Sisters told me. They are not afraid now that he has come. They were never afraid for themselves; it was for the children—the orphans. They said that little ones were dying all over the wilderness like frozen lambs."

"This new doctor is a most presumptuous person," said William Pressley, with the chilly deliberation which invariably marked his irritation. "He refuses to bleed his patients or to allow them to be bled. These unheard-of objections of his are levelled at the fundamental principles of the established practice and calculated to undermine it. Every physician of reputable standing will tell you that bleeding is the only efficacious treatment for the Cold Plague, and that it is entirely safe if no more than eight ounces of blood be taken at a time, and not oftener than once in two or three hours."[1]

[Footnote 1: "Medical Repository," 1815, p. 222.]

No one said anything for a moment. When William Pressley spoke in that tone, which he frequently did, there seemed to be nothing left for any one else to say. The subject appeared to have been done up hard and fast in a bundle and laid away for good and all. The judge was dozing again, Philip Alston was still gazing at Ruth, Miss Penelope was busy over the coffee-pot, and the widow Broadnax was watching every movement that she made. It was Ruth who replied after a momentary pause. She never lacked courage to stand by her own opinions, timid and gentle as they were; and she spoke now firmly though gently:

"But, William, just think! These were little bits of babies. Such poor, weak, bloodless little mites anyway. And it is said that the greatest pain and danger from the plague is from weakness and cold. The strongest men shiver and shiver till they freeze out of the world."

William Pressley bent his head in the courtesy that stings more than rudeness. He never argued. He had spoken; there was no need to say anything more. So that with this bow to Ruth he turned to Philip Alston and again took up the topic which he was so anxious to resume. It had already been interrupted, he thought, by far too much unimportant talk. Ruth looked at him expectantly when he started to speak, but he was looking at Philip Alston and spoke to him.

"You have, I suppose, sir, mentioned to my uncle what you so kindly suggested to me, in the event that the attorney-general should resign on going to Tippecanoe."

The deepest feeling that Ruth had ever heard in his voice thrilled it now. She involuntarily bent forward. Her eager lips were apart, her radiant eyes were upon him. Was he going with the attorney-general to Tippecanoe? She was afraid, glad, frightened, proud, all in a breath. She had forgotten the beautiful gifts that lay before her. The mere mention, the merest thought of the noble and the great, stirred her heart like the throb of mighty drums.

"No, but I will speak to him about it now," replied Philip Alston. "Judge, Judge Knox!" raising his voice.

The judge, aroused, sat up, looking round. But William Pressley spoke again before Philip Alston could explain.

"If the attorney-general really intends to go, he must resign. There will, of course, be many applicants for the place, and we can hardly be too prompt in applying for it, if I am to succeed him."

Ruth sank back in her chair. The fabric which she had held unconsciously now dropped unheeded from her hand. She could not have told why she felt such a shock of revulsion and disappointment. She had known something like it before, when this man who was to be her husband had shown some strange insensibility to great things which had moved her own heart to its depths. But the feeling had never been so strong as it was now; had never come so near revealing to her the real character of him with whom her whole life was to be spent; and she was still more bewildered and perplexed than shocked or distressed. She thought that she must have misunderstood; that he could not have meant thus to pass over this great national crisis,—this noble offering of a great man's life to the service of his country,—in unfeeling haste to grasp some selfish profit from it. She looked at him wonderingly, with all the light gone out of her face. Being what she was, she could not see that he was just as true to his nature as she was to hers; that he was following it with entire sincerity in looking at the noblest things in life and the greatest things in the world,

Nancy Huston Banks

solely as they affected himself and his own interests. It was not for a nature like hers ever to understand that a nature like his would, if it could, bend the whole universe to his own ends without a doubt that such was its best possible use.

Philip Alston, also, was regarding William Pressley with rather an inscrutable look. But his estimate and understanding were fairer than Ruth's, for the reason that he could come nearer to giving the young man his due. He knew that William Pressley was honest and sincere in his vanity and conceit, and was assured that these traits were the worst he possessed. Philip Alston knew men, and he had found that those who honestly thought highly of themselves usually had something, more or less, to found the opinion upon. He had never known a bad man who sincerely thought himself a good one. He knew that many dull men really believed themselves to be intelligent,— but that was a comparatively harmless mistake,—and he had never observed that a woman thought less of a man who thought well of himself. Aside from this surface weakness William Pressley was a most worthy young fellow; far more worthy to be Ruth's husband than any one else in that rough and thinly settled country. The nearer the time for the marriage approached, the more Philip Alston came to believe that he had chosen wisely in selecting William Pressley. Fully convinced at last that he could not do better for her future than to intrust it to this serious, conscientious young man, who was unquestionably fond of her and to whom she was much attached, he now rested content. He still found, to be sure, some amusement in the young man's estimate of himself; but he never doubted its sincerity or questioned its harmless-ness. It did not occur to him that Ruth might be troubled by these matters which merely made him smile.

There would have been a warning for him in the look which she now gave William Pressley had he seen it. But he was looking at the judge, who could not grasp the meaning of what had been said; and he tried again to put the facts before him, but the judge would not allow him to finish.

"Who says Joe Daviess is going away?" he demanded excitedly. "Why, he can't leave. It's out of the question. There is nobody to take his place. We can't spare him. It is preposterous to think of his going to be slaughtered by those red devils. A man like that! when there are plenty of no-account wretches good enough to make food for powder. He mustn't go. The country needs him more here than there—or anywhere. And I will see him to-morrow, for he is coming; tell him so, by —!"

"You will have your trouble for nothing, then, sir," said Philip Alston, quietly, interrupting him. "The attorney-general is not a man to let another man tell him what to do or not to do. And we are merely considering the probability of his going. If he should go, some one must, of course, take his place. In that case I can think of no one more fit than William here," laying his hand on the young man's arm. "With his qualifications, backed by your influence and mine, there should not be much difficulty. But we must press his claims in time; the notice will be short."

The idea was new to the judge and startling. He turned quickly and looked at his nephew blankly for a moment, and then his left eyebrow went up. His opinion was easy enough to read on his open, rugged face as it always was, and Philip Alston read it like large print; but it did not suit him to show that he did, and no one else saw it. Ruth's face was buried in her hands as she sat with her elbows on the candle-stand. William was looking at the floor with the quiet air of one who is calmly conscious of his own merits, and can afford to await their recognition, even though it may be tardy. The ladies were deeply absorbed in the duties binding them to the hearth. The coffee was now ready, and Miss Penelope lifted the pot from its trivet, and, carrying it to the table, called everybody to supper. No affairs of state ever were, or ever could be, of sufficient importance in her eyes to justify letting the coffee get cold.

Philip Alston went to her side with his deferential air, and told her that he could not stay for the evening meal. He explained that he was expecting several friends that night over the Wilderness Road. It was possible that they might already have arrived and were now awaiting him in his cabin. He must hasten homeward as fast as possible. So saying he took her bony little hand and bowed over it, and made another bow of precisely the same ceremony over the widow Broadnax's pudgy fingers. He always brought his finest tact to bear upon his acquaintance with these ladies.

He looked around for Ruth and held out his hand. She came to him, and went with him to the door. They stood close together for a moment, talking with one another while the others were settling around the table. When he had mounted his horse and set out, she still stood gazing after him till the judge's voice, exclaiming, caused her to turn.

"Call Alston back, if he isn't out of hearing!" he said.

Ruth shook her head. Philip Alston always rode very fast. He was already out of sight in the falling night.

"Pshaw! I never seem able to keep my mind on anything these days," the judge said, fretted with himself. "I fully meant to ask Alston to take that money to the salt-works. It wouldn't have been much out of his way. I don't know what makes me so forgetful lately—and always so drowsy. I promised faithfully to pay for that cargo of salt to-day, so that it would be on the river bank ready for loading when the flatboat comes to-morrow. The owner of the boat sent the money yesterday. I've got it here in my pocket. And the salt was to be delivered for cash; it will not be sent till it is paid for." He paused a moment in troubled thought. "David! Call that boy. He's always hidden off somewhere."

"Here, sir," said David, standing up and coming out of the shadow beneath the stairs.

"You will have to help me in this matter, my lad," said the judge, kindly, forgetting his momentary irritation. "I'll have to send the money by you."

He drew from his pocket a queer-looking roll which he called his wallet. It was a strip of thin, fine deerskin, bound with a narrow black riband and tied with a leathern string. The bank-notes were rolled in this, and the gold pieces and the "bits"— which were small wedges of coin cut from silver dollars—were in two pouches sewed across the end of the strip. It was very seldom that this wallet of the judge's contained so large a sum of money as on that night, for salt was dear in the wilderness. It required eight hundred gallons of the weak salt water and many cords of fire-wood, and the work of many men for many days, to make a single bushel of the precious article. It was still scarce and hard to get thereabouts at five dollars a bushel, so that a large sum was needed to pay for an entire cargo. Drops of perspiration stood on the judge's forehead as he counted out the bank-notes, the gold, and the cut money. He cared little for his own money, and he rarely had much at a time; but he was scrupulously careful in his handling of other people's. And he knew that his eyes were not very clear that night, and that his fingers were not so sure as they should be of anything that they touched. Ruth saw how it was with a tender pang at her heart, for she knew how honest he was and how good, and she loved him. She knelt down at his side and helped him count the money, over which his clumsy hands were fumbling pathetically, so that there might be no error in the counting.

"There!" he said, tying the string round the wallet, which was now almost empty, and putting it back in his pocket. "I want you, David, to take this and go over to the salt-works very early in the morning, as soon after daybreak as you can see your way. Take two of the best black men with you,—they will take care of you and the money, too," he added, with his easy-going laugh. And then he grew suddenly sobered with a touch of shame. "I wouldn't give you the money to-night, my boy," he said hesitatingly, "but—I am hard to wake in the morning. I am afraid you couldn't wake me early enough for me to give you the money in time to get you off by dawn. And my client will be here with his boat, waiting for the cargo, if you are any later in starting. But you can take just as good care of the money as I could. You are not so likely to lose it."

"I will do my best, sir," said the boy, quietly.

He took the money and put it away in his safest pocket. When he had eaten supper with the family, he went back to his shadowed corner under the stairs. But he could not read his book; his mind was too full of thoughts which were fast becoming a purpose. Ruth looked at him and at his book now and then, while she talked to the others, and her teasing glances hastened his decision. She would never laugh at him again for dreaming over romances, if he could prove that he was able to do an earnest man's part in the world. Yes, this was the chance which he had been wishing for. He would go to the salt-works at once—that very night—without waiting for daylight and without calling the black men. The judge would not care; he never cared for anything that did not give trouble, and he need not know until afterward. David stood up suddenly in the shadows under the stairs. He had decided; he would go as soon as he could get away from the great room and put his saddle on the pony. Even Ruth must acknowledge that a night's ride over the Wilderness Road was the work of a man—the work of a strong, brave man.

IV

THE NIGHT RIDE

He left the great room for his own cabin at the usual hour. No one but Ruth observed his going. She smiled at him as he passed, and caught his hand and gave it a little teasing, affectionate squeeze. He must leave "The Famous History of Montilion" unread for one night,—so she said,—and he must go to bed at once, since he was to be up before the sun. These little ways of Ruth's were usually very sweet to him, but he did not find them so that night. He made no reply, and looked at her gravely, without an answering smile. Had anything been needed to fix his purpose, this gentle raillery would have been more than enough.

He went straight from the door of Cedar House to the stable under the hill, stopping at his cabin only long enough to get his rifle. The stable was very dark within, but he knew where to find the pony that he always rode, and the saddle and bridle which he always used, without needing to see. And the pony knew him, too, for all the darkness, and welcomed him with a friendly whinny which said so as plainly as words. For the boy and the pony were good friends, and moreover they understood one another perfectly, which is rarely the case with the best of friends. And then they were both foundlings, and that may have made another bond between them. The pony had been a wild colt caught in the forest on the other side of the river. Nothing was known of his ancestors, although they were supposed by those who knew best, to have been the worn-out horses of good blood which had been deserted in the wilderness by the Spaniards. But then everything cruel was laid at the door of the hated Spaniards in those days, when they had so lately been forced to take their throttling grasp from the throat of the Beautiful River. The pony certainly bore no outward mark of noble ancestry. He was a homely, humble, rough-coated little beast. Yet David liked him better than all the other finer horses in the judge's stables, notwithstanding that some of these had real pedigrees; for good horses were already appearing in Kentucky. The judge allowed David to claim the pony as his own. Robert Knox was a kind man when he did not forget, and he never forgot any one without forgetting himself,—first and most of all,—as he did sometimes.

David always thought of the pony as an orphan like himself, and his own bruised feelings were very tender toward the friendless little fellow. He led him from the stable now as a mark of respect and because it was dark; for he knew that the pony, with a word, would follow him anywhere, at any time, like a faithful dog. It was not quite so dark outside, and springing into the saddle, the boy bent down and stroked the rough neck and the tangled mane that no brush could ever make smooth. The pony lifted his head to meet the caress, and then these two orphans of the wilderness looked out dimly, wondering, over this wonderful new country into which both were come, without knowing how or why or whence, through no will or choice of their own.

That portion of Kentucky rises gently but steadily from the river, and rolls gradually upward toward its eastern hills. On this October night so close to the very beginning of the commonwealth, these terraced hills were still covered with the primeval forest. Hill after hill, and forest after forest, on and on and higher and higher, till the earth and the heavens came together. Near the river on the natural open spaces, and where earliest the clearings had been made, the boy could see the widely scattered rude homes, the young orchards, and the new fields, which the first Kentuckians had won from the wilderness, from the savage, from the wild beast and the pestilence. Southward, and a long way off, lay the great Cypress Swamp. The wavering sable line of its tree-tops spread a pall across the starless horizon. The deadly white mists which shrouded its gloomy mystery through the sunniest day were now creeping out to enshroud the higher land. Through the mingled mist and darkness the sombre trunks of the towering cypress trees rose with supernatural blackness. The mysterious "knees," those strange, naked, blackened roots, so wildly gnarled and twisted about the foot of the cypress, appeared to writhe out of the swamp's awful dimness like monstrous serpents seen in a dreadful dream.

And thus these dark fancies swayed the boy's imagination as wind sways flame, till he suddenly remembered and turned from them more quickly and firmly than ever before. He had made up his mind to cease dreaming with his eyes open. He was resolved to see only real sights and to hear only real sounds from this time on. He did not deceive himself by thinking that this ever could be easy for him to do. He knew too well that in place of the cool, steady common-sense which should dwell in every man's breast, there dwelt something strangely hot and restless in his own. He had always felt this difference without understanding it; but he had hoped that no one else knew it—up to the cruel revelation of Ruth's laughing and kindly meant words. Well, neither Ruth nor any one should ever again have cause to laugh at him for romantic weakness, if he might help it by keeping guard over his fancy.

He therefore sternly kept his eyes away from the swamp where mystery always brooded. He would not look at the wonderful mound near the swamp, which he never before had passed without wonder. It was then—as it is now—such an amazing monument to a vanished race. It is so unaccountably placed, this mountain of earth in the midst of level lowlands; so astounding in size and so unmistakably the work of unknown human hands. Never till that night had David's fervid imagination turned toward it without his beginning forthwith to wonder over the secrets of the ages which lie buried beneath.

He had hitherto always thought of this mound in association with the mysterious blazed trail through the forest. But that was much farther off and more directly south, and no one but the boy had ever found any connection between the two. He, dreaming, would sometimes imagine that the same vanished race had marked the path through the forest by cutting the trees on either side—this marvelous blazed trail which De Soto is sometimes said to have found when he came, and again to have made himself, regardless of the fact that history does not mention his being anywhere near. The romance of the buried treasure which this mystic path was believed to lead to, perpetually held David under a spell of enchantment. But he would not allow himself to linger over these mysteries now. He also resisted the horrible fascination of the Dismal Slough— that long, frightful black pit—linking the swamp to the river. And most of all he shrunk from giving a thought or a glance toward the gloom hanging over Duff's Fort, which was still farther off, and the strongest, most bloody link in the long and unbroken chain of crime then stretching clear across southwestern Kentucky.

As these uneasy thoughts thronged, a faint sound borne by the wind caused him to turn his head with a nervous start, and he saw something moving in the deeper darkness that surrounded the swamp. He pulled up the pony, tightening his grip on the rifle, and strained his eyes, trying to make out what this moving object was. The wavering mists were very thick, and he thought at first that it might be nothing worse than a denser gathering of the deadly vapor creeping out of the swamp. The fog suddenly fell like a heavy curtain, and he could see nothing. And then lifting again, it gave him a fleeting glimpse of a body of horsemen riding rapidly in the edge of the forest, as if seeking the shadow of the trees. He could see only the black outline of the swiftly moving shapes, but he knew that they must be part of the band which was filling the whole country with terror, violence, and death. None other could be riding at night toward Duff's Fort. He thought of the money in his pocket, and felt the thumping of his heart as his hand involuntarily went up to touch it, making sure that it was still safe. He sat motionless—scarcely daring to breathe—watching the shadows till he suddenly realized with a breath of relief that they were going the other way, in the opposite direction from his own road. And then after waiting and watching a little longer, in order to make sure that they were out of sight, he rode on.

The courage and calmness which he had found in himself under this test, heartened him and made him the more determined to control his wandering fancy. Looking now neither to the right nor the left, he pressed on through the clearing toward the buffalo track in the border of the forest which would lead him into the Wilderness Road. Sternly setting his thoughts on the errand that was taking him to the salt-works, he began to think of the place in which they were situated, and to wonder why so bare, so brown, and so desolate a spot should have been called Green Lick. There was no greenness about it, and not the slightest sign that there ever had been any verdure, although it still lay in the very heart of an almost tropical forest. It must surely have been as it was now since time immemorial. Myriads of wild beasts coming and going through numberless centuries to drink the salt water, had trodden the earth around it as hard as iron, and had worn it down far below the surface of the surrounding country. The boy had seen it often, but always by daylight, and never alone, so that he noted many things now which he had not observed before. The huge bison must have gone over that well-beaten track one by one, to judge by its narrowness. He could see it dimly, running into the clearing like a black line beginning far off between the bordering trees; but as he looked, the darkness deepened, the mists thickened, and a look of unreality came over familiar objects. And then through the wavering gloom there suddenly towered a great dark mass topped by something which rose against the wild dimness like a colossal blacksmith's anvil. It might have been Vulcan's own forge, so strange and fabulous a thing it seemed! The boy's heart leaped with his pony's leap. His imagination spread its swift wings ere he could think; but in another instant he reminded himself. This was not an awful apparition, but a real thing, wondrous and unaccountable enough in its reality. It was Anvil Rock—a great, solitary rock—rising abruptly from the reckless loam of a level country, and lifting its single peak, rudely shaped like a blacksmith's anvil, straight up toward the clouds. It was already serving as a landmark in the wilderness, and must continue so to serve all that portion of Kentucky, so long as the levelling hand of man may be withheld from one of the natural wonders of the world.

Beyond Anvil Rock the night grew blacker. When David reached the buffalo track he could no longer see even dimly, the forest closing densely in on both sides of the narrow path, and arching darkly overhead. Instinctively he put up his hand again and touched the money in his breast pocket. His grasp on the rifle unconsciously grew firmer, but he loosed the bridle-rein for a moment to pat the pony. The little beast entered the shadows of the trees without a tremor; yet there were dangers therein for him no less than for his rider, and his excited breathing told that he knew this quite as well as his master. It was so dark that neither could see the path, and the boy was trusting more to the pony than to himself, as they went swiftly forward through the still darkness of the forest. The pony's unshod feet made scarcely a sound on the soft, moist earth. There had been no frost to thin the thick branches hanging low over their heads. The few leaves which had drifted down were still unwithered, and only made the hoof-beats more soundless on the yielding earth, so that there was not a rustle at the noiseless passing of the pony and his rider. Only a sudden gust of wind now and then sent a murmur through the dark tree-tops and gently swayed the sombre boughs. And so they sped on, drawing nearer and nearer to the Wilderness Road, till presently the wind brought the strong odor of boiling salt water. The woods became now still further darkened and entangled by many fallen trees which had been felled to make fuel for the furnaces, and by huge heaps of logs piled ready for burning. Here and there were great whitening giants of the forest still standing after they had been slain, as soldiers—death-stricken—stand for an instant on the field of battle. It seemed to the fanciful boy that the wind sighed most mournfully among these wan ghosts of trees, and that the dead boughs, moved by the sighing wind, smote one another with infinite sadness.

There was no sound other than this moaning of the wind through the forest and the muffled beating of the pony's feet on the leaf-covered path. Once a great owl flew across the dark way with a deadened beating of his heavy wings. Again wolves howled, but so far in the distance that the sound came as the faintest echo. A stronger gust of the fitful wind filled the forest with the sulphurous vapors arising from the evaporating furnaces. A moment more, and the vivid glare of the fires flared luridly through the wild tangle of the undergrowth. Against this red glare many black shadows—the dark forms of the firemen—could now be indistinctly seen moving like evil spirits around the smoking, flaming pits.

It was a wild, strange sight, wild and strange enough to fire a cooler fancy than David's. He forgot his errand, forgot the money, forgot where he was—everything but the romance of the scene which had taken him captive. Every nerve in his tense young body was strung like the cord of a harp; his young heart was beating as if a heavy hammer swung in his breast. And then, without so much as the warning rustle of a leaf or a sound more alarming than the sigh of the wind, two blurred black shapes burst out of the forest upon him.

V

ON THE WILDERNESS ROAD

The pony fell back almost to his haunches before the boy could draw the reins. The two horses recoiled with equal suddenness and violence. An unexpected encounter with the unknown in the darkness filled even the dumb brutes with alarm, and brute and human alike had reason to be alarmed; for this time and this place—stamped in blood on history—marked the very height and centre of the reign of terror on the Wilderness Road.

The boy strained his terrified gaze through the dark, but he could see nothing except those vague, black forms of two horsemen, looming large and threatening against the lurid glow of the furnace fires which faintly lit the forest. The men and their horses looked like monstrous creatures, half human and half beast, both as silent and motionless as himself. He felt that they also were listening and watching in tense waiting as he waited and watched, hearing only the frightened panting of the horses and the faint rustle of the sable leaves overhead. And so all held for an instant, which seemed endless, till a sudden gust of wind swung the boughs and sent the glare of the furnace flames far and high through the forest. The vivid flash came and went like lightning, but it lasted long enough for the boy to recognize one of the black shapes.

"Father!" he cried. "Father Orin!"

"Bless my soul—it's young David!" exclaimed the priest.

There was as much relief in his tone as in the boy's, and he turned hastily to the horseman at his side.

"Doctor, this is a young friend of mine—a member of Judge Knox's family. You have heard of the judge. And, David, this is Doctor Colbert. You, no doubt, have heard of him."

David murmured something. He had never before been introduced to any one; and had never before been so acutely conscious that he had no surname. The doctor sent his horse forward, coming close to the pony's side. He held out his hand—as David felt rather than saw—and he took the boy's hand in a warm, kind clasp. It was the first time that a man had given David his hand as one frank, earnest, fearless man gives it to another—but never to a woman, and rarely to a boy. David did not know what it was that he felt as their hands met in the darkness, but he knew that the touch was like balm to his bruised pride, which had been aching so sorely throughout the lonely ride. Father Orin now rode nearer on the other side, and although no more than the dimmest outline of any object could be seen, the boy saw that the priest continued to turn his head and cast backward glances into the dark forest. When he spoke, it was in a low tone, strangely guarded and serious for him, who was always as outspoken and light-hearted as though his hard life of toil and self-sacrifice had been the most thoughtless and happiest play.

"But how does it happen that you are here, my son?" he asked, almost in a whisper. "I can't understand the judge's allowing it. Can it be possible that he has sent you—on business? Why—! A man isn't safe on this part of the Wilderness Road at night, and hardly at midday, alone. For a child like you—"

There it was again, like a blow on a bruise! The boy instantly sat higher in the saddle, trying to look as tall as he could, and forgetting that no one could see. And replying hastily in his deepest, most manly voice, he said scornfully, that there was nothing to be afraid of with his rifle across the saddle-bow, declaring proudly that he knew how to deal with wild beasts, should any cross his path. As for the Indians, he scoffed at the idea; there were none in that country, and never had been any thereabouts, except as they came and went over the Shawnee Crossing.

"But you are mistaken; the Meek boys—James and Charles— were killed only a few weeks ago, just across the river," said the priest. "And they were better able to take care of themselves than you are, my child. Come, you must turn back with us. We cannot go with you, and we must not allow you to go on alone."

Saying this, Father Orin turned his horse and moved forward. David made no movement to follow. Tightening the reins on the pony's neck, he did not try to turn him. Something in the stiff lines of the boy's dark figure told the doctor part of the truth. He broke in quickly, speaking not as a man speaks to a child, but as one man to another.

"There are worse things than wild beasts or Indians to be met on the Wilderness Road," he said. "And the strongest and the bravest are helpless against a stab in the back, or a trap in the dark."

David felt a sudden wish to see the speaker's face. He longed to see how a man looked who had a voice like that. It stirred him, and yet soothed him at the same time. Every tone of it rang clear and true, like a bell of purest metal. All who heard it felt the strength that it sounded—strength of body and mind and heart and spirit.

David fell under its influence at once. He was turning the pony's head when Father Orin in his anxiety erred again.

"I am surprised at the judge," the priest said. "This isn't like him—forgetful as he is about most things. And what are you here for, my son? Where were you going?"

"The judge has nothing to do with my coming to-night. He merely told me to take this money—"

"Hush! Hush!" cried the two men in a breath. At the instant they pressed closer to the boy's side, as if the same instinct of protection moved them both at the same moment. "Come on! Let's ride faster," they said together. "It is not so dark or so dangerous in the buffalo track."

The pony, turning suddenly, pressed forward with the other horses, more of his own accord than with his rider's consent, and gallantly kept his place between them, although they were soon going at the top of their speed. Nothing more was said for several minutes, and then the doctor spoke to the boy.

"You will give us the pleasure of your company all the way, I trust, sir," he said ceremoniously, and as no one ever had spoken to David. "It is a long, lonesome ride, and my home is still farther off than yours."

David murmured a pleased, bashful assent. They had now reached the buffalo track, which was not wide enough for the three to ride abreast. It was therefore necessary for them to fall into single file, and David managed to get the lead. This made him feel better, and more of a man, for the darkness was still deep, and the black boughs overhead still hung low and heavy. Neither of the horsemen spoke again for a long time after entering upon the buffalo track. Once more the only sound was the steady, muffled beating of the horses' swiftly moving feet. The two men were buried in their own thoughts of duties and aims far beyond the boy's understanding, and he was not thinking of these silent companions by his side—he was scarcely thinking at all; he was merely feeling. He was held under a spell, dumb and breathless, enchanted by the mystery of the wilderness at night.

It was so black, so beautiful, so terrible, so soundless, so motionless, so unfathomable. There was no moon. The few pale stars glimmered dimly far above the dark arches of the trees. No bird moved among the sable branches, or even twittered in its sleep as if disturbed by the light, swift passing of the shadowy horsemen. No wild animal stirred in his uneasy rest or even breathed less deeply in his hunting dreams, at the flitting of the shadows across his hidden lair.

The mystery, the beauty, and the terror went beyond the black border of the forest. Out in the open and over the clearing, the mists from the swamp mingling with the darkness gave everything a look of fantastic unreality yet wilder than it had worn earlier in the night. Dense earth-clouds were thus massed about the base of Anvil Rock. Its blackened peak loomed through the clouds,—a strange, wild sight, apparently belonging neither to earth or to heaven. But far beyond and above was a stranger, wilder sight still; the strangest and wildest of all; one of the strangest and wildest, surely, that human eyes ever rested upon.

There across the northern sky sped the great comet. Come, none ever knew whence, and speeding none ever knew whither, it reached on that night—on this fifteenth of October—the summit of its swift, awful, arching flight. It was now at the greatest of its terrible splendor and appalling beauty. It was now at the very height of its boundless influence over the hopes and fears of the superstitious, romantic, emotional, poetic race which was struggling to people the wilderness. As it thus burst upon the vision of the three horsemen, each felt its power in his own way,—the man of faith, the man of science, and the fanciful boy,—each was differently but deeply moved. The men looked at the comet as the wise and learned of the earth look at the marvels of another world. The boy gazed quiveringly, like a harp struck by a powerful hand. He strove to cast his fancies aside, and to remember what he had heard before the comet had become visible to this country. He tried vainly to recall the talk about it—not the idle and foolish superstitions which Miss Penelope had mentioned, and which all the common people believed—but the scientific facts so far as they were known. Yet even his imagination failed to realize that this flaming head, with its strange halo of darkness, and its horrible hair of livid green light, was four million times greater than the earth; or that its luminous veil—woven of star-dust so fine that other stars shone through—streamed across one hundred million of miles, thick strewn with other stars.

"Listen!" cried the doctor. "Hear that!" A distant roaring, like the oncoming of a sudden storm, rolled upward from the mists and darkness lying thicker around the swamp.

"There it is again!" Doctor Colbert went on, as if he had been waiting and listening for the sound. "There must be great excitement at the camp-meeting on this last night. Does it still interest you, Father? It does me, intensely. This is not the usual peculiar excitement which seems to belong to a crowd, though that, too, is always curious, mysterious, and interesting. We all know well enough that for some unknown reason a crowd will do wild, strange, and foolish things, which the individuals composing it would never be guilty of alone. But this is something entirely different and still more curious and mysterious. Those people down yonder keep this up by themselves when they are alone—it attacks some of them before they have ever seen one of the meetings. It is certainly the strangest phenomenon of its kind that the world ever saw. It never loses its painful fascination for me. I can't pass it by. How is it with you?"

The priest hesitated before replying. "Any form of faith—the crudest, the most absurd that any soul ever staked its salvation upon—must always be the most interesting subject in the world to every thinking mind."

"It seems so to me," the doctor replied. "And I assure you that there is no irreverence in the scientific curiosity which I feel in this extraordinary epidemic of religious frenzy; for it is certainly something of that sort. It is unmistakably contagious. I have become more and more certain of that as I have watched the poor wretches who are shrieking down yonder. It is a mental and moral epidemic, and so highly contagious that it has swept the whole state, till it now sweeps the remotest corner of the wilderness. And it seems to have originated in Kentucky. It is something peculiarly our own."

"Yes," said Father Orin, "Kentucky is the pioneer in religion, as well as politics, for the whole West. But my church came first," he added with a chuckle. "Remember that! The Catholics always lead the way and clear up the brush, with the Methodists following close behind. I got a little the start of brother Peter Cartwright; but that was my good luck, and not any lack of zeal on his part. And I've got to stir my stumps to keep ahead of him, I can tell you."

"He is down there at the meeting to-night, no doubt. He is its leading spirit. I should like to know what he really thinks of it all. He is by nature a wonderfully intelligent young fellow. And what do you really think of it, Father?" the doctor pressed. "Is this the same thing that has come down the ages? Is it the same that we find in the Bible—making great men and wise ones do such wild things? Is it the same that made a dignified gentleman, like David, dance—as those fanatics are doing down there—till he became a laughing-stock? Is it the same that made a sensible man like Saul join his faith to a witch and believe that he saw visions? And then, just remember the scandalous capers—even worse than the others—that the decent Jeremiah cut."

"Tut! Tut! Tut!" exclaimed the priest, in a voice that betrayed a smile. "Those were holy men, my young friend. I cannot allow them to be laughed at."

"Oh, come now, Father, be honest," said the doctor, laughing aloud, but adding quickly in a serious tone: "I am quite in earnest. What do you make of it all? I should greatly like to have your opinion. Is there anything in the science of your profession to explain it? There isn't in mine. The more of it I see, and the longer I study it, the farther I am from finding its source, its cause, and its real character. There! Just hear that!"

"Well, well," said Father Orin, with a sigh of evasion, "if you are going on to the camp-meeting, Toby and I will have to leave you here. We have a sick call 'way over on the Eagle Creek flats. And it's a ticklish business, going over there in the dark, isn't it, old man?" he said, patting his big gray horse. "The last time we went in the night the limb of a tree, that I couldn't see, dragged me from the saddle." He laughed as if this were a joke on Toby or himself, or both. "But Toby is a better swimmer than I am. He's better at a good many things. He got me out all right that time and a good many other times. He always does his part of our duty, and never lets me shirk mine, if he can help it. Well, then, we must be moving along, Toby, old man." He turned suddenly to the boy. "Will you go with me, David? My way passes close to Cedar House."

"Perhaps, sir, you would like to go on to the meeting," said the doctor to David. "It would give me pleasure to have you with me—if you prefer to go with me. Afterward we can ride home together. My cabin is not far beyond Cedar House."

After a little more talk it was decided that the boy should go with the doctor, and the priest bade them both a cheerful good night.

"Now, Toby, we must be putting in our best licks. If you don't look out, old man, we will be getting into idle ways. Keep us up to the mark—right up to the mark, old man!"

And so, talking to Toby, and chuckling as if Toby made telling replies, the good man and his good horse vanished in the earth-clouds round Anvil Rock. But the doctor and the boy sat their horses in motionless silence, listening to the kind, merry voice and the faithful beat, beat, of the steady feet, till both gradually died away behind the night's heavy black curtain.

VI

THE CAMP-MEETING

As they turned and were riding on toward the camp-meeting, the doctor spoke of the priest and his horse. The boy listened with the wondering awe that most of us feel, when some stranger points out the heroism of a simple soul or an everyday deed which we have known, unknowingly, all our lives.

"Father Orin and Toby are a pair to take your hat off to," the young doctor said. "I have come to know them fairly well by this time, although I have not been here very long. It isn't necessary for any one to be long in the neighborhood before finding out what those two are doing. And then my own work among the suffering gives me many opportunities to know what they are doing and trying to do. The church side is only one side of their good work. I am not a Catholic, and consequently see little of that side; but I meet them everywhere constantly caring for the poor and the afflicted without any regard for creed. And they never have any money, worth speaking of, to help with. They have only their time and their strength and their whole laborious, self-sacrificing lives to give. The expedients that they resort to in a pinch would make anybody laugh—to keep from crying. They were out the other day with a brand-new plan. They travelled about fifty miles through the wilderness trying to find a purchaser for the new overcoat that a Methodist friend gives Father Orin every fall. He, of course, had given his old coat to some shivering wretch last spring while it was still cold, but that didn't make the slightest difference. He didn't even remember the fact till I reminded him of it. It is only October now—so that he can do without the overcoat—and a poor fellow who has come with his wife and baby to live in that deserted cabin near the court-house, is in sore need of a horse for his fall ploughing. Father Orin had suggested Toby's drawing the plough, thinking that some of his own work might be attended to on foot. But Toby, it seems, drew the line at that. It was a treat to hear Father Orin laugh when he told how Toby made it plain that he thought there were more important duties for him to perform, how firmly he refused to drag the plough. He was quite willing, however, to do his best to sell the overcoat, so that they might have money to hire a horse for the ploughing."

The doctor broke off suddenly. The roar coming from the darkness around the swamp rose high on the gusty wind. He and David were now riding fast, and the roaring grew rapidly more continuous and distinct. The vast volume of inarticulate sound presently began to break into many human voices. At last a single voice pierced all the rest. Its shrill cry of spiritual anguish filled the dark forest with the wailing of a soul in extremity.

"And it's a woman, too!" cried the doctor.

He spoke shortly, almost angrily, but something in his tone told David that he also was shivering, although the night was warm, and that his heart was full of pity. They were now drawing near the camp-meeting, but they could not see it, nor even the light from it. They had reentered the forest, which was here made darker and wilder by many fallen trees, blown down and tossed together by the fierce tempests which often rent the swamp. The torn roots, the decaying trunks, and the shattered branches of the dead giants of the ancient wood, were dank with water-moss. Rank poison vines writhed everywhere, and crept like vipers beyond the deadly borders of the great Cypress Swamp. Through such dark and tangled density as this the smoky torches, burning dimly around the camp, could cast their light but a little way. And thus it was by

Nancy Huston Banks

hearing and not by seeing, that they came at last upon the spot almost by accident. They had scarcely got hurriedly down from their horses, and hastily tied them to a swinging bough when the scene burst upon them—a wild vision revealed by the dim flickering torchlight.

There was a long, low shed of vast extent. It was covered with rough boards, and upheld by tree-trunks which still bore the bark. There was no floor other than the bare earth, and there were no seats other than unhewn logs. Here, under the deep shadows of this great shed, all darkly shut in by the black wilderness and dimly lit by a wide circle of smoking, flaring torches, there surged a dark, confused, convulsed, roaring, writhing mass of humanity. And there were many hundreds in that shadowy multitude—swaying, struggling, groaning, laughing, weeping, shouting, praying, dancing, leaping, and falling.

"It does not seem possible that there can be so many in all the wilderness," said the doctor. "But they come from long distances, from as far as fifty and sixty miles around. And they have been coming for weeks—day and night—just like this."

He spoke sadly, and with deep feeling. He laid his firm, gentle hand on David's shaking arm, knowing how the awful spectacle must affect the sensitive boy. David instinctively drew nearer to his side feeling the support of his calm, sane, strong presence, and began gradually to see with clearer eyes, so that this awful vision became by degrees a more awful reality.

"Listen!" cried the doctor. "They are beginning to sing!"

Ah, listen indeed! For a stranger, wilder chant than this which now went swelling up from that frenzied, swaying mass of humanity surely never stirred all that is most mystical in the soul of man! Pealing grandly, awfully upward through the star-lit spaces of a grander temple than ever was reared by human hands, it rolled heavenward, on and on, and higher and higher, to the very dome of the firmament.

With the wild chanting, the madness of the multitude increased. Many men and women—ay, and little children, too—all dropped to their knees, heedless of being trodden underfoot by the unfallen frenzied, and thus crept the length of the earthen floor to the foot of the rude altar. Here, before the pulpit of rough-hewn logs, great heaps of straw were strewn thick and broadcast. On these straw heaps men and women fell prostrate side by side, and lay as if they were dead. Others, both men and women, were suddenly seized with the unnatural, convulsive jerking which gave this mysterious visitation its best-known name. Under this dreadful tremor the long hair of delicate ladies poured unnoticed over the most modest shoulders and flew back and forth with the sound of a whip; for those so wildly wrought upon were not solely of the humble and the ignorant. The highest and the most refined of the whole country were there. The earth was strewn with costly raiment. Gentlemen rent the fine ruffles from their wrists and their bosoms; gentlewomen cast their richest ornaments to the winds. And all the while that this awful, majestic, soul-stirring chant was thus mounting higher and growing wilder, many were whirling and dancing.

David shrunk back, and the doctor drew him closer to his side, as a man suddenly burst out of the swirling mass of maddened humanity, and dashed past them into the forest. There, still within the wide circle of flaring, smoking, torchlight, the poor creature threw his arms around a tree, and uttering strange, savage cries like the barking of a dog, he dashed his head against the tree-trunk till the blood gushed out and poured down his ghastly face. David clung closer to the doctor's arm and turned his eyes away, feeling sick and faint with horror.

"Don't look at him. Turn your head. I must go to him and help him if I can," the doctor said, gently loosing the boy's grasp. "I shouldn't have brought you here. But—Good God! Who is that?" he cried sharply. "Look! Quick! Do you know that girl? Over there by the last pillar—yonder, yonder, with her face turned this way!"

In his eagerness he seized the boy, fairly lifting him from the ground, and held him up so that he could see over all the heads of the surging, swirling crowd. The girl was still there, and David recognized Ruth. She was standing not far off and near the edge of the shed. Close behind her the torches threw out gloomy banners of smoke and vivid streamers of flame, and against them she appeared a quiet, white spirit among many tossed dark shades. When David first saw her, he thought she was looking at him. But in another moment her beautiful face, which had been pale enough before, turned as white as her frock and her large eyes widened with terror. And then David knew that she was looking beyond him and had seen the horror by the tree. He forgot his own horrified faintness, he forgot where he was, the doctor—everything but Ruth and that look in her dear face. He sprang toward her with a piercing cry and outstretched arms.

"Ruth!" he cried. "Here I am, Ruth, dear. I am coming to you. I'll take you away!"

It was a single voice raised against the deafening roar of a hurricane. Only the doctor heard or heeded, and he laid a restraining hand on David's shoulder.

"You are right," he said. "Take her away as soon as you can. She should not have come. Is she your sister? Come this way. We will go round," he went on, without waiting for an answer. "We may be able to reach her from the other side of the shed."

The firm touch and calm tone partly brought the boy to himself, and he followed as closely as he could, but only to be beaten back again and again. That terrific chant was now at its highest and wildest, and he and the doctor were caught in the human maelstrom and swirled hither and thither like straws. They were swept far apart, and when they were quickly driven together again, they had lost sight of Ruth. They were tossed once more, and thrown outside the fiercest swirl. Standing still, they held to a tree, gasping, and searched the crowd with their gaze, trying to find her. She was nowhere to be seen. But while they thus paused, waiting for breath to go on, they saw a tall man near by, leaning against a pillar and quietly overlooking the wild scene. He stood within the circle of torchlight, and they could see him distinctly. Neither the doctor nor David had ever seen him before and neither ever saw him again, but they never forgot just how he looked that night.

He was a very tall man of more than six feet in height. He was very erect and very slender, with the slenderness that gives a look of youth as well as grace. There was no tinge of gray in his tawny hair, which fell heavily back from his high, narrow forehead, without any of the stiffness seen in his later portraits. He was not more than thirty-five years of age at this time, but his face was already lined with care and trouble and exposure. It was naturally pale and thin, almost haggard. Its sole redeeming feature was the wonderful brilliance of his blue eyes. The doctor and David could not see the color of his eyes, and yet he seemed to them a singularly handsome man, as he did to almost every one. There was something about him that may be called a presence, for lack of a better term, something which drew the gaze of the crowd and held it everywhere. Many eyes were upon him that night in the very height and centre of all the frenzy. Glances were cast at him even from the pulpit, which was not far away. One of the ministering preachers gave him a look of recognition, and then, bending down, whispered in the ear of another preacher, a very young man who stood below the pulpit among the fallen, exhorting them to repentance. The exhorter shook off the whisperer and went on with his impassioned plea. He, too, was well worth looking at, and better worth listening to—this inspired young backwoodsman, Peter Cartwright. His swarthy face was pale with the pallor of fanaticism, and his dark eyes were aflame with some mystic fire. His long black hair was wildly blown by the wind which bore his broken words still more brokenly:—

"Such a time as this has not been seen since the day of

Pentecost.... A sacred flame is surely sweeping sin from the earth.... Come all ye. Take up your cross and follow Him.... Heaven's gate stands wide to-night.... Praise the Lord!... Come in.... Come at once.... Do not delay—or the gate may close, never to open again. Come! Come with me to the mercy seat. I was once like you. My soul, like yours, was rent in agony. I wept, I strove, I prayed, I was in utter despair ... just as you are now.... Sometimes it seemed as if I could almost lay hold on the Saviour.... Then—all of a sudden—such a fear of the devil fell upon me that he appeared to stand right by my side ready to drag me down to hell. But I prayed on, and said, 'Lord if there be mercy for me, let me find it!' ... At last, in the midst of this awful struggle of soul, I came to the foot of the altar— here—where I am begging you to come.... And then it was as if a voice out of heaven said to me, 'Thy sins are forgiven thee.'...Glory! Glory! Delight flashed all around me. Joy unspeakable sprung up in my soul. It seemed to me that I was already in paradise. The very trees, the very leaves on the trees, seemed to be singing together and praising God.... Will you share this divine peace with me? Will you come with me this night to the foot of the cross?... Then come now—now—for this may be the accepted hour of your salvation.... Come.... If you wait, you are lost ... lost!"

But these simple, broken words are only the cold and lifeless echo of Peter Cartwright's fiery, living eloquence. Nothing can ever bring that back as it really was. None may hope to tell those who never heard him what it was like. No one, perhaps among the numberless thousands who did hear him, ever knew what the power was, by which this unlettered backwoodsman swayed multitudes at his will. Perhaps David afterward described it as nearly as any one could, when he said that the mere sound of Peter Cartwright's voice that night—when he could not hear the words—made him feel so sorry, so grieved, so ashamed, that he wanted to fall down on the earth and hide his face and weep like a woman, for his own sins and the sins of the whole world.

"There she is!" cried the doctor. "We can reach her now."

But another roaring wave of humanity dashed over them, sweeping them farther from Ruth and nearer the pulpit. They were so near that they could see the fire that flashed over the pale darkness of the young preacher's face as his brother preacher bent down for the second time and touched him warningly, and whispered again. Peter Cartwright, who was still bending over the men and women lying at his feet, suddenly stood erect. He threw back his long black hair, and flung a flaming glance at the tall man leaning against the pillar. And then his voice rang out like a trumpet calling to combat.

"What if it *is* General Jackson?" he cried. "What is Andrew Jackson but a sinner, too? Let him come with the rest of these poor sinners to beg for pardon before the throne of grace. And let him make haste—or a just and offended God will punish him as if he were the lowest of earth!"

The challenge sounded clear and far. It must have reached the ears of Andrew Jackson, the proud and feared hero of many battles. No man living was more intolerant of indignity or quicker to resent the slightest affront. An alarmed murmur circled through all the tumult; the doctor and David heard it distinctly, and turned with those about them to look at the man thus challenged. But Andrew Jackson himself stood quite still and gave no sign that he had heard. He barely bowed his head when a short, thick-set man pressed through the crowd and touched his arm. The man was a henchman of his, widely and not favorably known in the country, a gambler and adventurer whose name was Tommy Dye. He was leading the general's horse. There were a few words between them, and then the tall figure vaulted into the saddle and disappeared in the surrounding blackness of the forest.

"Now! Here she is. Quick!" cried the doctor.

So crying, he plunged into the storm-lashed sea of humanity like a strong swimmer. The boy followed as well as he could, using all his strength, but they were both dashed back again and again, till at last a wilder wave caught them up and cast them down beside Ruth. Instantly the doctor lifted her in his arms before David found breath, and held her as lightly as if she had been but a wreath of smoke blown across his breast. Holding her thus, and lifting her higher above those wild waves, he bore her through them as if they had been but rippling water. On and on he went to the border of the forest beyond the tumult where the torchlight was brightest, and there he gently set her down. And then all alone they stood silently looking at each other. They were still gazing down into one another's faces, when the boy ran up, panting. At the sight of him the wonder went out of Ruth's blue eyes, and the fright came back. The spell was broken, and she remembered where she was.

"David! Come to me. Take me away!" she cried. "Oh, what a fearful place! I can never forget it while I live. Where is William? We were separated by the crowd."

But even as she spoke, in tones that trembled with alarm, while yet her beautiful face was white and her blue eyes full of tears, there came one of the swift changes that gave her beauty its greatest charm. A vivid blush dyed her cheek, the long, wet lashes suddenly unveiled a coquettish glance, there was a dazzling smile, her hands went up to put her blown hair in order, and she drew on the forgotten gypsy bonnet which was hanging by its strings on her arm. She drew closer to the boy, but she looked at the doctor over her shoulder.

"Who is this gentleman, David?" she faltered. "And how—"

Paul Colbert spoke for himself, telling her his name.

"I am a doctor—the new doctor of the neighborhood," he said, adding with a smile, "I beg your pardon. There was no other way. This young gentleman—who came with me—saw you. We had been trying for an hour or more to reach you. We were afraid to lose the first chance to get you out of that dangerous crush."

His voice was drowned by a sudden roar which lifted the frenzy higher and brought it nearer. The color and smiles fled again from Ruth's face, and she clung to David in greater alarm.

"Take me home. Oh—oh—isn't it terrible! I can't wait to find William. I must go now. I wouldn't be afraid to go alone with you, dear. Not in the least afraid. Take me—take me!"

"Come, then," said David. "The pony's over here."

"But I don't know where my horse is. I don't know where William tied it. I am so turned round that I don't know anything." She was beginning to smile again at her own bewilderment.

"The pony can take us both," said the boy.

She was turning away with him when the doctor interfered with hesitating eagerness:—

"If you will permit me—I would suggest that your friend who came with you may be anxious. He will naturally try to find you. Not knowing that you are gone, he must be alarmed. If I knew him by sight, I could find him and tell him—"

Again his voice was lost in the rising roar of the multitude. The girl buried her face against the boy's shoulder, shudderingly and trembling, and burst into weeping.

"Tell me what to do, David! I can't bear this any longer," she sobbed. "Take me away. Tell me what to do! Oh! Oh!" putting her shaking hands over her ears to shut out the dreadful sounds.

The doctor touched her arm. "If you would allow me to take you home, perhaps this young gentleman could stay and find the person who came with you." He turned quickly to the boy. "You know him?"

"Yes," David replied unwillingly.

His heart had begun to beat high. Here was a better chance to prove himself a man than he had dared hope for. And now this bold stranger was trying to rob him of it. He struggled with himself for a moment, before he could give it up. But Ruth was crying and trembling and clinging to him.

"I will find William," he then said hastily. "Let the doctor take you home."

"But my horse is lost," Ruth lifted her head from David's shoulder and flashed a tearful, smiling glance at the doctor. "How can you take me?"

"Leave it to me," Paul Colbert said quickly, in the tone of a man used to meeting emergencies. "Come with me. I will find a way."

It seemed to Ruth and David that he was one to find a way to whatever he wished. They followed him like two children, to the spot where his horse was tied beside the pony. He untied the bridle with the quickness of constant practice, and sprang into the saddle with the ease of the practiced horseman. He threw the reins over the pommel, and then bending down, held out his arms.

"Now!" he cried. "Give the young lady your hand for her foot!"

David hesitated, not understanding what he meant. It was the custom for the women of the wilderness to ride behind the men; but it was plain that this was not the young doctor's intention. He sat far back in his large saddle, and when Ruth set her foot in the palm of David's hand, and fluttered upward like a freed bird, he caught her and seated her before him. A word to his horse and they were away. He was holding Ruth close to his breast, and her white garments were blown about him, as they vanished in the black wilderness.

VII

A MORNING IN CEDAR HOUSE

It was almost morning when the boy and William Pressley reached home. David did not go to bed, but set out at the first glimmer of dawn to do the judge's bidding, calling the black men to go with him, since there was no great glory to be won by going alone in the daylight. There was time for a little rest after coming back, and it was still very early when he arose from his bed and began to get ready for breakfast.

He looked from his cabin window at the river which always drew his waking gaze. It was sparkling like a stream of liquid diamonds under the flood of sunlight pouring over the dazzled earth. The fringing rushes rippled as gently as the water under the snowy breasts of many swans. The trees along the shore were freshly green and newly alive with the color and chatter of the paroquets. Looking and listening, he thought what a poetic notion it was that these vivid birds should carry the seed pearls of the mistletoe from one mighty oak to another, bearing the tiny treasures in the wax on their feet.

Far up the wide, shining river a great, heavy-laden barge was gliding swiftly down. Its worn and clumsy sail seemed as white and graceful as the wings of the swans in the sun. Its dull and tangled coils of cordelles caught an unwonted charm from the sunbeams. Its merry crew was singing a song, which came gayly over the flashing water:—

Nancy Huston Banks

"Hi-ho, the boatmen row,
The Kentuck boys and the O-hi-o.
Dance, the boatmen, dance,
Dance, the boatmen, dance;
Dance all night till broad daylight,
And go home with the gals in the mornin'."

Watching the barge pass out of sight beneath the overhanging trees, David turned to see a small dark object, leading two long verging lines of silvery ripples across the glittering current. This cleft the water near the Shawnee Crossing, and might, not long before, have been the plumed head of a warrior wanting his canoe. But since the warriors were all gone so strangely and suddenly, this brown speck now crossing the river must have been the antlered head of a deer swimming to the other side, thus giving the hunters warning that these green hills would soon be white with snow. If so, there was no other sign of nearing winter. The sombre forest stretching away from the opposite shore had not yet been brightened by a touch of frost. The leaves on the near-by trees, the great oaks and elms and poplars standing around Cedar House, were thinning only through ripeness, and drifting very slowly down to the green and growing grass. On the tall maples perfection alone had culled the foliage, so wreathing the bronze boughs with rarer garlands of fretted gold.

No dread of wintry storms had yet driven away any of the birds that Ruth fed every day on the sill of her chamber window. They were all there as usual—the whole feathered colony—as if they wished to be polite, even though they were not hungry on that sunny morning. The little ones, to be sure, pecked a crumb now and then with a languid indifference. The blue jays—as usual—were brazen in their ingratitude for any dole of commonplace crumbs, while spicy seeds were still strewn by every scented breeze. But shy and bold alike, they all flocked around Ruth's window, and sat on the sill within reach of her hand, and cocked their pretty heads as if it were feast enough only to look at her.

She had already been downstairs to fetch the birds' breakfast, and had gone into the garden where the sweetest and reddest roses of all the year were still blooming. She held a big bunch of them in her hand as she stood at the open window and waved it at David in a morning greeting, when she saw him crossing the yard. She came down the broad stairs as he entered the great room, and she was wearing a fresh white frock and her arms were full of the fragrant red roses.

The rest of the family were already in the room, and the table was laid for breakfast. Ruth greeted each one with a smile, but she did not speak, and began to move quietly about the table, giving those dainty little finishing touches which no true woman ever leaves to a servant. She put some of the roses in a vase, and rearranged this and that, moving lightly and softly about. Her footsteps were as soundless as the fall of tender leaves, and her garments made no more rustle than the unfolding of a flower. She threw one of the red roses at David, and wafted the judge a kiss. Once or twice she turned to speak to William, but forthwith smilingly gave up all thought of it for the time being.

There never was any use in anybody's trying to speak while Miss Penelope was in the height of the excitement of making the morning coffee. An opportunity for a word might possibly occur during the making of the coffee for dinner or supper. Miss Penelope did not consider this function quite so solemn a ceremony at dinner or supper time. Sometimes, at rare intervals, she had been known to allow the coffee for dinner or supper to be made by the cook in the kitchen. But the making of the breakfast coffee was a very different and far more imposing ceremonial. This must always be performed in the presence of the, entire assembled household, by her own hand, on the wide hearth in the great room of Cedar House. To have permitted the cook to make the morning coffee in the kitchen, would have been in Miss Penelope's eyes, to relegate a sacred rite to profane hands in an unconsecrated place. Her own making of the morning coffee had indeed much of the solemnity of a religious ceremony—or would have had, if those who looked on, had been unable to hear, or even slightly dull of hearing. For the sound of Miss Penelope's voice was charming when the listener could not hear what it said. And her dulcet tone always ran through the whole performance like the faint, sweet echo of distant music. But when the listener's ears were keen, and he could hear the things that this kind, caressing voice was saying, the threats that it was uttering!— They were alarming enough to curdle the blood of the little cup-bearers, black, brown, and yellow, who always flew like shuttles back and forth between the big house and the distant kitchen while Miss Penelope was making the breakfast coffee. It required much flying of small dusky legs, to and fro, before the cold water was cold enough, the hot water hot enough, and the fresh egg fresh enough, to satisfy Miss Penelope that the coffee would be all that it should be.

On this particular morning the usual excitement had reached its crisis as Ruth came down the stairs. There was usually a slight lull when the first slender and almost invisible column of steam arose from the long spout of the coffee-pot. That was the most critical moment, and it now being safely past, Miss Penelope hastily sent away all the cup-bearers in a body. But she still hovered anxiously over the pot, gravely considering how many minutes longer it should rest on its trivet over the glowing coals. Hers was a quaint little figure. She wore a queer little black dress, very short and narrow, made after some peculiar fashion of her own, and over it a queerer little cape of the same stuff. Her cap on the other hand was singularly large and white, and the ruffle around her face was very wide and very stiff. The snapping black eyes under the ruffle were never still, and the clawlike little hands were never at rest. David in his idle way used to wonder what she worried about and fidgeted over in her sleep. But it was hard to think of her asleep; it would have been easier to fancy a sleeping weasel. Nevertheless the boy liked Miss Penelope. Ruth and he had learned while they were little children, that there was no unkindness in the snapping of her sharp little black eyes, and that the terrible things she said were as harmless as heat lightning. Even the little cup-bearers, black, brown, and yellow, all knew how kind-hearted she was, and did not mind in the least the most appalling threats uttered by her sweet, soft voice. She always gave them something before she sent them flying back to the cabins. Everybody liked her better than the widow Broadnax who never scolded or meddled and indeed, rarely spoke at all to any one upon any subject. For the household had long since come to understand that this lady, like many another of her kind, was silent mainly because she had nothing to say; and that she never found fault, simply because she did not care. Indifference like hers often passes for amiability; and that sort of motionless silence conceals a vacuum quite as often as it covers a deep. Only one thing ever fully aroused the widow Broadnax; and this was to see her half-sister taking authority in her own brother's house. And indeed, that were enough to rouse the veriest mollusk of a woman. In the case of the widow Broadnax this natural feeling was not at all affected by the fact that she was too indolent to make the exertion to claim and fill her rightful place as mistress of the house. It did not matter in the least that she lay and slept like a sloth while poor little Miss Penelope was up and working like a beaver. No woman's claims ever have anything to do with her deserts; perhaps no man's ever have either; perhaps all who claim most deserve least. At all events, it was perfectly natural that the widow Broadnax should feel as truly and deeply aggrieved at her half-sister's ruling her own brother's house, as if she, herself, had been the most energetic and capable of housekeepers.

On that morning her dull eyes kept an unwavering, unwinking watch over the coffee making; as they always did over every encroachment upon her rights. Her heavy eyelids were only partially lifted, yet not a movement of Miss Penelope's restless little body, not a gesture of her nervous little hands was allowed to escape. Now that the coffee was nearly ready, Miss Penelope had become rather more composed. She still stood guard over the coffee-pot; she never left it till she carried it to the table with her own hands, but she was lapsing into a sort of spent silence. She merely sighed at intervals with the contented weariness that comes from a sense of duty well done. But her

Nancy Huston Banks

half-sister still eyed her as a fat, motionless spider eyes a buzzing little fly which is ceasing to flutter. Miss Penelope had not observed a large pewter cup resting on the floor near the widow Broadnax's chair. It had been left there by a careless servant, who had used a portion of the mixture of red paint and sour buttermilk with which it was filled, to give the wide hearth its fine daily gloss. Miss Penelope had not observed it because she was always oblivious to everything else while hanging over the coffee-pot. The widow Broadnax had seen the cup at once because it was slightly in the way of her foot; and she was quick enough to notice the least discomfort. But she had not immediately perceived the longed-for opportunity which it gave her. That came like an inspiration a few moments later, when Miss Penelope was off guard for an instant. Her back was turned only long enough for her to go to the table and see if the tray was ready for the coffee-pot, but the widow Broadnax found this plenty of time. With a quickness truly surprising in one of her habitual slowness, she swooped down and seized the cup of buttermilk and paint. In a flash she lifted the lid of the coffee-pot, poured the contents of the cup in the coffee, set the empty cup down in its place, and was back again, resting among the cushions as if she had never stirred, when poor little Miss Penelope, all unsuspecting, returned to her post.

"You really must get up, Sister Molly," that lady said resolutely, renewing an altercation. "I hid the pantry keys under your chair cushions at supper, last night. That's always the safest place. But I forgot to take them out before you sat down. And you must get up—there isn't enough sugar for the coffee."

"Let me," said Ruth, coming forward with a smile, in her pretty, coaxing way.

When the antagonism between the sisters broke into open hostility, it was nearly always she who managed to soothe them and restore a temporary semblance of peace—for beyond that no mortal power could go. She now prevailed upon the widow

Broadnax to rise with her assistance, thus securing the keys, and when that lady was once on her feet she was easier to move, so that Ruth now led her to her place at the breakfast table without further trouble. There was, however, always more or less trouble about the place itself. It was but woman nature to feel it to be very hard for a whole sister to sit at the side of the table while a half sister sat at its head. The judge always did what he could to spare her feelings, and Miss Penelope's at the same time. He was a bachelor, and held women in the half-gallant, half-humorous regard which sets the bachelor apart from the married man, and places him at a disadvantage which he is commonly unaware of. The judge thought he understood the distinctively feminine weaknesses particularly well, and that he made uncommonly large allowance for them, as the bachelor always thinks and never does. And then when the quarrel reached a crisis, and he was entirely at the end of his resources for keeping the peace, he could always threaten to take to the woods, and that usually brought a short truce.

"Ruth, my dear, what's all this about some stranger's bringing you home last night?" he inquired, taking his seat at the foot of the table. "Where were you, William? and what were you doing? You shouldn't have taken Ruth to such a place, or anywhere, if you couldn't take care of her," with unusual severity.

Ruth sprang to William's defence. She said that it was not his fault. They were separated by the crowd. He had done his best, and all that any one could have done.

"I made William take me. He didn't want to do it. And I am not sorry that I went, although I was so much frightened at the time. Without seeing it, no one can ever know what this strange and awful thing is like. No description can possibly describe it," she said, with darkening eyes and rising color.

"A most shocking and improper scene," said William Pressley, as one who weighs his words. "A most shocking and improper scene."

Ruth looked at him wonderingly.

"Shocking—improper!" she faltered, perplexedly. "What a strange way to think of it. To me it was a great, grave, terrible spectacle. The awe of it overwhelmed me, alarmed as I was. Why, it was like seeing the Soul universal—bared and quivering."

William Pressley said nothing more. He never discussed anything. Once he had spoken, the subject seemed to him finally disposed of.

"Great Grief!" cried Miss Penelope in the blankest amazement and the greatest dismay. "For the land's sake!"

As the faithful high-priestess of the coffee-pot she was always the first to taste her own brew. She now set her cup down hastily. Her red, wrinkled little face was a study. The widow Broadnax, whose cup was untouched, sat silent and impassive as usual, regarding her with the same dull, half-open, unwinking gaze.

"What under the sun!" gasped Miss Penelope, still more and more amazed and dismayed, and growing angry as she rallied from the shock.

"Come, come!—if I can't eat breakfast in peace, I'll take to the woods. What's the matter?" exclaimed the judge. "Didn't you get the coffee made to suit you, after all that rumpus? Isn't it good?"

"Good!" shrieked Miss Penelope. "It's poisoned, I do believe! Don't drink it, any of you, if you value your lives!"

"Oh, nonsense!" said the judge. "You are too hard to please, Sister Penelope. And you spoil the rest of us, making the coffee yourself. Never mind—never mind!"

He took a sip and made a wry face, but he hardly ever knew what he was eating, and pushing the cup back, forgot all about it. He was more interested in Ruth's account of the meeting, and asked many questions about her ride home.

"This young doctor must be a fine fellow," he said. "I have been hearing a good deal about him from Father Orin. They are already great friends, it seems. They meet often among the poor and the sick, and work together. I hope, my dear, that you thought to ask him to call. You remembered, didn't you, to tell him that the latch-string of Cedar House always hangs on the outside? I want to thank him and then I should like to know such a man. He is an addition to the community."

"Oh, yes, I thought of that, of course," said Ruth, simply. "I told him I knew you and William would like to thank him. He is coming to-day. I hope, uncle Robert, that you will be here when he does come."

"I shall be here to thank him," said William. "Uncle need take no trouble in the matter. I will do all that is necessary."

A woman must be deeply in love before she likes to hear the note of ownership in a man's voice when speaking of herself. Ruth was not at all in love—in that way—although she did not yet know that she was not. The delicate roses of her cheeks deepened suddenly to the tint of the rich red ones which she held again in her hands. Her blue eyes darkened with revolt, and she gave William a clear, level look, throwing up her head. Then her soft heart smote her, and her gentle spirit reproached her. She believed William Pressley to be a good man, and she was ever ready to feel herself in the wrong. She got up in a timid flurry and went to the door and stood a moment looking out at the sun-lit river. Presently she quietly returned, and shyly pausing behind William's chair, rested her hand on the back of it. There was a timid apology in the gesture. She was thinking only of her own shortcomings. Had she been critical of him or even observant, she would have seen that there was something peculiarly characteristic in the very way that he handled his knife and fork; a curious, satisfied self-consciousness in the very lift of his wrists which seemed to say that this, and no other, was the correct manner of eating, and that he disapproved of everybody else's manner. But she saw nothing of the kind, for hers was not the poor affection that stands ever ready to pick flaws. He did not know that she was near him until the judge spoke to her; and then he sprang to his feet at once. He was much too fine a gentleman to keep his seat while any lady stood. Ruth smilingly motioned him back to his chair, and going round the table, leant over the judge's shoulder. He had been examining a packet of legal papers, and he laid a yellow document before her, spreading it out on the table-cloth.

"You were asking the other day about the buffalo—when they were here, and so on. Now, listen to this old note of hand, dated the fifteenth of October, seventeen hundred and ninety-two, just nineteen years ago. Here it is: 'For value Rec'd, I promise to pay Peter Wilson or his Agent, twenty pounds worth of good market Buffalo Beef free from Boone, to be delivered at Red Banks on the Ohio River, or at aney other place that he or his shall salt beef on the banks of said river, and aney time in the ensuing fawl before this fawl's hunting is over.' There now, my dear! That would seem to prove that there were plenty of buffalo hereabouts not long ago. A hundred dollars in English gold must have bought a large amount of wild meat. If this meant Virginia pounds it was still a great deal. And the hunter who drew this note must have known how he was going to pay it."

"Rachel Robards says there were lots of buffalo when she came," said Miss Penelope, who was gradually recovering from the shock of tasting the coffee, and now prudently thought best to say no more about the matter. "I always call her Rachel Robards, because I knew her so well by that name. I am not a-disputing her marriage with General Jackson. If she wasn't married to him when she first thought she was, she is now, hard and fast enough. I have got nothing to say about that one way or another. As a single woman, it don't become me to be a-talking about such matters. But married or not married, I have always stood up for Rachel Robards. Lewis Robards would have picked a fuss with the Angel Gabriel, let alone a fire-eater like Andrew Jackson. Give the devil his due. But all the same, if Andrew Jackson does try to chastise Peter Cartwright for what he said last night, there's a-going to be trouble. Now mark my word! I know as well, and better than any of you, that Peter is only a boy. Many's the time that I've seen his mother take off her slipper and turn him across her lap. And she never hit him a lick amiss, either. But that's neither here nor there. His being young don't keep me from seeing that he has surely got the Gift. It don't make any difference that he hasn't cut his wisdom teeth, as they say. What if he hasn't?" demanded Miss Penelope, with the most singular contrast between her mild tone and her fierce words. "What has the cutting of wisdom teeth got to do with preaching, when the preacher has been given the Gift!"

So speaking, she suddenly started up from the table with an exclamation of surprise, and ran to the open door.

"Peter! Oh, Peter Cartwright!" she called. "Wait—stop a minute. To think of your going by right at the very minute that we were a-talking about you!"

She went out under the trees where the square-built, stern-faced, swarthy young preacher had brought his horse to a standstill.

"Now, Peter, you surely ain't a-going up to the court-house to see Andrew Jackson," she said in sudden alarm.

"No, no, not now," said Peter, hurriedly. "I am riding fast to keep an appointment to preach on the other side of the river."

"But you can stop long enough to eat breakfast. I lay you haven't had a bite this blessed day."

Peter shook his head, gathering up the reins.

"And ten to one that you haven't got a cent of money!" Miss Penelope accused him.

Peter's grim young face relaxed in a faint smile. He put his hand in his pocket and drew out two small pieces of silver.

"Ah, ha, I knew it!" exulted Miss Penelope. "Now do wait just one minute till I run in the house and get you some money."

"No, no, there isn't time. I'll miss my appointment to preach. I will get along somehow. Thank you—good-by."

Miss Penelope, reaching up, seized the bridle-reins and held on by main force with one hand while she rummaged in her out pocket with the other.

"There!—here are three bits—every cent I've got with me," she said indignantly, shoving it in his hand. "Well, Peter Cartwright, if your mother could know—"

But the young backwoodsman, whose fame was already filling the wilderness, and was to fill the whole Christian world, now pressed on riding fast, and was soon beyond her kind scolding.

"Well, 'pon my word! Did anybody ever see the like of that!" she cried, seeing that Ruth had followed her to the door. "That boy don't know half the time whether he has had anything to eat or not. And it's just exactly the same to him when he's got money and when he hasn't."

The girl did not hear what Miss Penelope said. Her heart was responding, as it always did, to everything great or heroic, and she looked after this boy preacher with newly opened eyes. She suddenly saw as by a flash of white light, that he and the other pioneer men of God—these soldiers of the cross who were bearing it through the trackless wilderness—were of the greatest. Her dim eyes followed the young man—this brave bearer of the awful burden of the divine mission—watching him press on to the river. She thought of the many rivers that he must swim, the forests that he must thread, the savages that he must contend against, the wild beasts that he must conquer, the plague that he must defy, the shelterless nights that he must sleep under the trees—freezing, starving, struggling through winter's cold and summer's heat, and all for the love of God and the good of mankind.

VIII

THE LOG TEMPLE OF JUSTICE

Most of those dauntless soldiers, who first bore the cross through the wilderness were as ready to fight as to pray—as they had to be. No power of earth or evil which he had been able to combat could have turned young Peter Cartwright that day or have held him back. Pressing on without rest or food, he was in time to preach. When this duty was done, he returned over the Shawnee Crossing and rode straight to the court-house. To go there was in his eyes the next service due the Word.

The court-house was a single large, low room built of rough logs, and standing in the depths of the primeval forest. Great trees arched their branches over its roof and the immemorial "Oh, yes, oh, yes, oh, yes," went up through their heavy dark tops. It must have been strange thus to hear this formal summons before the bar of human justice, strange indeed to see the precise motion of man's law in so wild a spot. Roundabout there still stretched the wilderness which is subject only to nature's law—the one immutable law which takes no heed of justice or mercy; which recks neither man's needs nor his deserts.

The court-house in the wilderness stood quite alone, with no other building near. There was not even a fence round it, nor so much as a hitching-post in front of the rude door which was rarely closed. Those who came—the judge, the jury, the lawyers, the clients, the spectators—all hitched their horses to the swinging limbs of the trees. The sole sign of man's handiwork, beyond the log walls of the court-house itself, was a crude attempt at bridge-building. A creek ran between the court-house and the home of Judge Knox, who was the judge of the court, and over this a few rough boards had been loosely laid across two rotting logs. The structure being both weak and unsteady, it was the judge's habit to dismount on coming to the bridge and to cross it on foot, leading his horse by the bridle. It was then but a stone's throw to the court-house, and as he was heavy, clumsy, and an awkward rider, he did not mount again, but walked on till he came to the spot where he always stopped to tie the bridle to the same limb. And there he invariably tied it in his absent-minded way, without ever thinking of looking round to see if the horse was tied with the bridle. Sometimes he was and again he was not, for this was as that sagacious and dignified animal himself thought best. He commonly made up his mind upon this point when they got to the bridge, where he could tell easily enough by the judge's gait in crossing over, whether or not it would be advisable to follow. If the horse then saw fit to turn back and go home, as a hint to the family to send for the judge at the proper time, he never hesitated to pull his head out of the old bridle which he could do very easily. So that the judge sometimes went on and tied the empty bridle in the usual place, never knowing the difference; while his horse calmly turned round and soberly walked back to the stable. Seeing him thus pass the windows, the good people of Cedar House sighed a little, and shook their heads, but they nevertheless always knew exactly what to do.

On this late October day, however, the horse followed the judge without demur, assured by his own observation that all was right. The judge, honest, simple soul, rarely failed to turn over a new leaf and make a fresh start on the morning after the meeting of the grand jury, which gravely and respectfully found an indictment against him almost as regularly at it met. He had already assessed and—gravely ordering it written up— paid his own fine on this occasion without a murmur, as he always did, and he was now quite sober and ready to resume his place on the bench. He had held it for a long time to the public satisfaction; and he continued to hold it for many years afterward with honor, ability, and distinction, notwithstanding these occasional lapses. His one weakness was of course well known but his profound knowledge of the law, and his unimpeachable integrity were still better known. It was said of him that he never had anything to say which could not be shouted out from the court-house door. And these qualities were sorely needed on the bench of the wilderness, more sorely needed at this time than ever before or since.

The whole country had lately been overrun by open and defiant lawlessness. It was fast coming to be known far and wide as "Rogue's Harbor." It had already become the recognized refuge and hiding-place of the outcasts from the older states. The breakers of all laws human and divine,—the makers of counterfeit money, the forgers of land titles, the stealers of horses, robbers, murderers, thieves and criminals of every sort and condition, the fine gentleman and the ruffian, the duelist and the assassin—all these were now flocking to Rogue's Harbor. Once there, they were not long content merely to find a hiding place from the wrath of broken law and outraged civilization. They were soon seeking and finding opportunity to commit other and worse offences. It was no longer a secret that regular stations of outlawry were firmly established between Natchez on the one side and Duff's Fort, on the other. The most dreaded of these were known to be within the new state's border along the line of the Wilderness Road, although the law had not been able to lay its hand upon them. And thus was southern Kentucky now bound, blinded and helpless, in a long, strong, bloody chain of crime.

It was knowing this and feeling his own responsibility and powerlessness that made the judge's good-humored face stern on that October morning. It was this which made his absent-minded eyes clear and keen as he drew near the court-house. He had come earlier than usual but others, equally anxious, were there before him. And then the court-house was in a way the mart of the whole region, especially for the sale of horses. Rough-looking men with the marks of the stable and the race-track upon them, were riding the best quarter nags up and down the forest path and pointing out the delicate leg, the well-proportioned head, and the elegant form, which made the traits of the first race-horses in Kentucky. Foremost among these first men of the turf was Tommy Dye, scanning the quarter nags with a trained eye. As soon as the judge saw him, he knew that General Jackson was not far away, for wherever the general went, there also was to be found his faithful henchman, Tommy Dye. It was he who arranged the cockfights in which the general delighted, declaring a game cock to be the bravest thing alive. It was he who was always trying to find for him a race-horse which could beat Captain Haynie's Maria. This famous racer had beaten the general's Decatur in that year's sweepstakes, and he had sworn by his strongest oath that he would find a horse to beat her if there was one in the world that could do it. But Tommy Dye and other eager, tireless agents of the general had already searched far and wide. They had gone over all the horse-raising states with a drag-net, they had sent as far as other countries. And no horse which even promised to beat Maria had yet been found, so that the general's defeat was still rankling bitterly, for it was the bitterest that he had ever met or ever was to meet. He did not feel his defeat in the first race for the Presidency nearly so deeply and keenly as this; and then that was afterward retrieved by a most brilliant victory. But, as a friend once said of him— although he went on achieving great victories of many kinds, overcoming powerful enemies, conquering the Indians, subduing the lawless, defying the Spanish and the French, vanquishing the British and slaying single-handed the Dragon of the Bank—he could never find a horse to beat Maria.

But he was still trying everywhere and under all circumstances however unpromising. On that day he cast anxious glances through the open door of the log court-house at the horses which Tommy Dye, in a forlorn hope, was having paraded up and down the forest path. He turned away with a sigh, and went on talking to the United States Attorney for Kentucky at whose request he had come to the court-house that day. He had done for his own territory in a lesser degree, the identical thing which Joseph Hamilton Daviess was desperately striving to do for this country; and he had consented to give him the benefit of his own experience, and to advise him as to ways and means. These were always strenuous with Andrew Jackson, and Joe Daviess himself was not a man of half measures. In mind and body he was quite as powerful as the man to whom he now listened with such profound deference. He was also a handsomer man and younger. He was fully as tall, too, with as lordly a bearing; the most marked contrast in their appearance being in their dress. General Jackson wore broadcloth of the cut seen in all his older portraits; Joe Daviess wore buckskin breeches and a hunting shirt belted at the waist, both richly fringed on the leg and sleeve. The suit was the same that he had worn when he rode over the Alleghanies to Washington, to plead the historic case before the Supreme Court. But the rudest garb could never make him seem other than the courtly gentleman that he was. He was a scholar moreover, and a writer of books. A great mind, and ever eager to learn, he now stood listening to General Jackson with the humility of true greatness. He bowed to the judge, seeing him enter, but he did not move or cease to listen. His grave, intent face brightened suddenly as if a light had passed over it, when he saw Father Orin's merry, ruddy countenance look in at the open door. He and the priest were close friends, although they held widely different faiths, and argued fiercely over their differences of opinion whenever they met—and had time—and notwithstanding that neither ever yielded to the other so much as a single hair's breadth.

Father Orin now came straight toward him, merely nodding and smiling at those whom he passed, and reaching Joe Daviess' side, he coolly ran his hand deep down in his friend's pocket, precisely as if it had been his own. The attorney-general made believe to strike out backward with his left hand—his right being full of papers. But he laughed, and he did not turn his head to see how much money the priest had taken and was calmly transferring to his own pocket. And then, chuckling and nodding his gray head, Father Orin quietly made his way round the court room, keeping close to the wall, and taking care to pass behind the jury which sat on a bench of boards laid across two logs. He was now making his way to the little platform of logs on which the judge was sitting. The judge saw him coming and hastily shook his head, knowing from long experience what he was coming for. But Father Orin only chuckled more merrily and drew nearer. When he put out his hand the judge surrendered, knowing how useless it would be to resist while a few Spanish dollars or even a few bits of cut money were left in his wallet, or there was want in the wilderness which the priest's persistence could relieve. But his left eyebrow went up very high in a very acute angle, as he leant far over to one side and ran his hand into the depths of his breeches pocket.

"There!" he said, handing over what he had. "I am glad I haven't got any more. Hereafter, when I see you coming, I'm going to take to the woods. Much or little, you always get all there is," he said, ostentatiously buttoning the flap over his empty pocket. "Oh, by the way, Father, somebody wants you over yonder in that corner. Those men, standing there, asked me just now if I knew where you were. They have got into some sort of a snarl, and they want you to straighten it out."

"Very well, I will go and see," said the priest, simply, being used to all sorts of calls, temporal as well as spiritual.

The two men had already seen him, and were standing to receive him when he came up. One of them was a member of his own church and known to him as a man of large affairs. The other, a lawyer and a Protestant, he had a much slighter acquaintance with. It was the lawyer who spoke after both had greeted him warmly, as if they felt his appearance to be a relief.

"We have been hoping you might come. We are in trouble and think you are the man to help us set matters right," said the lawyer.

"What is it?" laughed Father Orin. "I don't know anything about law."

The lawyer laughed too. "Well, you see, Father, it isn't law exactly. That is, not the kind of law that I know. That's just where you come in. It's this way. My client here has won a suit. He was bound to win it and I told him so before it came to trial. The law was clear enough. But you see, Father, law isn't always justice. You can keep within the law and do mighty mean things. And my client here doesn't want to do anything that isn't right. He, as you know, is a clean, straight man. He has scruples about the rights that this decision gives him. It's a knotty question. The other man thinks that he is being cheated, and my client isn't quite sure himself. I didn't know what to advise in such a case. I could tell him what the law of the land and the court—of this court—was, and I have told him. But I couldn't tell him anything about the law of that other land or that Higher Court. I don't know any more about those than you know about my laws and my court. And so we have decided to ask you, to leave the whole dispute to you, and the other man has agreed to let you decide it. He is a Protestant, as I am, but that has nothing to do with this business. We are all perfectly willing to leave it to you; we will all abide by your decision without another word."

Father Orin hesitated. "I don't know that I can see any more clearly than the rest of you. Well, call the other man," he then said. "We can try to find out what is right, anyway. We can't go far wrong if we do our best to treat the other man as we should like him to treat us. Come over here where we will be more to ourselves, and fetch the other man."

The judge was too busy to notice the consultation, but after a while he saw the four men leaving the court room together, with quiet, smiling faces. They all stopped for a moment in the doorway to allow Father Orin to shake hands with Peter Cartwright. The young preacher had been delayed on his way, and was just now entering the court-house. He did not smile when the priest said something which made the others laugh.

His square jaw was grimly set, and his fiery black eyes looked over the heads of the crowd at the tall figure of General Jackson which towered above every one else in the court room, with the exception of the attorney-general. These two great lawyers still stood absorbed in low-toned conversation. But the young preacher had no eyes for Joe Daviess nor for any one except Andrew Jackson. As soon as he could free his hand from Father Orin's clasp he entered the court room and went straight up to General Jackson and stood still in front of him, looking at him. Both the gentlemen turned in surprise at the young backwoodsman's abrupt approach. Both were much older and taller than he, and very different altogether from this square-built, rough-mannered youth. But they may have felt the power that was his as well as theirs, for neither gave a sign of the impatience that both were quick to feel and almost as quick to show. Peter Cartwright was gazing steadily up into General Jackson's eagle eyes—which few could face, which turned many a stout heart from a firm purpose—without swerving for an instant from what he meant to do.

"This is General Jackson, I believe," he said.

Andrew Jackson bent his haughty head. His gaze was now enough to make the bravest flinch. But the young preacher went on without the slightest flinching.

"I have been told, sir, that you wanted to see me. I am Peter Cartwright. I understand that you intend to chastise me for what I said at the camp-meeting. Well, here I am."

Andrew Jackson stared at him silently for a moment, as if he did not get the drift of the words. And then he suddenly burst into a great roar.

"The man who told you that was an infernal fool! I did say that I wanted to see you—to meet you. But I said so because I desired the honor of knowing you, sir. I wanted to shake the hand of a man like you. Will you give it to me now, sir? I shall take it as an honor. I am proud to know a man who is ready to do his duty in spite of anybody on God's earth—as a preacher should be. A minister of Jesus Christ should love everybody, and fear no mortal man. Give me your hand again, sir. By the eternal, if I had a few officers like you, and a well-drilled army, I could take old England!"

With the meeting of the two men's hands a shout rang out from the crowd now pressing in at the door. Shout followed shout, till the outcry sounded far through the forest. It reached the ears of Philip Alston and William Pressley, who were riding slowly toward the court-house. They spurred their horses forward, wondering what could be the cause of the unusual noise and excitement. When they had reached the court-house and learned what the shouting meant, Philip Alston smiled in approval.

"Very fine, very patriotic," he said.

But his real attention was not for the crowd; he cared nothing for its cries. He was looking at Joe Daviess and Andrew Jackson, the two famous attorneys, who were again absorbed in grave, low-toned consultation.

"Do you happen to know, William, what these distinguished gentlemen are discussing with such interest and gravity? It must be something of importance. But of course you know, my dear boy. You needn't tell me if it is any matter of state or any sort of a secret. I asked without thinking. Pardon me," said Philip Alston.

He spoke in a low tone of gentle indifference. There was nothing to indicate that he felt any special interest, but William Pressley answered the question at once, and without reserve. Nothing pleased that young man more than a chance to display his own first knowledge of political affairs, either local, state, or national. A single word of politics never failed to fire his ambition, to light that one spark in his cold eyes. And Philip Alston knew how to strike the flint that lit this spark, as he knew how to do almost anything that he wished to do. So that William now told him what it was that these two powerful guardians of the public peace and safety had met to discuss. He also told him everything that the judge had said of his own determination to do his utmost to aid Joe Daviess in carrying out the plans which were to be laid that day. Philip Alston listened in silence, with his eyes on General Jackson and Kentucky's attorney-general; looking first at the one and then at the other, admiring and appreciating both. He had a sincere, although purely intellectual admiration for any real greatness. Thus gazing at the two men he saw how great was the responsibility resting on them, and how ably and fearlessly they were meeting it. He realized clearly that these two grave, honest, earnest, fearless thinkers must find help for the whole country solely in the might of their own minds and in the strength of their own hands. He knew that no aid ever had been given, or ever would be given, by the government as none could know better than themselves. All this and much more came to Philip Alston, as he stood looking at Andrew Jackson and Joe Daviess while listening to William Pressley. Through his whole life this had been his attitude. He had always looked one way and rowed another, like the boatman in The Pilgrim's Progress.

"And doubtless you too are giving valuable assistance," he said, turning his inscrutable gaze on William Pressley, and speaking in the tone of deference which often covered his contempt. "You will, however, be in a position to make your services far more valuable and much more widely recognized, should the attorney-general resign. There can be no doubt of your succeeding him. No one else stands so close to the place. You shall have it without fail if any influence can aid you. And then, when things are as we wish them to be in this vicinity, we will send you to Congress to look after our larger interests. But in order to do this, we must both keep a keen lookout beforehand—there must be no mistakes. It might be well for you to meet me to-morrow at Anvil Rock. I shall pass there at twelve o'clock on my way to Duff's Fort. You can then tell me the plans which these able gentlemen are now making. You will learn them from your uncle. Take care to remember the smallest detail. Bear in mind, my dear boy, that you will soon have this whole responsibility on your own shoulders. You are now in excellent training for it. Everything that passes between these brilliant lawyers must be of personal value to you in the discharge of your future duties, and to me, also, in order that I may serve you."

William's chest swelled out with pride, and he held his head higher in conscious rectitude. He had not a doubt of his ability to fill the place, nor thought of doubting that he was doing what was right and wise in being perfectly candid with Philip Alston. He thought it most likely that he could secure the appointment without that gentleman's influence. He was quite sure that he would not require any one's assistance in filling it. Still, he was willing to pay all proper deference to an old friend, and to the foster-father of the girl who was to be his wife. These thoughts were an open book which Philip Alston read with another queer smile, while thanking him for the promise to come to Anvil Rock.

"I will leave you now," Philip Alston said. "I have business to-day, also, at Duff's Fort. And you, left alone, will be free to join your uncle and the distinguished gentlemen who are working with him."

The two great lawyers had not seen Philip Alston up to the moment that he turned to leave the court-house, when General Jackson's eagle eye fell upon him.

"Why, there's Philip Alston now!" he exclaimed in an undertone and with a frown. "The splendid audacity of the magnificent rascal! Think of his coming here—right under our noses—to-day, too, of all days! And he knows perfectly well that we know him to be the leader, the originator, the head and the brains of all this villany!"

"Yes. But how are we going to prove it?" asked the attorney-general. "Believing a thing and proving it are two different things. If I could only once get my hand on a particle of evidence.—Do you suppose he could have known what we were talking about?" with sudden uneasiness. "He is intelligent enough to guess, without hearing a word. It is scarcely possible that Judge Knox could have been so thoughtless as to speak of our plans to his nephew—that solemn, pompous young fool who was with Alston. Surely, even Robert Knox couldn't have been so indiscreet in a matter of life and death, such as this!"

"Not when he was sober; and he hasn't been drinking to-day. As for yesterday—that is another matter," said General Jackson. "Robert Knox always means to do exactly what is right, but what a man means is sometimes very different from what he does, especially when he doesn't know what he is doing."

IX

PAUL'S FIRST VISIT TO RUTH

None of this strife had yet touched Cedar House. Even the hazy sadness which had dimmed Ruth's bright spirits as she had watched the young preacher ride away, had passed as quickly as mist before the sun. For it is one of the mercies that happy youth never sees life's struggle quite clearly, and that it is soon allowed to forget the fleeting glimpses which may cloud its happiness for an instant.

Her thoughts were now solely of the young doctor's coming. He had not named the hour; the epidemic made him uncertain of his own time. But he had said that he would come during the day, so that it was necessary to be ready to receive him at any moment. And there were many pleasant things to do in preparation for his coming. More roses were to be gathered, and other flowers also, were blooming gayly among the sober vegetables as if it were mid-summer. So that the first thing Ruth did was to strip the garden, with David to help her and no one to hinder.

The judge and William had gone away from the house as soon as breakfast was over, saying they would try to return in time to see the visitor. Miss Penelope was busy in seeing that the coffee-pot was washed with hot water and rinsed with cold, and scoured inside and out till it shone like burnished silver. The widow Broadnax, too, was as busy as she ever was, sitting in her usual place in the chimney-corner, looking like some large, clumsily graven image in dark stone, and watching her half-sister's every movement without winking or turning her head. So that Ruth and David were left to follow their own fanciful devices, free to put flowers everywhere. They wrought out their fancies to the fullest and the more fantastic, as the artistic instinct rarely fails to do in its first freedom. When they were done, the great room of Cedar House was an oddly charming sight, worth going far to see. Never before had it been so wonderful, strange, and beautiful. It had now become an enchanted bower of mingled bloom and fragrance, shadowed within yet open to the sun-lit day and the flashing river.

"There!" cried Ruth, looking round, with her head on one side. "There isn't one forgotten spot for another flower. Now, I must run and dress. And you must wait here till I come back, David, dear, for the doctor may arrive at any moment, and somebody should be ready to welcome him. Why! aunt Molly has actually followed aunt Penelope clear to the kitchen, so that there is no one left but you. Don't go till I come back."

She went up the broad, dark stairs, turning on almost every step to look down over the room and drink in the beauty and sweetness. David, also, drank it in still more eagerly, taking deep intoxicating draughts, as the thirsty take cool, sparkling wine. He then sat quietly looking about and waiting. His book was in his pocket, as it nearly always was when not in his hand. But he had grown shy of reading "The Famous History of Montilion—Knight of the Oracle, Son to the true Mirror of Princes, the most Renowned Pericles, showing his Strange Birth, Unfortunate Love, Perilous Adventures in Arms: and how he came to the Knowledge of his Parents, interlaced with a Variety of Pleasant and Delightful Discourse," since Ruth had laughed at it, and had laid the blame for his weakness upon the romance. And then his craving for the romantic and beautiful was satisfied for the moment by gazing about this big, strange, shadowy, embowered room. Moreover, Ruth came back very soon. When beauty is young, fresh, natural, and very, very great, it does not need much time for its

Nancy Huston Banks

adornment. Ruth's toilet was like a bird's. A quick dip in pure, cold water—a flutter of soft garments as the radiant wings cast off the crystal drops—and she was ready to meet the full glory of the sunlight. When she thus came smiling down the stairs that day, with the dew of life's morning fresh upon her, David turned from the flowers.

"Yes, indeed! Isn't it a lovely frock!" she cried, running her hand lightly over the big, puffy, short sleeve. "It is one of the last uncle Philip had made in New Orleans, and fetched up the river. You might draw this muslin through my smallest ring. See this dear little girdle—way up here right under my arms— and so delicately worked in these pale blue forget-me-nots, that look as if they were just in bloom. See!"—lifting the gauzy skirt as a child lifts its apron—"Here is a border of the forget-me-nots all around the bottom. But you are such a goose that you don't know how pretty it is unless I tell you," pretending to shake him, with trills of happy laughter. "All the same, you shall look at the slippers, too! You shall see that the kid is as blue as the forget-me-nots,—whether you want to or not!" drawing back the skirt and putting out her foot.

And the boy gazing at her face, forgot his bashfulness far enough to admire the frock and the slippers as much as she thought they deserved. Neither of these children of the wilderness knew how unsuitable her dress was, that it had never been intended for wearing in the morning anywhere, or for the forest at any time. Ruth had worn only the daintiest and finest of garments all her life, without any regard for suitableness. From her babyhood to this day of her girlhood, it had been Philip Alston's pride and happiness to dress her as the proudest and richest father might dress his daughter, in the midst of the highest civilization. Ruth knew nothing else, and those who knew her would scarcely have known her, seeing her otherwise. It was only the few strangers stopping at Cedar House, on their way over the Wilderness Road, who gazed at Ruth in wondering amazement. Naturally enough, those who had never seen her before could not at first believe the evidence of their own dazzled eyes. To them this radiant young creature in her rich, delicate raiment could not seem real at first; she was too lovely, too like an enchanting vision born of the dim green shadows of the forest, a bewitching dryad, an exquisite sprite.

Some such thoughts as these crossed the mind of Paul Colbert as he looked at her through the open door. He had ridden up unheard, had dismounted, tying his horse to a tree, and had then stood for several minutes without being seen by Ruth or David. When he spoke, they thought that he had just arrived. Ruth went forward to welcome him with the ease and grace that marked everything she did. Nature had given her a pretty, gentle dignity, and Philip Alston's cultured example had polished her manner. She now did all the graceful offices of the hostess, quietly and simply. She said how sorry she was that neither her uncle nor her cousin was at home. They wished, she said, to be there when he came, so that they might try to thank him for his kindness to her. But one or the other would return very soon; both had hoped to do so before his arrival.

"It is early for a visit," Paul Colbert said, in a tone of apology; "but I couldn't come at all to-day, unless I stopped now in passing."

"Oh, no!" said Ruth, quickly. "It isn't very early."

"And then I thought you might like to see this," he said.

Rising, he stepped to her side, and gave her a sheet of paper torn from his note-book and covered with writing. He did not return to the chair which he had arisen from, but took another much nearer her own.

"Poetry!" she said. "Is it something that you have written?"

He smiled. "I have merely copied it. I saw the poem for the first time an hour or so ago at Mr. Audubon's. It is new and has never been printed. It was written by the young English poet, John Keats, to his brother George Keats, who is a partner

Nancy Huston Banks

of Mr. Audubon in the mill on the river. Mr. Keats and his wife are here now, the guests of Mr. Audubon. The poem came in a letter which has just been received. I have copied a part of it, and a few words from the letter, also. Mr. George Keats was kind enough to allow me, and I thought you would like to see them. I hadn't time to copy the entire poem, though it isn't very long."

"It was very kind," said Ruth. "I am so glad to see it. May I read it now? This is what the letter says," reading it aloud, so that David also might hear. "If I had a prayer to make for any great good ... it should be that one of your children should be the first American poet?"

"The first English hand across the sea!" said Paul Colbert.

Ruth read on from this letter of John Keats to his brother: "I have a mind to make a prophecy. They say that prophecies work out their own fulfilment." And then she read as much of "A Prophecy" as the doctor had copied.

*   *   *   *   *

"Though, the rushes that will make
Its cradle are by the lake—
Though the linen that will be
Its swathe is on the cotton tree—
Though the woollen that will keep
It warm is on the silly sheep—
Listen, starlight, listen, listen,
Glisten, glisten, glisten, glisten,
And hear my lullaby!
Child, I see thee! Child, I've found thee!
Midst the quiet all around thee!
Child, I see thee! Child, I spy thee!
And thy mother sweet is nigh thee.
Child, I know thee! Child no more,
But a poet ever-more!
See, see, the lyre, the lyre!

In a flame of fire
Upon the little cradle's top
Flaring, flaring, flaring,
Past the eyesight's bearing.
Wake it from its sleep,
And see if it can keep
Its eyes upon the blaze—
Amaze, amaze!
It stares, it stares, it stares,
It dares what none dares!
It lifts its little hand into the flame
Unharmed and on the strings
Paddles a little tune and sings,
With dumb endeavor sweetly—
Bard thou art completely;
Little child,
O' the western wild...."

Ruth looked at Paul with shining eyes. "I thank you again for thinking that I would like this," she said.

"A little chap whom I saw last night made me feel like making a prophecy that he would be the first Kentucky astronomer," said Paul, with a smile. "He was hardly more than a baby, not much over two years old—a toddling curly-head. Yet there he stood by the roadside, looking up at the heavens, as solemn as you please. And he said that 'man couldn't make moons.' I didn't hear him say this, but his brother repeated what he said."

"Yes, I know. You mean' little Ormsby MacKnight Mitchel. His people live near here, over on Highland Creek. His father came there from Virginia. He intended to bore for salt water, meaning to make salt. But he found more interest in the wild multiflora roses that bloom all around the Lick, and the bones of unknown animals buried fifty feet beneath the surface of the earth—though the bones were not found just there—but farther off at another Lick."

"Then Master Ormsby MacKnight Mitchel is the true son of his father," smiled Paul Colbert. "Neither seems commonplace enough to be content with what everyday people find between heaven and earth."

He said this idly, as we all speak to one another when casting about for mutual interests before really knowing each other. Thus the talk drifted for a few moments, with a shy word now and then from David. And presently a chance reference to the epidemic brought a new light into the doctor's eyes, and a new earnestness into his voice.

"The fathers and mothers of the country are much alarmed for their children," he said. "But there is far more need to be alarmed for themselves. The Cold Plague attacks the strong rather than the weak. But all the people, young and old, everywhere through the wilderness, are almost frantic with terror. They fear infection from every newcomer. There was a panic throughout this vicinity a few days ago, over the landing of a flatboat, and the coming ashore of the unfortunates who were on it. They were in a most pitiful plight. I hope never to see a sadder sight than that poverty-stricken little family. But they were not suffering from any disease more contagious than want; they were only cold, wet, tired, hungry, and disheartened. The poor mother was sitting on the damp sand near the water's edge, with her little ones around her, when I found them. They were merely stopping to rest on their way from another portion of the state, to the wild country on the other side of the river."

"We saw them, too, poor things," said Ruth, quickly, with pity in her soft eyes. "Father Orin and Toby came by to tell us, and David and I went at once to do what we could. I can't forget how the mother looked. She was young, but had such a sad, haggard face, with such a prominent forehead, and such steady gray eyes. She held a strange looking little child on her lap. She said that her name was Nancy Lincoln, and she called the baby 'Abe.' He couldn't have been more than two years of age, but he looked up at Father Orin, and from his face to ours, like some troubled little old man."

"Yes, Father Orin and Toby were first to the rescue, as they always are. I can't imagine when those two sleep, and I am sure they never rest when awake."

And then, seeing her interest and sympathy, he went on to tell of three little ones, orphaned by the plague, and left alone and utterly helpless, in a cabin on the Wilderness Road. As he spoke, he remembered with a pang of self-reproach, that Father Orin was with them now and waiting for him. He rose suddenly, saying that he must go, but a slight noise at the door caused him to pause and turn. It was William Pressley coming in, and Ruth went forward to meet him, and introduced him to the doctor, who sat down again for a few moments. The two young men then talked with one another as strangers do, of the current topics of the day and the country, speaking mostly of the Shawnee danger—the one subject then most earnestly and universally discussed throughout the wilderness. The nearest approach to a personal tone was in William Pressley's formal expression of thanks. Paul Colbert put these aside as formally as they were offered, and in a moment more he got up to take leave. Yet in that brief space the two men had begun to dislike each other.

This was natural enough on the part of William Pressley. It is indeed the first instinct of his kind toward any equal or superior. When a man's or a woman's vanity is so great that it instinctively and instantly levies on all within reach—demanding incense—nothing can be so dislikeful as a bearing which refuses to swing the censer. From its very nature it must instantly resent any such conscious or unconscious claim to equality, to say nothing of superiority. Those so afflicted must of necessity like only their inferiors and must have only inferiors for friends, if they have any friends at all. So that this is maybe the real reason why many reasonably good and perfectly sincere men and women go almost friendless through useful and blameless lives. And this was William Pressley's natural feeling toward Paul Colbert. The honest, sincere young lawyer could have forgiven the honest, sincere young doctor almost any real sin or weakness and have liked him well enough; but he could not forgive the polite indifference of his manner toward himself, or his looking over his head at Ruth, or turning from him to speak to David. Least of all could he forgive him for being at that moment the most conspicuous figure in the whole region, on account of his single-handed struggle with the mysterious disease, which, defying the other doctors, had been devastating the new settlements of the wilderness. Nor could the difference in their aims affect this feeling in the least. To a nature like William Pressley's, anything won by another is something taken from himself. Yet the dislike for Paul Colbert, which thus hardened within him, had no taint of jealousy in the ordinary sense of that term. He did not think of Ruth at all in the matter. It did not occur to him to associate her with this stranger, or with any one but himself. It was in keeping with his character for him to be slower than a less vain man to suspect her—or any one whom he knew—of personal preference for another than himself; for vanity of this supreme order has its comforts as well as its torments.

On the part of Paul Colbert, the feeling was wholly different, and largely impersonal. It was merely the dislike that every busy man feels for a new acquaintance which promises no interest, even at the outset. Had he been less busy, and his mind more free, he might perhaps have found some amusement in trying to find out how far this serious young man was mistaken in his high estimate of himself. He thought at a first glance that he was a good deal in error, but he also saw that he was sincere in his conviction; so that the young doctor was tolerantly amused at the lofty air of the young lawyer, without the slightest feeling of real resentment. He made one or two straightforward, friendly efforts to thaw the ice of William Pressley's manner. His own was naturally frank and cordial. He always wished to be liked, which is the natural wish of every truly kind nature. And then, above and beyond this, was the right-minded lover's instinctive desire to secure the good-will of all who are near the one whom he loves; for Paul

Colbert had fallen in love with Ruth, and he knew it, as few do who have fallen in love at first sight. He could, indeed, have told the very instant at which love had come—like a bolt from the blue.

He was therefore more than willing to be friendly with William Pressley, and already seeking a pretext to come again. He now said, turning to Ruth with a smile:

"Since you are fond of poetry, perhaps you will allow me to fetch you a new volume of poems by a young Englishman, Lord Byron. A friend sent it to me from London. He says it is being severely treated by the critics. They say that they never would have believed that any one could have been as idle and as worthless generally, as those 'Hours of Idleness' prove the author to be. But I think you will like the poems, especially one called 'The Tear.' It is said that the poet means to write something about Daniel Boone."

"There should be many tears in that poem," said Ruth, a shadow falling over the brightness of her face. "To think of the poor old hero as he is now makes the heart ache."

"It should make us all ashamed," said Paul Colbert. "He gave us the whole state, and we are not willing to give him back enough of it to rest his failing feet upon, nor a log cabin to shelter his feeble body, worn out in our service. It is the blackest ingratitude. It is a disgrace to the commonwealth."

"Pardon me," said William Pressley, with his cool smile; "but as I look at the matter, there is no one but himself to blame. It is solely the result of his own negligence and ignorance. He did not observe the plain requirement of the law."

"But, William," said Ruth, impulsively, with a brighter color in her cheek, "just think! How could he know—a simple old hunter, just like a little child, only as brave as a lion!" There was a quiver in her voice and a flash in her soft eyes.

"We can but hope that the state will remember what it owes," said the doctor, moving toward the door.

He felt that he had been tempted to linger too long. Father Orin was still waiting for him in the desolate cabin where the Cold Plague had left the three orphans. His conscience smote him for lingering, and yet he could not leave, even now, without speaking again of the poems, and saying that he would fetch the book and leave it the next time he rode by Cedar House.

When he was gone, Ruth looked at William Pressley in silent, troubled perplexity. She was wondering vaguely why she had felt so ashamed—almost as if she had done some shameful thing herself—when he had spoken as he had done before the doctor about Daniel Boone. It must have been plain to the visitor that she did not think as William thought. And yet she flinched again, recalling the doctor's glance at William, and wondered why it should have hurt her, as if it had fallen upon herself. She was not old enough or wise enough to have learned that the mere promise to marry a man makes a sensitive woman begin forthwith, to feel responsible for everything that he says and does; and that this is one of the deep, mysterious sources of the misery and happiness of marriage.

X

FATHER ORIN AND TOBY MEET TOMMY DYE

Under the spur of his conscience the young doctor rode fast. He was not the man to let duty wait even on love, without trying to make amends. But a sharper pang stung him when he reached the desolate cabin in which the Cold Plague had left the orphans.

It seemed to him that Toby, standing by the broken door, gave him a look of reproach. Toby had not failed or been slow in doing his part; Father Orin and he had already done all that they could, though this was piteously little. The one had cut fire-wood from the near-by fallen trees, and the other had drawn it to the cabin door, so that there was a good fire blazing on the earthen hearth. But the rotting, falling logs of the cabin's walls were far apart, the mud which had once made them snug having dropped out; and the chilly, rising wind blew bitterly through the miserable hut. The covers on the bed were few and thin, although Father Orin had spread Toby's blanket over them. The three little white faces lying in a pathetic row on the ragged pillows, lay so still that the doctor was not sure they were alive, till the oldest child, a boy of three, languidly opened his eyes, looked up unseeingly, and wearily closed them again.

There was a tightening in the doctor's throat when he turned away, and he was glad to smile at Father Orin's housekeeping. The priest certainly had left nothing in his power undone, to keep life in the frail little bodies. On the hearth was such food as he had been able to prepare, carefully covered to keep it warm. As the young man's gaze thus wandered sadly about the cabin, his eyes encountered the old man's. The laughter with which he was fighting emotion died on his lips, and their hands met in a close clasp.

"The poor little things!" the young man said. "Ah, Father, it is wild work—this making of a state. The soil of Kentucky should bear a rich harvest. It is being deeply sown in pain and sorrow, and well-watered with tears and blood."

They stood silent for a moment, looking helplessly at the bed and the little white faces.

"What shall we do?" then asked Father Orin. "These children can't stay here through another night. That wind blows right over the bed, and there is no way to keep it out. They could hardly live till morning. And yet they may die on the way if we try to take them to the Sisters at once."

"That is their only chance. We are bound to take the risk. We must do our best to get them to the Sisters as quickly as possible. Women know better than doctors how to take care of babies. What is there to put round them—to wrap them in?"

There were no wrappings, nothing that could be used for the purpose, except the bed covers and Toby's blanket. The men took these and with awkward tenderness covered the helpless, limp little bodies as well as they could. Father Orin then went out of the cabin, and with a nod summoned Toby to do his part. When the priest was seated in the saddle, the doctor turned back to the bed, and lifting one of the three limp little burdens, carried it out and carefully placed it in Father Orin's arms.

"But you can't carry both of the others," said the priest, in sudden perplexity. "And we can't leave one here alone while we take the others and return. Maybe it would be better to take one at a time. I can either stay or go."

"Oh, no, indeed! I can take these two easy enough—one on each arm. They weigh nothing—poor little atoms—and I don't need a hand for the reins. My horse often goes in a run with them thrown over the pommel. He went on a bee-line with them so last night."

With both arms thus filled with the helpless morsels of humanity, he had no trouble in seating himself in the saddle. He laughed a little, thinking what a spectacle they must make; and Father Orin laughed too, with the shamefacedness that the best men feel when they do such gentle things. And then the strange, pathetic journey through the wilderness began.

"Steady, Toby. That's right, old man," said the priest, now and then.

The doctor kept a close, anxious watch over the child in Father Orin's arms, and frequently glanced down at the two little faces lying in the hollow of his own arms. Any one of the three,—or all of them—might cease to breathe at any moment. It seemed to both the anxious men that they were a long time in going to the Sisters' house, although the distance was but a few miles. When the log refuge first came in sight through the trees, they breathed a deep sigh of relief in the same breath. The Sisters, who had been warned, saw them coming, and ran to meet them, and took the babies from their arms. When the little ones had been borne in the house and put to bed, the doctor sat down beside them to see what more might be done. But the priest, without rest or delay, set out on another errand of mercy. Toby, needing no word or hint, at once quickened his pace, knowing full well the difference between this business and that which was just finished, so far as they were responsible.

"You're right, old man. Keep us up to the mark, right up to the mark," chuckled Father Orin. "I'm mighty tired, and I'm afraid I might shirk if you would let me."

As he bent down with a bantering chuckle to pat the horse's inflexible neck, a man's voice suddenly hailed them from the darkening woods lying at their back.

"Hello! Hello! Hold on!" the unseen man shouted.

They turned quickly and stood still, looking in the direction from which the shouting came. A horseman soon appeared under the trees and came galloping after them, and when he had drawn nearer, the priest saw, with some annoyance, that it was Tommy Dye. As he reined up beside them, Toby turned his head slowly and gave the horse precisely the same look that Father Orin gave the rider. Toby wanted to have nothing more to do with a tricky race-horse than Father Orin wished to have to do with a shady adventurer.

Tommy Dye looked at them both with a grin. "I saw you just now—you and the new doctor—a-toting them there youngsters."

Father Orin straightened up, feeling and showing the embarrassment and indignation that every man, lay and clerical alike, feels and shows at being seen by another man acting as a nurse to a child.

"Well, what of it?" he retorted, as naturally as if he had never worn a cassock.

Tommy Dye grinned again, more broadly than before. He took off his hat and rubbed his shock of red hair the wrong way. The humor of the recollection became too much for him, and he roared with laughter. Toby of his own indignant accord now moved to go on, and Father Orin gathered up the reins saying rather shortly that he had urgent business, and must be riding along.

"I say—wait a minute. What makes you in such an all-fired hurry?" Tommy Dye called after them.

Toby stopped reluctantly, and he and Father Orin waited with visible unwillingness, until Tommy Dye came up again and stammeringly began what he had to say. He did not know how to address a priest. He had never before had occasion to speak to a churchman of any denomination. So that he now plunged in without any address at all:

"I say—who pays for them there youngsters, yonder?" he blurted.

Father Orin merely looked at him in silence for a moment, and then gathered up the reins once more.

Tommy Dye saw that there was something amiss, that he had made some mistake, and not knowing what it was, he resorted to the means which he usually employed to set all matters right. He hastily plunged his hand in the outer pocket of his coat, and then dropped the bottle back in its place still more hastily, after another glance at the priest.

"Well, I thought you might like it," he said with a touch of defiance, feeling it necessary to assert himself. "When a man's face is as red as yours, I don't see why a fellow mightn't ask him to take a drink."

Father Orin laughed with ready good humor.

"My face is red, my friend. I can't deny that fact; but the redness comes from a thin skin and rough weather. What is it you want? I haven't time to wait."

"Say, I kinder thought, seeing you and the doctor with them babies just now,"—grinning again at the comical recollection—"that maybe you would let me come into the game. I'd like to take a hand in the deal, if there's room for another player. I'll put up the stakes right now." His hand went into his breeches pocket this time. "Here's the roll I won on the fall races. Put it all up on the game. What's the odds? Come easy, go easy."

He held out the money. "I saw you at the court-house, too," he added sheepishly, as if trying to excuse what he did.

"I beg your pardon, sir," said Father Orin, gravely. "I didn't understand. I've done you great injustice."

"Hey? What did you say?"

"The Sisters would be only too glad to use this money for those children, and for other little ones just as helpless and needy," murmuring something about the use purifying the source. "But I want you to take it to them yourself, and give it to them with your own hands."

"Me! Old Tommy Dye!"

The coarse face actually turned pale under its big freckles. Its dismay was so comical that Father Orin laughed till the woods rang with his hearty, merry voice. Toby turned his head in sober disapproval of such unseemly levity, and Tommy Dye was a good deal miffed.

"'Pears to me you are mighty lively—and most of the time, too," he said, in a tone of offence, tinged with wonder.

"Why not?" said the priest, still chuckling. "Why shouldn't I be lively?"

Tommy Dye hesitated, more puzzled now than angry. "Well, you see, your job has always seemed to me just about the lonesomest there is."

Father Orin began to laugh again, but he was hushed by the soft, sweet pealing of the Angelus through the shadowed forest. The gambler also listened, with a softening change in the recklessness of his face.

"The sound of that bell always makes me feel queer," he stammered. "It sets me to thinking about home, too,—and home folks. I'm blamed if I can see how it is. I never had any home, and if I've got any kin-folks, I don't know where they live. But anyhow, that's the way the ringing of that bell always makes me feel. Say! there's lots of things about your church that come over a fellow like that. Now there the very name of that little house back yonder amongst them trees—Our Lady's Chapel.

That's just it—just to the notch what I mean—there's something kind of homelike in the name itself. And that's the very difference between your church and the other churches. The Protestant church seems real lonesome, like a sort of bachelor's hall. The Catholic church makes you feel at home, because there's always a mother in the house."

"Take care!" exclaimed the priest. "But I am sure you don't mean to be irreverent, my friend. And about your generosity to the orphans. Here, let me give the money back. I am in earnest in asking you to give it to the Sisters with your own hands. When they see you and you see them, you will both understand each other better than if I were to try ever so long and hard to explain."

He looked at Tommy Dye for a moment with a returning smile, but the pity of it all put the humor aside.

"The doctor will be coming along in a moment—ah, there he comes now! I will ask him to go with you to see the Sisters. I am sorry that I cannot turn back with you myself. I should be glad to."

It did not take long to state the case to the doctor, who readily agreed to do what the priest asked. Tommy Dye was by this time so thoroughly cowed by the situation in which he thus found himself that he no longer resisted. There was one uncertain instant when, seeing the Sisters appear in the door, he was undecided whether to run away or go on. But he was afraid to flee, with the Sisters' eyes upon him, and the doctor led him into the house. The ladies had been frightened by the doctor's unexpected and speedy return; but he soon quieted their fears, and made them happy by telling them the reason of his turning back. Sister Teresa, the Lady Superior, keenly touched, quickly turned to Tommy Dye and he handed her the money in awkward haste.

"How good of you! How generous—how noble! Ah, you don't know how much good this will do," she said, with her eyes full of tears. "We thank you with all our hearts for ourselves and for the children."

"Thank *you*,—ma'am," stammered Tommy Dye, scarlet, and almost dumb.

None of the many sins of which he had been suspected had ever made him feel nearly so uncomfortable as he felt now. None of the many sins of which he had been convicted had ever made him look half so guilty as he looked now.

"You mustn't call me 'ma'am,'" said Sister Teresa. "You must call me Sister, and Sister Elizabeth and Sister Angela are your sisters, too. You must always think of us as your real sisters, and the little ones belong to you after this, as much as they do to us. You must always remember that. Will you come into the other room and see them? Or I will fetch—"

But Tommy Dye could not endure any more. He turned with hardly a word, and fled in desperate haste. The Sisters gazed after him in surprise, and with a good deal of alarm, until Paul Colbert told them about him, who and what he was, of his meeting with Father Orin, and the whole story of the money.

"The poor fellow," said Sister Teresa, softly. "We will pray that the gift may bring him some of the good that it will do the children. Yes, we will hereafter remember him, also, in the prayers for our benefactors," turning her gentle, smiling gaze on the young doctor.

And then he reddened almost as suddenly as Tommy Dye had

done, and he likewise was hastening to make his escape when Sister Teresa called him back, to ask if he would not be passing Cedar House on the way home. He said that he would, reddening again. Whereupon the Sister begged as a favor, that he would stop at the door and tell Ruth to come on the next day, if possible, to look at the sewing which Sister Angela was doing for her.

"Sister Angela is a wonderful needle-woman," Sister Teresa could not help adding with modest pride. "She learned to sew and to do the finest embroidery while she was studying in a convent in France. She could earn a great deal of money for the little ones if we were where there were more patrons who wished to have such fine sewing done. But nobody in this wild country ever wants it except Mr. Alston for Ruth."

"Mr. Alston for Ruth," Paul Colbert repeated, wonderingly.

"Oh, yes. He thinks nothing is fine enough for Ruth," said Sister Teresa, simply. "And he pays anything that Sister Angela asks. He never says a word about the price. Sometimes I fear we ask too much. But then, the children need so many things, and we have so few ways of earning money. You won't mind stopping to tell Ruth, doctor? Ask her to come early to-morrow morning, please. And another thing, if it isn't too much trouble. Tell her to bring more of the finest thread lace."

This was the first time that Paul Colbert had heard Philip Alston's name associated with Ruth. It was a shock to hear the names called in the same breath, for he already knew as much of Philip Alston as any one was permitted to know. He was aware of the suspicion which blackened his reputation. He had learned this on first coming to the country. Father Orin, when asked, had told him something of the reasons for the general distrust and fear of the man. But the doctor himself had never seen him, and, naturally enough, thought of him as the usual coarse leader of lawlessness, only more daring and cunning, perhaps, than the rest of his kind. Thus it was that trying to understand only bewildered the young man more and more, so that he was still filled with shocked wonder when he came within sight of Ruth's home.

The day was nearing its close. In the forest bordering the bridle-path, dark shades were noiselessly marshalling beneath the great trees. But the sunset still reddened the river, and the reflected light shone on the windows of Cedar House. He glanced at her chamber window before seeing that she stood on the grass by the front door, giving the swan bits of bread from her fingers while the jealous birds, forgetting to go to roost, watched and scolded from the low branches overhead. But she had seen him a long way off and looked up as he approached.

"Isn't he a bold buccaneer?" she said, with a smile, meaning the swan. "We thought at first that he couldn't be tamed—Mr. Audubon, too, thought he couldn't—and we clipped his wings to keep him from flying away. And now he wouldn't go. See! He is the most daring creature. Why, he will go in the great room before everybody and walk right up to aunt Penelope when she's making the coffee, without turning a feather!"

It was not till he was leaving that Paul remembered the Sister's message which had served him as a pretext for stopping. And he was sorry when he had given it, for a shadow instantly came over the brightness of Ruth's beautiful face. Riding on to his cabin he wondered what could have cast the shadow.

XI

THE DANCE IN THE FOREST

She did not go on the next morning. That day had been chosen for the dance in the forest, one of the two merry-makings dearest to the hearts of those earliest Kentuckians. The May party came first, with its crowning of the queen of love and beauty and its dance round the May-pole; and after that this festival of dancing and feasting under the golden trees.

Both of these were held as regularly as the opening of the spring flowers and the tinting of the autumn leaves. No one ever asked why or when they were first begun; it was never the way of the Kentuckians to ask any questions about anything that they had always been used to. And indeed, had they tried ever so hard, they could hardly have found in their own history the origin of these ancient customs. Those must have been sought much farther back than the coming of those first settlers into the wilderness,—as far back, perhaps, as the oldest traditions of the purest stock of the old English yeomanry from which these people were sprung. For in their veins throbbed the same warm red blood, which, having little to do with the tilling of the soil or the building trade, had everything to do with the fighting of battles and the making of homes. For in their strong simple hearts was the same love of country that bore England's flag to victory, and the same love of the fireside that made peace as welcome as conquest.

And as these old English fighters had danced with their sweethearts on the greensward in the intervals between wars, so these fighters of the wilderness now went on with the dance in the forest just as if there had been no fierce conflict at hand. They might be called to fight to-morrow and they would be ready, but they would dance to-day, just as their forefathers had done. To go elsewhere than to the dance on the morning selected for it was, therefore, not to be thought of by any young person of the neighborhood. Ruth had asked David to take her, explaining that William Pressley could not accompany her quite so early as she wished to go. He had business which would detain him, she explained with a painful blush. And then, when she had said this with a troubled look, she flashed round on the boy, demanding to know why William should not do whatever he thought best.

"William always has a good reason for everything he does, or doesn't do. He is never neglectful of any duty. Never!" with her blue eyes, which were usually like turquoises, flashing into sapphires. "He takes time to think—time to be sure that he is right. He isn't forever rushing into mistakes and being sorry, like you and me!"

In another moment she laughed and coaxed, patting his arm.

"Do be ready, David, dear, and wear your nicest clothes," she said, in her sweetest way. "And no girl there will have a handsomer gallant than mine, than my Knight of the Oracle, my—"

The boy teased but smiling ran away to do her bidding, as he always did. He had no clothes besides the worn suit of homespun which he was then wearing, except one other of buckskin, gayly fringed on the sleeves and on the outer seam of the breeches. This had been his pride till of late. But he now took it down from its peg behind his cabin door and eyed it with new dissatisfaction. Fashions were changing in the wilderness. Gentlemen no longer clothed themselves in the skins of wild beasts, nor even in the coarse homespun. Not many, to be sure, were dressed like Philip Alston; but David had lately seen Mr. Audubon hunting in velvet knee-breeches and white silk stockings, with fine ruffles over his hands. That gentleman had laughed at himself for doing it, but the sight had pleased the boy's taste and gratified his craving for everything refined and beautiful. It humiliated him to have no choice between the shabby homespun and the fantastic buckskin. But he tried to find comfort in thinking that he would have a boughten suit before very long. The judge had given him a calf. The master of Cedar House was always kind when he did not forget, as has already been said, and he was most generous at all times. The calf was now ready for sale to the first passing buyer of cattle. Nevertheless, David sighed as he put on the buckskin suit, wishing, as only the young can wish for what they desire, that he had the boughten suit then to wear to the dance in the forest.

Yet Ruth smiled at him as if she were well pleased with his looks. There were, to be sure, certain tangles in the gay fringes for her deft fingers to untangle. There were, of course, many swift little touches to be given here and there, the caressing touches that no true woman can withhold from the dress of a man whom she is fond of. So that David's buckskin suit suddenly seemed to him just what it should be—as all that a man wears or has or is always does seem, when a woman's caressing touches have convinced him that everything is right. Indeed, David forgot to think any more of his own clothes or of himself. Looking at Ruth he thought only of her.

He did not know what it was that she wore. He did not know that the muslin of her dress had cost an hundred francs the yard. He did not know how charmingly odd the mode of its make was, since Ruth's little hands had planned it out of her own pretty head in enchanting ignorance of the fashion. He knew nothing of the value of the three-cornered kerchief of white lace which tied down her gypsy hat. He did not notice that the flowers on her hat were primroses, or that the long gloves meeting the short sleeves and the slender little slippers peeping from beneath her skirt, were both of the finest primrose kid. He saw only the beauty of her face smiling at him from under the gypsy hat, the sweetness of her red lips, and the charm of her blue eyes. And she seeing only the look that she had seen in every man's eyes ever since she could remember, was not made vain thereby, as a less beautiful girl might have been. She took it all for granted and thought no more about it. Rising on the tips of her toes, she put back an unruly lock of David's hair with a last loving little pat.

"There now! We are all ready," she said, with a happy sigh.

"Yes, the coffee is the first thing on the top of the basket," said Miss Penelope, coming in from the kitchen. "That's it in the biggest bottle. You can have it warmed over the campfire. I shouldn't like to drink warmed-over coffee, myself. But then nobody in this house ever thinks as I do about anything. It isn't my notion of what's right and proper—to say nothing of Christian—to be a-dancing when everybody ought to be a-praying. Not a day passes without something in the way of a warning. Now there is the big hole that they've just found in the earth right over yonder—a hollowness without end or bottom, and as dark as the bottomless pit. That's what it ought to be called, too—instead of the Mammoth Cave. For if that don't show that there is nothing but a dreadful, empty shell left of this awful world, I don't know what any true sign is. But all the same, I know very well that nobody in this house pays any attention to what I say. Howsomever, the works of the light-minded who are a-dancing on the edge of perdition don't make any difference in my plain duty. And I am a-going to do it as near as I can so long as I breathe the breath of life. When my cold, stiff hands are crossed under the coffin-lid, nobody left 'pon top of this mournful earth ever can say that I sat by, like a bump on a log, and never said a word when I saw all these awful calamities a-coming."

Thus voicing these vague alarms in her sweetest tones, Miss Penelope turned nervously and glanced at her half-sister. She was always afraid of her, as very talkative, restless people often are of those who say little and watch a great deal. But the widow Broadnax seemed to be dozing among her cushions, and Miss Penelope felt it quite safe to go on with the softly uttered threats which scattered the small dark servitors, who were still flying about her like a flock of frightened blackbirds, although the basket was packed.

"No," said Miss Penelope, "it don't make any difference in my duty. If folks won't listen to what I am bound to say, that is no fault of mine. My duty is to give warning when I see true signs of what's a-going to happen. For a true sign is as plain as daylight to me. I never had a caul, and I don't lay any claim to second sight. But I know what it means when I hear the dogs a-baying the midnight moon. I know, too, what's a-coming to pass when the death-watch goes thump, thump, thumping in the wall right over my head the whole blessed night. And more than that, I was a-looking for both these true signs of bad luck before I heard 'em. That big black ring round the comet's head that I've seen for a night or two back told me plain enough what to expect. And look at the things that have already happened—all over the country. Nobody in this world of trouble surely ever saw the like. Just look at the twins!"

This was the chance that the widow Broadnax had been waiting and watching for in motionless silence. She seized it as suddenly as a seemingly sleepy cat seizes an unwary mouse.

"I don't see any sign of bad luck in twins, or triplets either, for my part," she said hoarsely and loudly. "They are every one of 'em bound to be whole brothers and sisters. To my mind, it don't make any difference how big a family is so long as it ain't mixed up."

Ruth and David seized the basket, and escaped—laughing and running—carrying it between them.

The spot chosen for this Indian Summer dance in the forest was near Cedar House. It was one of the natural open spaces, of which there were many in the wilderness, and it overlooked the river. High walls of thick green leaves enfolded it upon three sides, and it had a broad level floor of greener sward. It was sun-lit when the shadowed woods were dark. In the spring the greensward was gay with wild flowers; for it was in these open spaces between the trees that Nature displayed her most brilliant floral treasures which would not bloom in the shade. In the fall the leafy walls were more brilliant than the flowery sward, and they now rose toward the azure dome, gorgeously hung with bronzed and golden vines, blossoming here and there with vivid scarlet leaves. Below ran a dazzling border of shrubs—the sumac, which does not wait for the coming of the frost king to put on its royal livery; the sassafras already gleaming with touches of fire; the wild grape as red as the reddest wine, and rioting over all the rich green; the bright wahoo with its graceful clusters of flame-colored berries overrunning its soberer neighbors; the hazel, the pawpaw, the dog-wood, the red-bud, the spice-wood, the sweet-strife, the angelica. On the west the velvet turf began to unroll gently downward toward the river. The quiet stream ran with molten silver on that flawless October day, and deep shadows of royal purple hung curtains of wondrous beauty above the water. Back under the trees the shadows were darkly blue, bluer even than the cloudless sky arching so high above the tall tree-tops.

Nature indeed always made more preparations and much finer ones, for the dance in the woods than the simple people of the wilderness ever thought of making. The word merely went from one log house to another, fixing the day for the dance. The hunters' daughters with the help of their mothers, filled the big baskets with simple good things on the night before; for the young hunters came very early to go with their sweethearts to the festival, and there was no time to spare on the morning of the dance. The dancing sometimes began at nine o'clock in the morning. The three black men from Cedar House who played for the dancing were in their places long before that hour, with their instruments already in tune. One had an old fiddle, another the remnant of a guitar, and the third a clumsy iron triangle which he had made himself. Nevertheless they were famous for their dance music and known throughout the wilderness to all the dancers. Those old-time country fiddlers—all of them, black or white—how wonderful they were! They have always been the wonder and the despair of all musicians who have played by rule and note. The very way that the country fiddler held his fiddle against his chest and never against his shoulder like the trained musician! The very way that the country fiddler grasped his bow, firmly and squarely in the middle, and never lightly at the end like a trained musician! The very way that he let go and went off and kept on—the amazing, inimitable spirit, the gayety, the rhythm, the swing! No trained musician ever heard the music of the country fiddler without wondering at its power, and longing in vain to know the secret of its charm. It would be worth a good deal to know where and how they learned the tunes that they played. Possibly these were handed down by ear from one to another; some perhaps have never been pent up in notes, and others may have been given to the note reader under other names than those by which the country fiddlers knew them. This is said to have been the case with "Old Zip Coon," and the names of many of them would seem to prove that they belonged to the time and the country. But there is a delightful uncertainty about the origin and the history of almost all of them—about "Leather Breeches" and "Sugar in the Gourd" and "Wagoner" and "Cotton-eyed Joe," and so on through a long list.

On this day the musicians sat in a row on a fallen tree, and the grass beside it was very soon worn away, and the earth before it beaten as hard as any ballroom floor under the gay and ceaseless patting of their feet. On the other side of the wide level space was a green bower made of freshly cut boughs. This was a retiring room, intended for the use of any fair dancer whose hair might fall into disorder or whose skirt might be torn in the dancing. The baskets were all put out of sight till wanted, hidden beneath the bushes that bordered the open space. But now and then, when the soft warm breeze swayed the leafy screen of green and gold and crimson, there were tantalizing glimpses of the folded table-cloths covering the baskets, like much belated or very early snowdrifts.

Most of the hunters' daughters came to the dance riding behind their sweethearts, after the pleasant custom of the country. They were fine girls for their station in life, and well fitted for the hardships which must be their portion. They were large, strong, brave, simple, good—healthy in body and mind, warm in heart, and cool in courage, with pleasing faces roughened by exposure, and capable hands hardened by work. They were dressed in homespun as became their looks, their means, and manner of living. In all things these future mothers of a great state were the natural and suitable mates for the gallant young state-makers. And each one of the young hunters now standing beside them, held his head high as he led out the girl of his choice, feeling his own right to be prouder and happier than any of his fellows.

The dancing had begun before Ruth and David came, although they were so early. The spot being near, they had walked through the forest swinging the basket between them like two happy children, and coming to the open space, they stopped for a moment and looked on, thinking what a pleasing scene it was. The girls, tripping through the dance, smiled at Ruth as they passed. They knew her very well, and had seen her so often that they no longer looked at her as plump brown partridges might look at an exquisite bird of paradise. And then, they felt that Ruth was unconscious of any difference between herself and them. There was a sweet, cordial friendliness about her, an innate warm-hearted, magnetic charm which won women as well as men. The hunters' daughters liked her because they knew that she liked them for, after all, most of us get what we give in our larger relation to humanity—seldom, if ever, anything else, either more or less. Those who truly love their kind can never be really hated: those who hate their kind can never be really loved. The balance may waver one way or the other at times, but it cannot fail to weigh truly at last.

Ruth danced first with David and then with one of the bashful young hunters. But all the while she was looking toward the opening in the undergrowth, expecting to see Paul Colbert. He had said that he would be there, and presently she saw him standing in the opening between the trees, with the shining river at his back. He was wearing his best and Ruth thought with a leap of her heart, that she had not known till now how handsome he was. His hair was fairer than she had thought, as fair as hers was dark, and she liked it all the better for that. His eyes were gray and clear and steady and fearless. He had a proud way, too, of throwing up his head, as if he tossed away all petty thoughts. She saw him do this as he crossed the greensward, coming straight to her side. It pleased her that he did not stop for a single glance round. She felt his unlikeness to another man, when she saw that he had no thought of any eyes that might be upon himself. And because of this comparison, and the pang of uneasiness and self-reproach which it brought, she blushed when her eyes met his as she had not done heretofore.

There is little use in trying to put into words what he thought of her, or what any true lover thinks of the beloved. The rose of the dawn, and the breath of the zephyr were not glowing or delicate enough to portray Ruth as she was to Paul that day. The beauty of her face under the gypsy hat; the witchery of her dark blue eyes smiling up at him; the pink roses blooming on her fair cheeks; the red rose of her perfect mouth—all this gave him at a glance a likeness of her to lay away in his memory: a vivid flashing, imperishable treasure to keep forever.

*   *   *   *   *

The gayety of the Indian Summer dance was now at its height. The mellow sunlight fell straight down through the arching green branches of the bordering trees. The earth, still warm with the summer's fires, lifted a cool face to the soft breeze. The dancers growing tired and hungry about noon, sat down on the greensward in little groups, while the baskets were taken from their hiding-places and the simple feast was soon spread. The black men served it with the coffee which they had heated over the campfire built at some distance in the forest. The homespun linen of the table-cloths looked very white on the

Nancy Huston Banks

dark green of the rich grass. But the single square of fine damask from Ruth's basket was not whiter than its humble neighbors, and she did not think of her finer linen or richer food. With Paul Colbert seated on the grass at her right hand, and David at her left, she took what was given her, knowing only that she was quite content and perfectly happy. She was indeed so happy that she was less gay than usual, for the greatest happiness makes least noise. She listened to all that was said, saying almost nothing herself. Paul's eyes hardly left her face, and he instantly observed that a shadow suddenly clouded it, the same shadow which had fallen over it on the evening before. Turning his eyes in the direction of her gaze, he saw William Pressley standing not far away. He did not know that the white-haired gentleman who stood beside the young man was Philip Alston, but he noted that the shadow quickly left Ruth's face at sight of the older man, when, brightening and smiling, she beckoned the newcomers to approach. And he also saw what she seemed not to see, that the older man turned a frowning face on the younger, and said something which was not cordially received. Had he known William Pressley better, he would have seen the dignified protest that was in every line of his large slow-moving figure as he followed Philip Alston across the wide open space to Ruth's side. To her, William's very step said as plain as words could have spoken that he was used to being misunderstood, but none the less sure of having done his whole duty. She looked up with the little uneasy flutter which this manner of his always caused her. She so craved love and approval that a dark look made her tender heart ache, even though she was unconscious of having done anything to deserve it. This was nearly always the state of feeling between her betrothed and herself, but up to this moment she had never doubted that her own shortcomings were wholly to blame. She hurriedly drew her thin skirt closer about her, nervously trying to make room for him between David and herself. The boy and doctor rose to their feet as the two men approached. Ruth sat still on the grass, lifting her blue eyes to William Pressley's face with a timid, wistful, almost frightened glance.

"You have met Doctor Colbert, William," she said quickly, and then she turned with a smile that was like a flash of light. "And uncle Philip—Mr. Alston—this is the doctor."

Paul Colbert in his utter amazement took the hand which Philip Alston held out. He could not have refused it had there been time to think, for her eyes were on him, and there was no doubting her affection for Philip Alston; that shone like sunlight on her face and thrilled in every tender tone of her voice. The young doctor could scarcely believe the evidence of his own eyes and ears. This Philip Alston! It was incredible, impossible; there was certainly some mistake. Nevertheless he hastily withdrew his hand and Philip Alston noted the haste, understanding it as well as Paul Colbert himself. His own manner was quiet and calm, showing none of the irritation which he felt at William Pressley's negligence. He lost none of his graciousness through seeing the young doctor's involuntary recoil. His intuitions were unerring; he knew instantly that this newcomer was already acquainted with the stories told about himself, but he cared little for that. He was considering the interference with his plans which might come from the sudden appearance of a young man of this young doctor's looks and intelligence. Hardly half a dozen commonplace remarks had been exchanged between them before he had recognized the unusual power of mind and body which he might soon have to contend with. He turned and looked at William Pressley and then back at Paul Colbert with a clouded brow, but he glanced down with a smile when Ruth touched his arm.

"Dearest uncle Philip," she said, "I am so—so—glad that you have come. You are just in time to dance with me. You did once, you know, at the May party, and none of the other girls had so courtly a partner. They couldn't have because I wouldn't let them have you. I should be jealous if you were to dance with any one else, and there is no one anywhere like you."

Looking up with her eyes full of affection she took his hand and pressed it against her pink cheek. At the sight a stab of pain and a thrill of fear went through the doctor's perplexed thoughts. He suddenly realized that the girl's life was closely bound up with this man's. He felt that any distrust of him must wound her, and although he still knew nothing of the bond between them, he saw that there could be no question of its being very close and strong. His first impulse was to try to persuade himself that the suspicion against Philip Alston might be unfounded; as it was certainly unproven. And then, finding himself unable to do this, he felt tempted to put the whole problem of the man's guilt or innocence aside, as no concern of his own. It is always the lover's temptation to shut his eyes when he must choose between the neglect of duty and the wounding of the woman he loves. And alas! this is a choice that comes sooner or later, in one form or another, to all who love. The woman sometimes can find an invisible thread leading through the labyrinth of the feminine conscience which may help her to follow a middle course. The man never has any such subtle resource and he knows, from first to last, that he must do what is wrong if he does not do what is right.

Paul Colbert's troubled perplexity grew deeper as he continued to look at Philip Alston and to listen as he talked. The softness of his voice, the culture that every word revealed, the intellectual quality of each thought, the clear, calm, steady gaze of his fine eyes, the noble shape of his distinguished head—all these things taken together almost made the young doctor feel that Philip Alston was the victim of monstrous calumny. And yet some unerring intuition told him that the terrible things which he had heard were true. His gaze wandered from Philip Alston to Ruth, and he grew sick. A sudden cold dampness gathered on his forehead under all the mellow warmth of the sun. He began to wish that he could get away long enough to clear his mind—to think. It was rather a relief when Philip Alston suggested that William Pressley should lead Ruth out for the next dance. Paul Colbert's gaze followed them as they walked away across the sun-lit grass, but he scarcely knew that he was looking at them till Philip Alston spoke.

"They are a handsome, well-matched young couple, are they

not?" he said with a smile, and with his eyes on the young doctor's face. "You know, of course, that they are to be married on Christmas Eve."

XII

THE EVE OF ALL SOULS'

Ruth saw Paul Colbert when he passed Cedar House for the first time without stopping. He was riding very fast, and she feared that the Cold Plague must be growing worse. Still, a glance at her chamber window would not have delayed him, and she wondered why he did not turn his head. She was almost sure he must know that she always gave the birds their supper on the window-sill at that hour. She did not know that he had seen her without looking, and had borne away in his heart a picture of her slight white form, framed by the sun-lit window, and surrounded by the fluttering birds. Disappointed, wondering, and vaguely troubled, she gazed after him as long as he was visible amid the green gloom of the forest path. And then when he was lost to sight, she turned sharply on the boldest blue jay.

"Go 'way, you greedy thing! You startled me. I wasn't thinking about any of you. How tiresome you all are! To teach you better manners, I am going to throw this down to Trumpeter," leaning forward to see the swan which stood on the grass below, anxiously watching everything that went on above. "There! That is the last nice fat crumb."

The day had seemed endlessly long. She went wearily down the stairs again, as she had done many times since morning. Neither the judge nor William was at home. Miss Penelope and the widow Broadnax were in their accustomed places, and matters around the hearth were going forward as usual. Miss Penelope had asked fiercely in her mildest tone, what anybody could expect to become of any country, when one of the biggest towns in it built a theatre before building any kind of a church, as Louisville had done. The widow Broadnax had replied in her loudest, roughest voice, that she supposed the people there, as well as elsewhere, could keep on getting married two or three times, and mixing up families that otherwise might have lived in peace, just as well without a church as with one. But the girl listened listlessly and unsmilingly, hardly hearing what was said. Going out of the room she sat for a long time on the doorstep, watching the forest path with patient wistfulness. But there was no sign of the young doctor's coming back and it was a relief when David came up the river bank. He reminded her that she had asked him to go with her to the Sisters' house, and she arose and went indoors to get her bonnet.

"You'd just as well take the orphans one of the biggest fatty gourds of maple sugar," sighed Miss Penelope. "Ten to one none of us will ever live to eat much of anything, with that comet a-hanging over us. It's just as well to get ready as soon as you can, when you've been warned. I know what to look for when I've dreamt of wading through muddy water three times a-hand-running. Tell the Sisters that all the maple sugar that was ever poured into fatty gourds couldn't hurt the children's teeth now. The poor little things, and all of us, will have mighty little use for teeth—or stomachs either, for that matter—if things don't take a turn for the better a good deal sooner than I think they will. For my part, I don't see what else anybody can expect with that big black ring round the comet's head a-getting bigger and blacker every night of our miserable lives."

She called all the small cup-bearers,—for some unknown reason she never called one or two without calling all,—and sent them running to the smoke-house to fetch the fatty gourd. She threatened them fiercely in her dovelike tones, saying what she would do if they loitered, or stopped to put their little black paws in the sugar. But the cup-bearers knew Miss Penelope quite as well as she knew them, and when they came back with the fatty gourd they waited, as a matter of course, till she gave each one of them a generous handful of the sugar, before handing the gourd to David.

The Sisters' house was within walking distance, and Ruth and David had gone about half the way when they met Father Orin and Toby. These co-workers were not moving with their usual speed on account of an unwieldy burden. Tied on behind the priest's saddle was a great bag, containing the weekly mail for the neighborhood. He went to the postoffice oftener than any one else, and it had become his custom to fetch the mail to the chapel once a week, and distribute it after service on Sundays. When possible, he sent the letters of those who were not of his congregation by some neighbor who was present; but he often rode miles out of his way to deliver them with his own hand. It was in carrying the mail on a bitter winter's day, when the earth was a glittering sheet of ice, that he had fallen and broken his arm. It was a serious accident, and would have disabled any one else for a long time, but he was out again and as busy as ever within a few days, though he had to carry his arm in a sling for several weeks. He now hailed the two young people with his kind, merry greeting.

"There's a great letter up at the convent," he said, when he came up beside them. "The Sisters have got it, and they will show it to you. Ask them to read it to you. That letter will have a place in Kentucky history. This is where we must turn out. No, Toby, old man, there's no time for you to be listening and enjoying yourself, nor for nibbling pea-vine, either. Move on, move on! Good-by, my children. Don't forget to ask the Sisters to show you the bishop's letter."

Sister Teresa held it in her hand when she came to the door to meet them. Both the girl and the boy had been her pupils, and she had formed an attachment for them which had not been weakened by their leaving the little school. Sister Elizabeth also hastened to receive them most cordially. Sister Angela merely waved her hand through the window, but the little faces peeping over the sill, and the tops of the little curly heads bobbing up and down at her side, told why she could not come with the others to meet the welcome guests. Sister Teresa did not wait to be asked to read the letter, she was too much excited over it to forget it for a moment; its coming was the greatest event that the convent had ever known.

"This, my dear children," she began almost as soon as they were within hearing, "is a letter from Bishop Flaget, the first bishop of Kentucky, the first bishop of the whole northwest. Of course you must know, my dears, that this is far too important a letter to have been written to an humble little community like ours, or even to Father Orin, much as he is esteemed. This is merely a copy of the letter which Bishop Flaget is sending back to France, and the original was addressed to the French Association for the Propagation of the Faith. It was written in June of this year, soon after the arrival of his Reverence in Kentucky, but our copy has reached us only to-day. Listen! This is what he says about his coming to Bardstown: 'It was on the 9th of June, 1811, that I made my entry into this little village, accompanied by two priests, and three young students for the ecclesiastical state. Not only had I not a cent in my purse, but I was compelled to borrow nearly two thousand francs in order to reach my destination. Thus, without money, without a house, without property, almost without acquaintances, I found myself in the midst of a diocese, two or three times larger than all France, containing five large states and two immense territories, and myself speaking the language, too, very imperfectly. Add to this that almost all the Catholics were emigrants, but newly settled and poorly furnished.' Ah, but he was welcomed with all our hearts!" cried Sister Teresa, with tears springing to her gentle eyes. "Listen to this, from another letter, telling how he came to St. Stephen's. It is like a beautiful painting—you can see how it looked! 'The bishop there found the faithful kneeling on the grass, and singing canticles in English: the country women were nearly all dressed in white, and many of them were still fasting, though it was four o'clock in the evening;

they having indulged the hope to be able to assist at his Mass, and receive the Holy Communion from his hands. An altar had been prepared at the entrance of the first court under a bower composed of four small trees which overshadowed it with their foliage. Here the bishop put on his pontifical robes. After the aspersion of the holy water, he was conducted to the chapel in procession, with the singing of the Litany of the Blessed Virgin; and the whole function closed with the prayers and ceremonies prescribed for the occasion in Roman Pontifical.' Ah, yes; we did our best for him!"

Sister Teresa's soft eyes were shining now behind her tears.

"And hear this, also written by the same dear friend who sends us the bishop's letter. The priest, M. Badin, to whom this letter refers, is in charge of St. Stephen's, so that it was his duty as well as his pleasure to make preparations for the bishop's coming. This letter says that: 'M. Badin had for his lodgings one poor log house ... and it was with great difficulty that he was enabled to build and prepare for his illustrious friend, and the ecclesiastics who accompanied him, two miserable log cabins, sixteen feet square: and one of the missionaries was even compelled to sleep on a mattress in the garret of this strange Episcopal palace, which was whitewashed with lime, and contained no other furniture than a bed, six chairs, two tables, and a few planks for a library. Here the bishop still resides, esteeming himself happy to live thus in the midst of apostolic poverty.'" The Sister broke off suddenly. "But I must not allow you to stand out here, my dear children. It soon grows chilly on these late fall evenings. Come indoors at once, my dears. And then, Ruth, Sister Angela is very anxious to show you the sewing which she has finished."

"Oh, I know how beautiful it is without seeing it," said Ruth, with a sudden shrinking; but she added hastily, "There is no such needle-woman as Sister Angela anywhere."

She followed the Sister into the larger of the two rooms which the house contained. David bashfully stayed behind, lingering on the threshold, and keeping man's respectful distance from the mysteries of feminine wear. But the three white caps and the flower-wreathed bonnet drew close together over the dainty garments, all a foam of lace and ruffles and embroidery. David heard the terms rolling and whipping, and felling and overcasting and hemstitching and herring-boning which were an unknown tongue to him. Ruth praised everything, till even Sister Angela was quite satisfied. That pretty young sister was indeed so elated that she turned to admire Ruth's dress but the Sister Superior gently reminded her that it was the eve of All Souls', when they and every one should be thinking of graver things.

"This year the souls and the safety of the living, as well as the repose of the dead, will need all our prayers," said Sister Teresa. "There seems no doubt of the war with the Shawnees. Ah me, ah me! And the Cold Plague growing worse every day!"

"But Doctor Colbert is curing that," said Ruth, eagerly.

"As God wills, my daughter," said the Sister, making the sign of the cross. "More recover, certainly, since he came. Before, the little ones always died."

"He told me that three babies were coming to you yesterday. Are they here? The poor, poor little things! And may I see them, Sister? I should like to help take care of them, if I might," Ruth said timidly, not knowing that her pink cheeks bloomed into blush roses.

The Sister led the way into the other room—the first orphan asylum in the wilderness—and Ruth smiled and talked to the desolate little waifs of humanity as brightly as she could with dim eyes and quivering lips. She, herself, and David, also, had been like this. He had followed her into the room, and was now standing by her side, so that she could clasp his hand and hold it close.

Walking homeward through the darkening shadows of the

forest, she still held his hand. Both were thinking sadly enough of their own coming into this wild country, they knew not—whence or how or wherefore—and were never to know.

"Fathers and mothers must go suddenly when they leave their children so," said Ruth, musingly. "Ours must have died—"

"Or have been murdered!" David broke out fiercely.

"No, no!" cried Ruth, shrinking closer to his side. "I could not bear to think that."

But the boy went on, as if speaking thoughts which had long rankled in bitter silence. "It isn't so bad as to believe that they deserted us, or died without leaving a word. Fathers and mothers who love their children well enough to bear them in their arms through hundreds of weary miles over high mountains and down long rivers, and into the depths of the wilderness, would never desert them at the hard journey's end. Fathers and mothers who loved their children so dearly could hardly be taken away by lightning so quickly that they would not leave behind a single token of their love. And we have never seen a sign showing that ours ever lived. There is something wrong—something unaccounted for—something that we have not been permitted to know!"

"David, dear, dear David!"

"I have always believed it—ever since I have been able to think. As soon as I am old enough to speak like a man, I mean to demand the truth from Philip Alston!"

She dropped his hand and drew away from him with a look of wondering distress. It was the one thing over which they had ever disagreed.

"You must never again say anything of that kind to me, David," she said firmly. "I beg that you will never say it to any one, never even think it. For in thinking it, let alone saying it, you are not only unjust, but ungrateful. What possible object could Philip Alston have in concealing anything that he might know about you and me? Hasn't he always been our best friend?"

And then the quick anger which had flashed out of her loyalty turned to gentle pleading.

"I can't bear a word said against him, dear. And it grieves me to see you making yourself unhappy over such useless brooding. What does it matter, after all—our knowing nothing about ourselves, who we are, or where we came from? We are happy, everybody is kind and good to us."

They started at the sound of a voice calling her name, and they saw William Pressley come out of the dark shadows beneath the trees, and stand still, waiting for them to approach.

"It is late, my dear, for you to be roaming about the woods like this," he said, when they were near enough.

He used the term of endearment in the tone of calm, moderate reproof which a justly displeased, but self-controlled husband sometimes uses. And Ruth felt the resentment that every woman feels at its unconscious mockery.

"Why, there isn't any danger," she said. "We haven't been out of sight and hearing from Cedar House."

"I was thinking of seemliness, not of danger," William Pressley replied coldly. "And then Mr. Alston is waiting for you."

Ruth moved nearer, and laid her hand on his arm, smiling rather timidly, with conciliatory, upward glances. Her first effort, whenever they met, was always to make something right—often before she could remember what it was that she had done or not done to displease him. This feeling was the natural attitude of a gentle, loving nature toward a harsh, unloving one, and it was the most natural thing of all that he should mistake her gentleness for weakness; that he should mistake her fear of giving offence for a lack of moral courage. This is a common mistake often made by those who care little for the feelings of others, about those who care, perhaps, too much. And as the three young people walked along toward Cedar House, Ruth gave David her left hand, and spoke to him now and then, just as affectionately and freely as she had done while they had been alone. William Pressley did not speak to the boy at all or notice him in any way. He did not dislike him, for he never disliked anything that was not of some importance. He disapproved of his impractical, visionary character, and thought that it might have rather an undesirable influence over Ruth. For this reason he tacitly discouraged all intimacy between them, but he did not take the trouble to express it and merely ignored the lad. And David, seeing how it was, felt instantly and strongly, that being overlooked was harder to bear than being misused—as most of us are apt to feel.

"We have been at the Sisters' house," said Ruth, shyly, breaking a strained silence. "They sent for me—to see the sewing that Sister Angela has been getting ready for Christmas Eve."

William Pressley looked down at her uplifted, blushing face, and smiled, as the most self-centred and serious of men must do, when the girl who is to be his wife speaks to him of her wedding clothes.

XIII

SEEING WITH DIFFERENT EYES

It was on the boy's account that they had their first and last serious quarrel a few hours later. This was by no means the first time that they had openly disagreed, and had come to rather sharp words. Their views of many things were too far apart for that to have been the case, but there had never before been any great or lasting trouble by reason of their difference of opinion. Ruth, gentle and yielding, was ever most timidly fearful of being at fault; William, hard and unyielding, was always perfectly certain of being in the right. It was therefore to be expected that his opinions should generally rule, and that he should construe her readiness to yield and her self-distrust, as proofs that he was not mistaken. Rock-ribbed infallibility could hardly be expected to comprehend the doubts that assail a sensitive soul.

William, naturally enough, had never noted that in giving way, Ruth had not turned far or long from anything involving a principle. The truth was that she had merely evaded his intolerance of any and all difference of opinion—as a deep stream quietly flows round an immovable rock—only to turn gently back into its own course as soon as might be.

And even in doing this, she had put aside only her own opinions and feelings and rights, never those of any one else. But this present dispute over David was wholly unlike any that had gone before. This concerned the boy's feelings and rights, so that she suddenly found herself forced to take a firm stand—affection, justice, and even mercy, now forbidding her to yield. Yet it was, nevertheless, just as clear to her in this as in everything else, that William sincerely thought he was right. That was the trouble. That is always the trouble with people like William Pressley, who are often harder to deal with and sometimes harder to live with, than those who knowingly do wrong.

The three had scarcely entered the great room of Cedar House that evening, when the judge asked the boy to go on an errand to a neighbor's. This was to take some seed wheat which the judge had promised to send for the fall sowing. The growing of wheat was still an interesting and important experiment which was exciting the whole country. There had been good corn in abundance from the first; on those deep, rich, river-bottom lands the grains had but to reach the fertile earth to produce an hundred bushels to the acre. But the settlers were tired of eating corn-bread; their wives and children were pining for the delicate white loaves made from the sweet fine wheat which they had eaten in their old Virginia homes. So that the culture of the best wheat had lately become a vital question, and this new seed was making a stir of eager interest throughout the region. Philip Alston had given it to the judge, and he, in turn, was dividing it among the neighbors. Each grain was accordingly treasured and valued like a grain of gold, and the judge cautioned the boy to be careful in tying the bag; wheat in the grain is a slippery thing to handle, and he wished none of this to be lost.

"You must have a good, strong string—one that can't slip," said Ruth, in her thoughtful, housewifely way. "Let me think—what kind would be best?"

"Here!" the judge drew out his wallet, and took off the string that bound it. "You may use this, David, but take care not to lose it. This is the strongest, finest strip of doeskin—"

Ruth's sweet laughter chimed in, "It looks like minkskin—it's so black!" touching it gingerly with the tips of her fingers.

The judge laughed, too. Everything that she said and did pleased him. But he cautioned the boy again not to lose the string, and to be careful to bring it back. William Pressley looked on in grave, indifferent silence. A slight frown gathered on his brow when he saw Ruth trying the knot, to make sure of its firmness, after the bag was tied. His gaze darkened somewhat and followed her when she went to the door to see the boy set out; and he watched her stand looking after him, with her hands raised to shield her eyes from the rays of the setting sun. It displeased William to see her show such regard for any one of so little importance—the personality of the boy did not enter into the matter. While gazing at her in this cold disapproval, he noted with increased annoyance that she then turned and looked long and wistfully toward the forest path. It did not occur to him that she might be expecting or wishing to see some one riding along the path. He was merely irritated at what seemed to him an indication of unseemly restlessness and empty-mindedness. To his mind the unusual and the unseemly were always one and the same. And it was eminently unseemly in his eyes that the woman who was to be his wife should wish to look away from the spot in which he was sitting. And then, his displeasure turned to anger when Ruth, after standing still and gazing up the forest path, till he felt that he must go out to her and utter the reproof that was on his lips, did not come back to her seat by his side, but began instead to play with the swan.

He sat motionless and silent, calmly biding his time to express the disapproval which such childish behavior made incumbent upon him. Cold, hard anger like his can always wait; and waiting only makes it colder and harder; there is never heat enough in it to melt its merciless ice.

A sudden darkening of the sky sent her into the house at last, and even then she did not return to her proper place by his side. She did not even look at him, but spoke to the judge who was just leaving the great room to go to the cabin which he used as his bedroom and office. Ruth begged him not to start out, saying that the storm seemed so near that it might break before he could reach the cabin. But he went on with a smiling shake of his head, after a glance at the dark clouds which were gathering blackly on the other side of the river behind the spectral cottonwoods, now bare of leaves and ghostly white.

"Did David have to go through the big deadening, William?" she asked suddenly, speaking over her shoulder, without leaving her anxious post in the doorway, though the wind was whipping her skirts about her slender figure and loosing her long, black hair. "I wish he would come. He should be back by this time. I am afraid—the great trees fall so in a storm. Father Orin and the doctor, too, often ride through there. And it is such a dangerous place when the wind blows. Oh!" with a cry of relief, "there's David now! Here he comes. David, David dear—I am so glad!"

She sprang down the steps and ran to meet the boy. The rush of the rising storm kept from hearing William Pressley's call for her to come back. He stood still for a moment, hesitating, and then, seeing that she flew on, he followed and overtook her just as she reached David, who was getting down from the pony and taking the empty bag from the saddle. The wind was now very violent, and the darkened air was thick with the dead leaves of the forest swirling into the river which was already lashed into waves and dashing against the shore. Waterfowl flew landward with frightened cries; a low, dark cloud was being drawn up the stream over the ashen face of the water—a strange, thick, terrible black curtain, shaken by the tempest and bordered by the lightning—pressed onward by the resistless powers of the air.

There was a lull just as William Pressley reached Ruth's side. It was one of those tense spaces which are among the greatest terrors of a storm by reason of their suddenness, their stillness, and their suspense. He grasped her hand, and she clung to his as she would have clung to anything that she chanced to touch in her fright. He said rather sternly that she must come to the house at once, and she turned obediently, following the motion of his hand rather than the meaning of his words. He spoke to David also, without looking at the boy, but she was clinging to him and hiding her face on his arm whenever the lightning flashed, and did not notice what he had said until he repeated his words:—

"You have of course brought back the doeskin string."

Ruth suddenly lifted her face from his arm, loosed her grasp upon it and stood away from him. Yet in that first dazed instant she could not believe that she had heard aright. It was impossible for her, being what she was, to understand that he had never in all his life done anything more true to his nature, more thoroughly characteristic, than to ask this question at such a time. She forgot the lightning while she waited till he asked it for the third time. And then, straining her incredulous ears again, she heard the boy murmur something, and she saw him hurriedly and confusedly searching his pockets for the string.

"I can't find it," he stammered. "I must have dropped it when I poured out the wheat. I am so sorry—I will go to-morrow—"

"You will go now;" said William, calmly. "The string will be lost by to-morrow. And then," judicially, "you will remember a needed lesson better if you go at once."

"William!" burst out Ruth almost with a scream. "You can't mean what you say. Listen to the roar of the coming storm. It's almost here. Surely you don't know what you are saying. Send David through the deadening in the very teeth of a tempest like this, for a bit of string!"

"Come to the house, my dear. It is beginning to rain. I am afraid you will take cold. You, sir, will go back at once," turning to the boy. "You know, of course, that the string itself is of no importance in this matter. It is absurd to speak of such a thing. But it is my duty to teach you, as far as I can, to perform yours. I tell you again to go at once. That is all I have to say, I believe, concerning this matter. Come, Ruth, it is beginning to rain."

She shrunk away from his hand as if its touch horrified her. Her tears were falling faster than the heavy, isolated drops that fell on her bare head. But her courage was rising at need, as it always rose, and she was not too much blinded by tears to see that the boy was getting on the pony again. She ran to him and caught his sleeve, and turned upon William Pressley with the reckless fierceness of a gentle creature made daring in defence of what it loves.

"You are cruel," she said, speaking calmly, steadied by the very extremity of her excitement and distress. "You have no more heart than a stone. You feel nothing that does not touch yourself. You have always been unkind to David. But you shall not do this. I will prevent you—defy you. You shall not send him to his death for some narrow, tyrannical notion. He is like my brother. I love him as if he were. And I wouldn't allow you to treat a stranger so. It's inhuman! It shall not be!" panting, and clinging to the boy.

William Pressley stared at her as if he thought she had suddenly lost her senses. Could this be Ruth speaking like that—and to himself? Instinctively he threw into his voice the whole weight of his heavy, cold rage, which had never yet failed to crush all life and spirit out of her most fiery resistance.

"This is truly shocking. I scarcely know what to say. I am merely trying to do my unpleasant duty in a perfectly simple matter. If I didn't try to do it, I should always think less well of myself—"

"Think less well of yourself!" she cried. "Nothing in the world could ever make you do that! Nothing! Whatever you think and say and do is always right; whatever anybody else thinks or says or does is always wrong. I have given up in almost everything because I loved peace more than my own way, and because I am not often sure that I know best. But I will not give up in this!" shrinking and quivering at a peal of thunder, but clinging closer to the boy's arm.

William Pressley came nearer and laid his hand on her shoulder.

"Come to the house, my dear," he said quietly. "It is beginning to rain harder. You will certainly take cold. Come at once. When you have time to think, you will see how childish and foolish all this is. We will say no more about it. You, sir, know what is right for you to do. You know as well as I do what the judge's positive orders were. You have disregarded them—"

"But uncle Robert never meant anything like this," she said. "He is kind and tender-hearted. I will call him. He would not—"

The boy had turned proudly and silently, meaning to get back in the saddle, but she would not loose her hold on his arm. And then came the first furious blast of the tempest, and the greatest trees—the mightiest giants of the ancient forest—bent and crouched before it, bracing themselves for the fierce conflict with the elements in which they must gain or lose centuries of life. The rain now began to fall heavily, and William abruptly told the boy to come in the house till the storm was over. In yielding thus far, he was not influenced by Ruth's threat to appeal to his uncle. He had scarcely heard what she said, and he was never in awe of the judge's opinion, and never looked for opposition from any source, because he could not anticipate an opinion different from his own. He merely dropped the argument for the moment because he saw the urgent necessity of bringing an undignified scene to a speedy close, and could not see any other or better way of doing it.

When they had gone indoors and had gathered around the fire, so that their damp clothes might dry, he was by far the most composed of the three. The boy was deeply agitated and suffering as only the supersensitive can suffer from harshness, whether merited or not. Ruth was still quivering with excitement and distress, and very soon her tender conscience also was aching. She could not recall very distinctly all that she had said, but she knew how bitter her words must have been, and was already wondering how she ever could have uttered them. How they came in her mind and heart she could not comprehend. She had always thought William a good man, and worthy of all respect, and she now felt that there had been much truth in what he had said. David was a dreamer, poor boy, and it would be well if he could be taught to remember, to be practical and useful like other people. She still could not think it right for him to have been forced to go back through the storm to correct an error; but she now thought that William had not really intended to send him. It seemed suddenly plain that William's sole intention must have been to impress him with the necessity of doing what he was told to do. She had scolded the boy herself about that very thing many a time. The fault was hers, she had been too hasty, too excitable, too impetuous. Ah, yes, that was always her fault! She looked at William with everything that she thought and felt clearly to be seen on her transparent face. But a ray of comfort shone through the cloud which darkened her spirits. Surely this and everything else would be well when she had told him how sorry she was, and how plainly she saw her mistake. They had been such good friends as far back as she could remember; the bond between them had been such a close and strong one that it certainly could not be broken or even strained by a few hasty, passionate words, repented at once. Her lovely eyes were already seeking his face and silently appealing to this old and faithful affection.

But William's gaze did not meet hers. He was looking into the fire and seeing what had occurred with wholly different eyes. To him everything was altered, and nothing could ever make the relation between them what it had been. No tenderness of affection, no length of association, no faithfulness of service, could stand for an instant against a single one of the many blows that his morbid self-love had received. For self-love like his is an incurable disease of sensibility, a spreading canker which poisons the whole character, as an unsound spot in the flesh poisons the whole body. To those who have not come in close contact with this form of morbidity, it may seem impossible that William Pressley's love for Ruth, which had been real so far as it went, should have hardened into dislike almost as soon as the words that wounded it had left her lips. Yet that was precisely what had taken place, quite naturally and even inevitably. He had loved her as much as he was capable of loving, mainly because of the deep gratification which he found in her great esteem for himself. No one else had ever come so near granting his self-love all that it demanded. Her sweet presence, always looking up to him, had been like the perpetual swinging of a censer perpetually giving the fragrant incense that his vanity craved. And now all this was changed. The gentle acolyte was gone, the censer no longer swung, and instead there was a keen critic armed with words as hard as stones. No, there was nothing strange in the fact that, when William Pressley finally turned his gaze on Ruth, he looked at her as if she had been a stranger whom he had never seen before; an utter stranger, and one moreover whose presence was so utterly antagonistic to him that there was not the remotest possibility of any liking between them. But he said nothing, and gave no indication of what he felt. No feeling was ever strong enough to cause him to say or do an unconsidered thing. In this, as in all things, he waited to be sure that he was doing what would place himself in the best possible light. While he had never a moment's doubt of being wholly in the right, he thought it best to wait and consider his own appearance in the matter. And then, just at that time, political affairs were claiming his first attention, for that was a period of intense public stress.

XIV

A SPIRITUAL CENTAUR

The whole wilderness, the whole country, the whole heart of the nation, was now aflame over the coming conflict at Tippecanoe.

Father Orin, like every one else, was thinking of this, a day or so later, as he rode along the forest path. There was a heavy weight in his merciful breast as he looked across the river. Over there, beyond those spectral cottonwoods and on the banks of its tributary, the Wabash, the white and the red races were about to meet in a supreme struggle now close at hand. He had just been told that Joe Daviess had offered his sword, and the news had brought the public trouble home to his own heart, for he loved the man.

And thus it was that, seeing Tommy Dye riding toward him, he had only a grave word of greeting, without any of the merry banter that the adventurer had come to expect. He stopped, however, feeling that Tommy had something to say, but he listened in rather abstracted silence, till Tommy spoke of having been to see the Sisters in order to tell them good-by.

"For I am going to Tippecanoe, too. I leave to-night. The general can't go. It looks like the wound from that infernal duel with Dickinson never would get well. But I like to be where things are stirring, and I am going, anyhow. So is Joe Daviess."

"Yes, I know," said Father Orin, sadly. "Good men as well as bad must go, I suppose, if wars must be fought."

Tommy Dye looked hard at him for a moment, and taking off his hat, rubbed his red hair the wrong way till it stood on end. His stare gradually turned to a sort of sheepish embarrassment before he spoke;—

"I'll swear some of the babies up yonder ain't much bigger than my fist!" he finally blurted out. "I took the Sisters the wad I won on the last chicken fight. 'Twasn't much, but there ain't any use taking it over the river for the red devils to get, if they get me—and maybe they will—for they say the Prophet is a fighter. If the Shawnees don't get me, I can make plenty more, so it's just as broad as it's long. Anyhow, the Sisters will know what to do with the wad. Say! I wish it had been bigger. They took me into the room where the youngsters stay," he said huskily, rubbing his head harder than ever. "They said—them real ladies said—that they would raise up the children to love me, and pray for me. When I come away they cried—them real ladies—about me, old Tommy Dye, that ain't even a heretic."

"You are kind, my friend; you have a good heart, and you are generous," said Father Orin; "but I wish you could earn your money in another and a better way. Somehow it grates—"

"Now, look here!" cried Tommy Dye, bristling at once, and jamming his hat back on his red head. He was always cowed at the very sight of the gentle Sisters; but as man to man—even though one be a priest—he was up again at once, and quite ready to hold his own. "Every man to his own notion," he blustered and swaggered. "I've got mine and you've got yours. That's my way of making a living, and I dare anybody to say it ain't honest. Just let any man come out flat foot and tell me so, face to face. I play fair, and I bet as square as the next one. I take my chances the same as the other man. I may fight rough and tumble, but I always give warning, and I never gouge. If any man's got anything to say against my honesty or fairness, he's only got to come on and say it."

"Come, come!" said Father Orin, too sad to be amused at the outburst, as he might have been at another time. "I beg your pardon if I have offended you. I had no thought of doing that. But I wish I could induce you to think before you go into danger. All who go over yonder will not come back. The Shawnees have been getting ready for this test of strength for a long time. There is great danger. I beg you, my friend, to think. Will you come back with me to the chapel? Just for a little while. There is no one there, and we can have a quiet talk."

"Now, what's the use of raking all that up again? We've gone over all that—and more than once—haven't we? You thought one way and I another, when we had it out the other day. And we've both got the same right now that we had then, to think as we like about something that neither of us knows the first blamed thing about, haven't we? Well, I think just the same now that I did then, and I reckon you do, too. I haven't seen any reason to change, have you? I haven't had any fresh news from up yonder"—pointing heavenward—"and I don't suppose you have either. So you see one of us is bound to be most damnable mistaken—"

"Shut up," shouted Father Orin, "you unmannerly rascal! I have a great mind to jump down and pull you off that horse and give you a thrashing to teach you some respect for religion, and how to keep a civil tongue in your head. And you know I could do it, too!"

They looked fiercely at each other for a moment. Father Orin was of a fiery spirit, and all his goodness could not always subdue it. Tommy Dye was a ready and a good fighter, but he paused now, and silently regarded the priest. He looked at his large, sturdy form, at his brawny shoulders, at his deep chest and his long arms, remembering suddenly that he had seen him roll, with his own hands, the largest logs in the little chapel which no one else could move.

"I reckon you could," Tommy Dye finally conceded frankly.

Father Orin burst into his good-humored, chuckling laugh, and Tommy Dye grinned, but their faces sobered instantly. The pity of it touched and moved the priest through his sense of humor. The gambler was softened and ashamed, he hardly knew why. With one simultaneous impulse they sent their horses forward, and coming closer together clasped hands.

"God bless and guard you, my friend," said Father Orin. "You can't keep me from saying that, and you can't help my praying for your safety," trying to smile.

Tommy Dye found nothing more to say and, laughing very loud, he put spurs to his horse and galloped away through the darkening forest. Father Orin and Toby stood still looking after him till he had passed out of sight. And then they turned to go on their way. They went along in silence for a while, and at last Father Orin began the conversation with a heavy sigh. "Well, old man, there's another bad failure that we have got to set down in our book—you and me. That was another of the times when we didn't know what to do. That is to say, I didn't. I suppose you did—you always do. You never make mistakes and lose your temper like I do nearly every day. If I could do my part as well as you do yours, we wouldn't fail so often, would we, old man?"

Toby quickly turned his head with a friendly, encouraging whinny, as if he saw his co-worker's trouble and wanted to give him what comfort he could. He always seemed to know as well when his friend needed encouragement as when he required to be kept up to his duty. It is a wonderful, wonderful thing, this bond between the good rider and the good horse! It is so wonderfully close and strong; the closest and strongest binding the human being to his brute brother. It is infinitely more subtle too, than that which binds any other, even the kindest master to the most faithful dog; for the man and his horse are not merely master and servant, they are friends and even equals in a way. Neither is nearly so complete or powerful without the other; but together—with body and spirit coming in living, throbbing contact—they form the mightiest force in flesh and blood. Along the marvelous electric currents of life there flashes from the man to the horse, intelligence, feeling, purpose, even thought perhaps, so that to the true horseman the centaur can never be wholly a fabulous creature.

One of the greatest things about this wonderful bond is that it reaches all classes of riders and horses. Every good rider and every good horse may rely upon it, no matter which of the many roads through life they may travel together: all may trustingly rely upon it till one or both shall have breasted "Sleep's dreamy hill." The horse of the fox-hunter, of the race-rider, of the mounted soldier—every one of these noble beasts has the fullest understanding of his rider's calling, and gives it his completest sympathy with the greatest assistance in his power. Who that has known the horse at his best can have failed to observe and recognize and be moved by this fact? We have all seen that the hunter hardly needs the touch of his rider's knee to be off like the wind and to go without urging from whip or spur on to the end of the chase; never flagging, no matter how long or hard it may be; never flinching at the deepest ditch nor fouling at the highest fence; straining every sinew to the last, for his rider's defeat is his own failure, his rider's success his own victory. And we have all seen the gallant response of the race-horse to every movement of his rider's body—a loyal gallantry that ennobles even the merely mercenary; and the sight of these two—now one—flying toward the goal, always makes the heart beat faster and grow warm with its brave showing of this magical bond. And above all, we have seen the trooper's horse, which comes closer to him than the comrade fighting by his side; for it is to his horse more than to his sword that the soldier must owe any glory that he may hope to win; and when strength and courage can no longer serve, it is his horse that often gives his own body to shield his rider from death.

And if all this be true, as all horsemen know it to be—even when the bond is strained by cruelty and tainted by gain and stained by blood—how much closer and stronger must have been the tie between this priest of the wilderness and his friend. Toby's loyalty was never tried like the hunter's by seeing some dumb brother tortured and slain—and that the hunter feels the test keenly, no one can doubt after seeing the horror in his eloquent eyes. Toby never had to suffer from a broken heart because of a lost race, or because he shared the disgrace of his rider's dishonesty, and many noble beasts have seemed to suffer something strangely like this. Toby never had to lend his strength to the taking of human life, like the trooper's horse; and the soldier's horse does not need the power of speech to tell that he suffers almost as much in the spirit as in the flesh from the horrors of the battle-field. Toby and his friend worked together solely for peace, kindness, and mercy, for the relief of suffering, and the saving of bodies and souls; all and always, solely for the good of the world, of their fellow-creatures, and the glory of God.

Think of what it was that Father Orin and his partner did! They had ecclesiastical jurisdiction over a strip of country which was more than fifty miles wide and little less than four hundred miles long. This lay on both sides of the Ohio River, much of it being the trackless forest, so that Father Orin and Toby used the Shawnee Crossing oftener than the Shawnees themselves. They went unharmed, too, where no other pioneers ever dared go. Some mysterious power seemed to protect them, as the rude cross drawn on a cabin door is said to have saved the inmates from the savages. Father Orin and Toby thus travelled about two hundred miles each week all the year through, without stopping for heat or cold. There was only one church when they first began their labors, and this was the little log chapel; but the members of that small and widely scattered congregation were served with the offices of their religion by the priest at many private houses which were far apart and called "stations." There were about thirty of these in Kentucky, several in Indiana and Illinois, and one or two in Tennessee, and Father Orin and Toby visited them all, some as often as once a month and the others as often as possible. To say Mass and to preach constituted but a part of the duty which called them from place to place. They went wherever the priest was needed to administer baptism to infants or older persons; they went wherever any one, old or young, required instruction in religion; they went wherever the priest was needed to hear confession; they went far and wide, so that the priest might solemnize marriage for Protestants as well as Catholics; they visited the sick, no matter how distant, in summer and in winter alike, and Toy day or by night; they went at any summons to bury the dead; and they tried to go again, so that the priest might do what he could to comfort the living. Yet with all this untiring zeal for the soul's welfare, there was also a ceaseless care for the body's welfare, and a divine disregard of any narrow line of faith; for wherever Toby carried Father Orin that good man's heart was always moved by compassion for any distress of mind, body, or estate, always overflowing with a deep, wide pity infinitely greater and more Christian than any creed.

It is not strange, then, that the good man and the good horse had become almost one in mind and body, and that they were quite one in spirit. It is not in the least strange, certainly, that Toby came to know the nature of their errand almost as well and nearly as quickly as Father Orin himself. He easily knew a sick call by the haste with which they set out, and he knew its urgency by their going with the messenger. He seemed to be able to tell unerringly when they were bearing the Viaticum, and it was plain that he felt the responsibility thus resting upon his speed and sureness of foot. Then it was that he would go like the wind, through utter darkness, through storm and flood and over an icy earth, without a pause or a misstep. Many a time, after such a struggle as this, has Toby turned his head, as if trying to see why Father Orin was slow in doing his part when the rain, freezing as it fell, had frozen the priest's poor overcoat to the saddle, and his ragged leggins were heavy and clumsy with icicles. But the apologetic tone in which Father Orin always said, "Well, here we are, old man," and the explanatory pat that he always gave Toby's neck, after going through the respectful form of hitching him, never failed to make this right. And when the priest came out of the house, he always had something in his pocket for Toby, if any one had remembered to give himself anything to eat.

But their errands were not all so sad as this. Sometimes there were weddings to attend, and Toby entered into the happy spirit of that lively business quite as heartily as Father Orin. The only thing that Toby was strict about then, was that his friend should not forget to wear his best clothes, which he was too apt to do, even if he had not given them away, and that there should not be a speck of mud on his own coat, which had to be neglected in more urgent cases. Father Orin used to declare that Toby eyed him from top to toe when he knew they were going to a wedding; and that if there were a spot on his cassock, or a hole in it, Toby's eye never failed to find it. At such leisurely times he was indeed so exacting as to his own proper appearance that he would not budge until the last "witch's stirrup" had been combed out of his mane and tail. He was only a degree less particular when he knew they were going to the christening of an infant. It was then plainly Toby's opinion that, while they might not take quite so much time to christen as to marry, there was still no need to rush off with the priest's vestments out of order and his own fetlocks weighted with mire. The two had many friendly contests on these occasions, but Toby's will was the stronger, and his temper was not quite so mild; and as it is always the less amiable who wins, it was commonly he who won, in the long run.

Whenever the way before them was not quite clear, Father Orin would let Toby lead, and only once in all their long pilgrimage together did he ever fail to lead aright. It was on a wild winter's night, and neither could see either heaven or earth; yet on against the bitter wind went the priest and his horse, Toby stretching his fullest length at the top of his speed, and Father Orin bending low to escape the boughs of unseen trees; and thus they sped through the stormy blackness. Faster still they went, up hill and down hill, leaping fallen trees, flying across the hollows made by the uptorn roots, swimming swollen streams, while the priest knelt on the saddle, holding the Viaticum high above the rushing water which dashed over his knees. At last they stopped, utterly exhausted, only to find that they were lost in the icy, dark wilderness; and they went on groping blindly for any kind of shelter under which to wait for the first glimmer of dawn. They finally came upon a ruined cabin, and although the whole front of it was gone, some of the roof and a part of the walls were left, and Father Orin led Toby into the driest, corner. Taking off the wet saddle and the soaked, half-frozen blanket, he laid them on the ground. He patted Toby as he did this, and Toby's responsive whinny said it was all right, just as plain as if he had been able to talk. But Father Orin was not quite satisfied, and moving a little farther over in the corner, where it was so dark that even Toby could not see what he was doing, he pulled off his poor old overcoat, from which the water was dripping, but which was still warm and partly dry on the inside. Stealing back to Toby, he laid the coat over his shivering shoulders, chuckling to think that Toby would never know that it was not the saddle-blanket. Feeling now that he had done his best for his friend, he buttoned his cassock closer and laid down on the freezing ground, with the frozen saddle for a pillow, and tried to get what rest and sleep he could.

At times like this—and they were not a few—it was hard for Father Orin to believe that Toby had no soul. It was indeed so hard now and then, as on that night, that he could not believe it; that he could not think there would be no reward of any kind for such service as Toby was giving the Faith. It was service as faithful as his own; he could not have given his without Toby's help. Looking upward toward his own reward, even this bitter, black winter's night became as nothing; but Toby—what was there for Toby? He did not remember that he often gave Toby the food which he needed himself, as he had just given him the warmth from his own shivering body. He thought only of the things that Toby did for him and for the Faith. And so thinking, very strange fancies about Toby would now and then come to him with the profoundest reverence. And on that dreary night, when their dauntless spirits seemed to touch, while their exhausted bodies thus dozed side by side, a pleasant vision vaguely blended Father Orin's half-conscious dreams with his perplexed waking thoughts.

Of a sudden, all was bright and warm, and he felt himself going up, up, up, through flawless blue space. He thought he had no wings, but he did not miss them, nor even think about them; he was missing and thinking about Toby, and wondering, where he was, and what he was doing. But ah! there he was all ready and waiting close to the gate of paradise. Yes, there was Toby after all! There he was, standing by a celestial manger overflowing with ambrosia, already blanketed with softest zephyrs, saddled with shining clouds, and bitted with sunbeams—quite ready and only waiting for the touch of his friend's hand on the bridle—to canter up the radiant highway walled with jasper and paved with stars.

XV

THE WEB THAT SEEMED TO BE WOVEN

The fancy pleased Father Orin, and he spoke jestingly to Toby about it, reminding him, however, seriously enough, that it was only in visions that there could be any such direct passing from earth to heaven.

"For you see, old man, there's a place on the way where most of us must tarry a while. Maybe you might be able to pass by and go straight on. I am afraid there wouldn't be much of a chance for me."

But they were both still far from their long, hard journey's end on that gloomy November evening. They were merely turning a little aside from their usual broad path for a still wider service to humanity. They had not seen the doctor that day, and there was always reason to fear that he might at any moment fall a victim to the epidemic which he was ceaselessly fighting, so that they were now going in some anxiety to see what had kept him away from the places in which they were used to seeing him. They were both very tired, yet Toby, nevertheless, quickened his weary pace at a gentle hint from Father Orin, and they got to the doctor's house just as the sun went down behind the cottonwoods on the other shore.

The cabin stood near the river bank. It was a single room of logs, rough without and bare within. The doctor was not very poor, as poverty and riches were considered in the wilderness, having inherited a modest fortune. But he was generous and charitable, and had gone from Virginia into Kentucky with an earnest wish to serve his kind. And then his acquaintance with Father Orin had brought him in close contact with want as well as suffering, and would have given him good uses for larger means than his own. Yet rude and empty as the cabin was, there were traces of refinement here and there, as there always must be wherever true refinement dwells. A miniature of his mother, whom he could not remember, hung against the logs at the head of his bed. There were a few good books on a rough shelf, and a spray of autumn leaves lay on the table. The beauty of the leaves had drawn him to break the spray from the bough and bring it home. But he had forgotten it as soon as he had laid it down on the table, and the leaves were withering as he sat beside them with his head bowed upon his hands.

The man of conscience, who cares for the bodies of his kind, bears almost as heavy a burden as he who cares for their souls. He must everywhere, and unrestingly, fight ignorance and prejudice with one hand, while he strives to heal with the other, and this double strife was fiercer in the wilderness, just at that time, than almost anywhere else within the furthest reach of science. On first coming he had found more people being killed by calomel and jalap than by the plague. At every turn he encountered this bane of the country which was called callomy-jallopy, and at that moment he was utterly worn out, body and soul, by a struggle to save the life of a man who had ignorantly poisoned himself by drinking some acid after taking the dose. This was not his first experience of the kind; but he had met the other trials with the high courage of a light heart and a free mind. It was only within the last two days that he had been weighed down by discouragement, by heaviness of heart, and depression of mind. He was so weary and absorbed now in disheartened thought, that he did not hear Toby's approach, and he was startled when Father Orin appeared in the open door. He greeted him with a warmly outstretched hand, but did not say that he was glad to see him; they were too good friends for empty phrases, such good friends that they sat down silently, neither needing a word to know the other's sadness. It was the priest who finally broke the silence.

"You are troubled, my son," he said, quietly and gently. "I see there is something besides the trouble which touches us all—this terror of what is coming on the other side of the river. I see that there is something else—some closer trouble of your own. If you wish to tell me about it, I will do what I can to help you; but you know this without being told."

He had spoken at the right moment, for there are moments in the lives of the most reserved and self-reliant when the heart must speak to ease the mind. Paul Colbert was a Protestant, and so firm and strong in his faith that he was ready at all times to defend it, to fight for it; yet this moment, which has nothing to do with any creed, had come to him, and he spoke as one man speaks to another whom he trusts and knows to be his friend. He told what he was suffering, and the cause of his wretchedness. He spoke of his first meeting with Ruth, and of the love for her that had leapt up in his heart at the first glimpse of her face, before he had heard her voice, before he knew her name. He said how happy he was when chance put her in his arms through that wild night's ride. He described his visit to her on the next day, and said how far he was from suspecting that William Pressley was more than a member of the same family. He went on to speak of the other visits which he had paid to Ruth, telling how fast his love had grown with every meeting. He ended with the revelation at the dance in the woods.

"But it wouldn't have made any difference had I known sooner. It couldn't have made any difference in my loving her," he said. "I must have loved her just the same no matter when or how we might have met. Nothing ever could have altered that. I am afraid that I couldn't have helped loving her had she been another man's wife. I am keeping nothing back, you see, Father. I am telling you the whole truth. But perhaps it wouldn't have been quite so hard to bear, had I known at the very first. It can hardly be so hard to give up happiness when we have never dared long for it. And I knew no reason why I might not try to make her love me. As it is, from this time on, every thought of her must be like constantly trying to kill some suffering thing that can never die!"

He dropped his head on his arm which lay on the table. The priest gently laid his hand on the thick, brown hair.

"My son," he murmured.

"If the man that she is to marry were only different," Paul groaned. "If he were only more worthy, if I could only think that she would be happy."

He did not know that he was merely saying what every unfortunate lover has thought since love and the world began; and it was a sad smile that touched the sympathy of Father Orin's face.

"William Pressley is not a bad young fellow," the priest said. "He means well. He lives uprightly according to his dull, narrow ideas of right. And none of us can do any better than to live up to our own ideals. It's a good deal more than most of us do. I am afraid he is selfish," with the hesitation which he always felt in pronouncing judgment upon any one; "but then most of us men are, and maybe he will not be selfish toward her, for he must be fond of her. Everybody loves the child."

"But about her—is she fond of him? How can she be?"

"I can't answer for that. There's no telling about a girl's fancy; in fact, I have never given the engagement a thought. It was all settled; it seemed a good, suitable arrangement—"

"Arrangement!" groaned Paul.

Father Orin shook his head. "It was most likely Philip Alston who brought it about. He doubtless thought it a wise choice for both the young people. He certainly never would have consented if he had not believed it to be for Ruth's happiness—that always comes first with him in everything."

Paul Colbert sat up suddenly, throwing back his hair, and looked at the priest with a clearing gaze. All the questions which he had been wishing to ask now rushed to his lips. What was Ruth's relation to Philip Alston? What right had he to choose her husband? What was his influence over William Pressley? What was his hold upon Judge Knox? What was this power that he wielded over the whole family of Cedar House?

"He is no relation to her, is he? He isn't even her guardian. And William Pressley is an honest man, isn't he, even though such a solemn, pompous prig? He can hardly be a confederate of counterfeiters, forgers, robbers, and murderers. And a single look at the judge's face shows him to be the most upright of men; his open, unswerving honesty of thought and deed, cannot be doubted. How is it, then, that Philip Alston can move all these honorable and intelligent people to suit his villainous purposes, as if they were pawns in a game of chess?"

"Ah, you don't know much about Philip Alston. You have met him only once—yet that must have made you feel the wonderful charm of the man, his singular power. You have seen how he looks," laughing at some recollection. "Sometimes when he has talked to me, looking me straight in the face with his clear, soft, gentle, blue eyes, I have doubted everything that I ever had heard against him. Things that I know to a moral certainty to be true seemed a monstrous slander. You must have felt something of this, though you have seen him but once; and the more frequently you meet him the more you will feel it. The power of the man is past words and past understanding. Did you know that he once held a high office under Spain? Oh, yes, for years he controlled the arrogant, treacherous, local government of Spain as absolutely as he controls the simple family of Cedar House. He was living in Natchez then, and was apparently a very devout Catholic, too, about this time. But the church which he attended was mysteriously robbed; its altar was stripped of everything precious,—gold, jewels, paintings,—when none but himself had had access to the church unobserved. That is the story. I do not vouch for its truth. There was no evidence against him—only suspicions in this as in everything else. It was shortly afterward that he suddenly appeared in this country a stanch Protestant; and then almost immediately the present reign of crime began. Yet he has never been seen in the company of any known law-breakers. Many mysterious visitors are said to come to his house over the Wilderness Road, and to go as mysteriously as they come. But no one claims to know who or what they are, where they come from, or where they go. It is said that these men who carry out his orders hardly know him by sight, that he sees only the leaders, and that they never dare go to his house unless they are sent for. It is believed that he rarely goes into detail, and does not wish to know what they do in carrying out his wishes. It is said that he is sickened by the slightest mention of bloodshed or cruelty, like any delicate, sensitive woman, but is perfectly indifferent to all sorts of atrocity that go on out of his sight and knowledge. There is, indeed, a general opinion that he actually does not know half of the time what his tools are guilty of; that he purposely avoids knowing. I have heard it said that the boldest of the band would no more venture to tell him of the crimes they commit while executing orders, than he would put his head in a lion's mouth. It is understood that Alston simply points to a thing when he wants it done, leaving all shocking details to his tools. But this is mere hearsay. No one really knows anything about him; that is to say, no one outside his band—if he actually has one. It is very generally believed, however, that he has only to blow a single blast on a horn at any hour of the day or night, and that from fifty to a hundred armed men will instantly appear, as if they had sprung out of the earth. It is also generally believed that he makes all the fine counterfeit money with which this country is flooded, and that he does the work with his own delicate, white hands. Yet not a dollar has ever been traced to him, although its regular sale goes steadily on at a fixed rate ofsixteen bad dollars for one good dollar. It is generally believed, too, that he keeps his money, both the good and the bad, buried somewhere in the forest near his house, presumably for the double purpose of guarding against robbery by his tools and against surprise by the officers of the law. This, of course, is also mere speculation; nobody really knows anything about what he does. I only know that his house is a bare log hut, which is singular enough, seeing what a fine gentleman he is, and what luxury he has surrounded the girl with. But I know that to be true, because accident once took me to his house, and greater courtesy I never found anywhere, though I was not invited to come again. It is known that he owns a fleet of flatboats, and one of them is usually seen waiting near Duff's Fort when horses are stolen, and it is always gone before the dawn of the next day; but there is no proof of this, either. Boats belonging to other people have a hard time getting past Duff's Fort. More often than not, they are never seen or heard of after reaching that fatal point, and the passengers vanish off the face of the earth. That is what happened to Ruth's parents, as nearly as any one but Alston knows. Most likely he knows nothing more."

"And knowing this, she loves him, and the judge and his nephew trust him?"

"The child doesn't know anything about it. Who would tell her? He is like her father—he could not have been more tender of her had she been his own child. There is nothing strange in her loving him; it would be far more strange if she did not. She is a gentle, loving nature, and he has done everything to win her love, and you know what he is."

"How can any creature in human form be so utterly unnatural—so wholly a monster? How can he endure to see her, much less profess fondness for her, knowing what he has done?"

"I have thought a good deal about that, and I have never been able to make up my mind. You see we don't know that he has done anything wrong. Yet it may be an unconscious expiation. Who knows? The human heart is a mysterious thing. But it is most likely that he simply began to love her when she was a baby, just because she was so lovely that he couldn't help it. She won all hearts in her cradle—the little witch. I remember very well how she used to keep me from my work, by curling her rose leaf of a hand around one of my rough fingers, before she could talk."

"But why—loving her—should he wish to marry her against her will?"

"We do not know that it is against her will. That is to say, I know nothing of the kind, and I have no reason even to think it."

There was a silence after this. Paul Colbert was suddenly realizing that he also had no reason to think her unwilling; but this did not comfort him or change his feeling. It is the delight and misery of love never to have anything to do with reason.

"It is not likely that Alston would approve anything that he did not believe was for her happiness," Father Orin went on after a brief silence. "But there may have been other inducements. With the judge's nephew under his thumb, he need not have much fear of the law or the court. That was the reason most generally assigned for his patronage of William Pressley in the first place, before there was any engagement between the young man and Ruth. But that will, as a matter of course, bind him closer to Alston's interests, through her fondness for him. And on yesterday I heard of a scheme to put Pressley in Joe Daviess' place. It has been kept quiet, but is said to be well on foot, and I should not be surprised if it were true. Pressley is politically ambitious above anything, so that there are several reasons why he and Alston should hold together. In the event of Pressley's securing the appointment, there would not be much danger of the law's interference with any unlawful plans that Alston might have. Mind you, I don't say that he has any. I don't know that he has, and I am not even sure that I am right in telling you these things, which are merely rumor, after all. Well, at all events he has his good points. He is very generous, and always ready, open-handed, to help any good work of the Sisters. I have had scruples about letting them accept his gifts, but I have hesitated to speak for they know nothing against him, and there is always danger of doing injustice. We have no right to accuse anyone of anything that we cannot prove."

Paul was not listening to his friend's scruples. He had risen from his chair, and was walking up and down the room. Presently he paused and faced the priest with the air of a man who sees his way and has made up his mind. His voice rang clear with decision.

"Then this is the net that has been woven about her—the innocent, helpless little thing! She is to be made a victim through her tenderest and most natural affections. It's like seething a kid in its mother's milk. And how utterly unprotected she is! Think of her father! Look at the judge—for all his kindness! What is there to expect from him? And Philip Alston, who pretends to love her? He is using her affection for himself to bring about this marriage, so that she may bind this dull tool—this pompous fool, Pressley—to the service of an organized band of robbers and assassins."

"You are rushing to conclusions, my son. There is no reason, is there, to think that she doesn't love the young man? We haven't the slightest right to assume that. I certainly have not—have you?"

Father Orin spoke with a keen look at the pale, agitated young face, which flushed painfully. Seeing this the priest went on more gently without waiting for any reply.

"And I must again remind you that we do not know that Philip Alston has anything to do with the lawlessness of the country,—we merely suspect him. Suspicion and evidence are different things; so widely different, indeed, that I may have done grave wrong in even mentioning the first to you."

"Then we must try to find out the truth—try to lay our hand

on the evidence which will prove Alston's innocence or his guilt. Doing that cannot harm her—if she is happy in this engagement," with a strong effort, "and it may help her—if she is not."

The priest shook his head. "You forget that many able men have already tried hard to do what you suggest, and that every attempt has failed."

"That hasn't a straw's weight with me. I shall not fail, because I am going to try harder than any one else ever can have tried," with the confidence and courage that belong to love. "I think I can do something to aid the officers in gathering evidence. My work, carrying me over the whole region where these villains do theirs, gives me opportunities to know what is going on. I shall speak to the attorney-general early to-morrow morning. Every honest man owes it to the state to give such help as he can in this extremity."

"Take care," said Father Orin, gently. "I am doubting more and more the wisdom and right of having told you these stories about Philip Alston. Remember, they are merely rumors, widespread and generally believed, it is true, yet still wholly unsupported by evidence. We must be careful.

There is a bare possibility that we may be wrong, that we may be doing a terrible injustice to an innocent man. I do not believe that anything can be long believed by a great many honest people unless there is some truth underneath for it to rest upon; and this about Philip Alston has been believed by the best men of this country for a good many years. But the fact that it hasn't been proven remains, nevertheless. There has never been a shadow of real evidence, and we, as fair-minded men, are bound to remember that." He hesitated for a moment, and looked at the young doctor as if uncertain whether to say something else that was in his kind, wise thoughts. "There is another thing that you would do well to bear in mind, my son. Any one bringing any charges, supported or unsupported, against Philip Alston, will break that little girl's heart. She would never credit the strongest proof. A woman like that,—a tender, soft, clinging, unreasoning little thing,—who is all affection and trust, could not be reached by testimony that would convince any jury. That is one of the merciful dispensations; that is one of the reasons why men get so much more mercy here below than they deserve. This gentle girl not only would never believe, but she would never, never forgive you for breathing a word against Philip Alston. That is the way with women of her kind. And you would not wish to hurt her, even though—"

"No! No—no!"

"And then you must not forget that the young man whom she is to marry is also more or less involved. And you must remember that he is essentially an upright, well-meaning, well-trained young fellow. There is no reason to think she doesn't love him. His conceit is the only thing against him, and she may not mind that. A gentle, yielding nature like hers is often attracted by a dominant, overbearing one like his. I have often noticed it. Maybe it is intended by nature and providence to keep the balance of things. What would become of the world if all the strong ones or all the good ones were to come together, and leave all the weak ones or all the bad ones by themselves? You can see at once that that would never do—everything would be at once unbalanced. It's hard on the good and the strong; but then, many of nature's provisions are hard on the individual, and yet they all work for the welfare of creation."

He said this with a smile and a chuckle, hoping to win his friend to the half-earnest, half-jesting talk with which they sometimes tried to lighten the heavy burdens that both were constantly bearing. But he saw that Paul could not respond, and he went back at once to the grave sympathy with which he had been speaking.

"At all events, this young couple have chosen one another for better or worse, and we, as honest men, and Christians, cannot allow ourselves to discuss, or even think of anything else. I wish I could help you, my son, but I can only beg you to hold to your own road in life, to press straight on upward as steadily and as bravely as you can. And you must put all thought of Philip Alston, too, out of your mind. You and I must work for the saving of men's bodies and souls—we have nothing to do with their punishment. Work, my son! Work, work for others, that is the secret of happiness! And if we work hard enough for the help and the healing of others, it may be that after a while we will be allowed to find help and healing for ourselves."

And the young man looking sadly in the face of the old man promised that he would try—that he would do his best.

XVI

LOVE'S TOUCHSTONE

Ruth, meantime, was still waiting and watching the forest path, and wondering why he did not come back. He nearly always passed Cedar House more than once during the day, but he did not return now, although she waited and watched from early morning till the sun went down. She was tired of hearing the old ladies wrangling over the hearth, and going outside the door she had played with the swan, and had grown tired of that. Looking listlessly about for something else to do, she caught sight of David sitting alone under the willows on the river bank. He thought himself safely hidden for the reading of his book, but the foliage was thinner now on the slender golden wands; some of them were quite bare, and hung like long silken fringes of shining yellow. The first frost had touched them on the night before; the soft breeze was freighted with drifting leaves, and there was a fresh sparkle in the crystalline air.

She had put on a long coat of dove-colored cloth—one of the fine garments that Philip Alston was always finding for her— on account of the cool weather, and she was wearing her gypsy bonnet tied down with its three-cornered handkerchief of white lace, so that she was all ready for going further from the house. In another moment she was skimming down the river bank toward the boy. He saw her coming; but she moved so like a darting swallow that he barely had time to hide his book under the mossy log on which he was sitting before she fluttered into a seat beside him, nestling against his arm.

"There now!" she sighed, smoothing down her skirts. "Now we can have a nice long talk about love."

The boy moved with the uneasiness that every boy feels at any abstract approach to the great topic. The girl went straight on, with all the serenity of the least experienced of her sex. Her big blue eyes were gravely fixed on his reddened face. Her own was quite calm, and very serious indeed. Her soft lips were set as firmly as one rose leaf may be folded against another. The tips of her little fingers met in wisdom's gesture.

"Listen, David, dear. Listen well, and think hard. I have been thinking a great deal about love lately. It is right, you know, that all young people should. I will tell you everything that I have thought, and then you must tell me what you think. For there are some things that I can't find out by myself, though I have tried and tried. And boys ought to know more than girls about love. But I don't believe they do!"

The blue eyes gazed at him rather severely from under the gypsy hat. It was the woman arraigning the man with the eternal challenge. The boy looked down at the ground, and tried not to feel guilty, as the challenged always do. Ruth saw how it was, and relented, as the woman always does. She ran her arm through David's, and gave it an affectionate teasing little squeeze.

"You can't help not knowing anything, can you, poor dear?" she said, with sweet laughter. "Well, then, never mind. We will try to find out together. There are only three things that I really must know—that I can't possibly do without knowing."

The smile faded. She sat silently gazing across the wide, quiet river.

"Only three really very, very important things," she presently went on. "The first is this: How may a girl tell what people call

Nancy Huston Banks

'true love' from every other kind of love? You see, dear, there are so many kinds of love, and they are all true, too. When a girl like me has loved every one ever since she could remember—because every one has always been so good and loving to her that she couldn't help it—she knows, of course, when another kind of love comes; but she doesn't know whether it is truer than all the rest. How can she tell? That is one of the things I want to find out—the first of the three really important things that I most wish to know," checking it off on her small forefinger.

Resting her elbow on her knee, and her chin in the palm of her hand, she fell suddenly silent again, and sat gazing across the river. Her blue eyes seemed to be wistfully seeking the secret of love among the rosy mists which the sunset had left beneath the shadowy trees. She did not observe that the boy made no reply. Her lovely head was intently bent to the other side, as if listening to hear some whisper from her own heart. When she spoke, it was in a low, absent tone, as though she were whispering to herself, or thinking only half aloud.

"And what are the signs of true love? That is the next thing. What are the sure signs that true love may be known by, so that there can be no danger of making a mistake, no risk of taking one kind of love for another? That is the question. How do the signs of true love look? How do they feel, I wonder? Can it be one of the sure signs of true love to feel at the first sight of a face that it is the one you have most wanted to see all your life? Can it be one of the sure signs of true love to have your heart leap at the first sound of a voice, so that you are glad to be alive—glad—glad as you never were before, although you have always been happy? I wonder—I wonder! And can it be another of the sure signs of true love to feel utter content in one presence, to feel that, walled in with it forever away from all the rest of the world, there would be nothing left outside on the whole, wide earth to wish for? Do you think so, David? I wonder if it can be. And then can it be yet another of true love's sure signs to have a warm, sweet glow come around the heart, as it never did before, and to have something tell you that it will grow warmer and sweeter and brighter as long as you live? I wonder—wonder—wonder. And could it be the surest sign of all, that you don't know why any of all these things are so; that you only know that everything some one is and says and thinks and does—satisfies and delights your eyes and mind and heart and soul."

Two heavy tears, like sudden drops from a summer shower, fell on her clasped hands, although her lips were smiling and she was still softly thinking aloud.

"And yet there is another kind of love—quite, quite different from this—and that, too, must be true. A feeling that you have had ever since you could remember must be true, surely. And you are always thinking about this one—always arguing with yourself about how right and reasonable it is. There isn't any trouble in finding one the reasons for this love. The only trouble about this kind of love is in your own unworthiness. It's somehow disheartening and tiring to be always looking up, higher than you can see, as though you stood all the time on your tiptoes. And then when you are always feeling how unwise and childish you are, it is hard to love wisdom and dignity as they deserve to be loved."

Saying this, Ruth turned suddenly upon David. Her soft eyes were flashing through her tears.

"Why do you sit there like a stone and never say a word!" she demanded. "I knew you didn't know the first earthly thing about love, but I didn't know you were dumb. Why don't you speak? Can't you say what a fine fellow William is? You know it, just as well as I do! Everybody knows it. Everybody respects William and looks up to him. Everybody is bound to do it. He always does what is right and sensible. He isn't forever doing and saying things that he has to be sorry for, as I am. He always goes steadily straight ahead. He isn't moved by every heart-beat and swayed by every fancy like you and me. Why even uncle Robert defers to William, because he is so dignified and right-minded. He always knows just what to do and say.

Nancy Huston Banks

Uncle Philip often speaks of it. *He* appreciates William. *He* never criticises him for being serious when other people are joking. And I've seen you do it many a time, when you didn't know I was looking. Yes, and uncle Robert, too. I've seen his eyebrow go up when he didn't know that it did. And I won't have it! Do you hear? I won't have people laughing at William, just because he never laughs. I like him all the better for it. I think all the more highly of him because he never understands my silly, light little ways. I do—I tell you I do!"

She sprang up and stamped her foot, and then, sitting down again, burst into helpless sobbing, and laid her head on the boy's shoulder. He could only draw her closer, and hold her in silent tenderness, having no words that he dared utter. After a time her sobs ceased, and lifting her head, she looked round, dimpling and smiling through the tears which were still heavy on her dark lashes.

"Well, then, since you don't know anything about love, sir, look and see what your silly old book says. Oh, you needn't pretend that you haven't got it," she said gayly. "If it isn't in your hand, it is in your pocket, or you have hidden it. Get it instantly," pretending to shake him.

The boy bashfully drew the book from beneath the log, while Ruth bantered him with sweet, bubbling laughter that made him think of awakening birds and blossoming orchards. He turned the leaves in embarrassed haste.

"I don't find anything about love," he stammered. "But here is something about marriage."

"As if they weren't one and the same!" cried Ruth. "Read it. Let's hear what it says. Read every word carefully and distinctly."

David then read aloud what the Knight of the Oracle said to the Most Fair Constantia:—

"They are truly married that have with united hearts plighted promise of perpetual friendship, electing one another by true love and not by outward ceremony; for where true love is not there can be no perfect marriage, though the outward ceremony be never so well performed."

"As if everybody didn't know that already!" scouted Ruth. "Any gosling of a girl knows that without having to be told. There isn't a single word there to tell what true love is, and what its signs are. If I didn't love you so dearly, David, I couldn't love you at all when you are so dull. What do you mean by reading anything so tiresome out of that foolish book? I think worse of it than ever."

Her smiles vanished like watery sunbeams. David trembled for fear she might begin crying again. But she looked fondly up in his face, and beamed brightly when she saw how frightened he was.

"But you know I do love you, David, dear. You know that you are all I have, of my very own," she said. "I am unreasonable— I know that well enough; but I couldn't help being hurt at your injustice to William. Could I, dear?"

"Oh, no! No indeed!" responded the boy, with vague eagerness.

"Well, then, I will forgive you if you promise never to do it again. And do you know any more about birds than you do about love, you poor dear? Look at that one flying over the river. Why do they always cross the stream in a slanting direction? Why do they never fly straight across? And why do birds sing so seldom in the depths of the forest? And is it true that none of the singing birds were here till the settlers came? It is said that they came with the settlers. I've heard many persons state that as a fact. But how does anybody know? Did any bird say so? Those paroquets could tell if they would; but they never will. They only chatter to scold one another. Just listen! I am sure they could tell lots of things if they liked.

They are not so green as they look—not half so green as you, my dear. I shall have to ask Mr. Audubon if there were any birds here before the settlers came. He will know; he doesn't go round all the time with his head in the clouds, as you do. You don't even know how old a snow-goose has to be before it turns from gray to white. And you really ought to know that, because you are a goose yourself. I saw a pure white snow-goose the other day on the pond back of Cedar House, and when the snow-goose comes, then winter is here, and it isn't long till Christmas."

She suddenly stood up shivering, and said she was cold; but it was the thought of Christmas Eve, not the frost in the air, that sent the chill to her heart.

XVII

THE ONCOMING OF THE STORM

On entering the great room of Cedar House they found the rest of the family in a most unusual state of excitement. The lamps and candles had not been lighted, as it was not yet quite dark, but the firelight was bright, and they could plainly see the anxiety on every face.

Miss Penelope was in her accustomed place, which she could no more get away from than a planet could leave its orbit. But her attention was wandering, as it rarely did, and she was silently casting uneasy glances at the judge and his nephew who sat on the other side of the room, talking to each other in a loud, excited tone. The widow Broadnax, also, was in her usual seat in the chimney-corner, yet looking now and then at the two men; and the mere fact that she thus allowed her gaze to stray for a moment from what her half-sister was doing, indicated the uncommon disturbance of her mind.

Ruth and David hardly knew the judge as he looked and spoke now, for it was he who was speaking as they came in. He had just motioned his nephew to silence with a sternness which was not to be disobeyed. His voice rang with a decision and severity, such as none of the household had ever heard from him, who was commonly so carelessly mild and abstracted.

"No one shall, with my consent, or even my knowledge, go from my house to Duff's Fort on any account whatever."

"Pardon me, sir," began William, stiffly.

He was keeping his self-control with the air of one who does it under great provocation, and who has scant respect for those who lose it; but his face was flushed, and his eyes were angry. The strained coldness of his tone and manner were like oil to the flame of his uncle's wrath. The judge's hand went out in a gesture that had almost the force of a blow.

"Stop!" he shouted. "I refuse even to discuss the matter. It is enough for me to tell you again that no one shall go from under my roof to the place where robbers and cutthroats congregate. It's a disgrace that I haven't been able to break up their den. I have done my best, and I am still doing it, but the reproach of this band's existence, here at my very door, nevertheless rests on me more than on any one else. I am the representative of the law—the law, good God! with the country in the murderous clutches of that lawless gang! Keep away, I tell you! And I will ask Alston what he means by even seeming to give countenance to those scoundrels by going nigh them. Business! What business can he or any other decent man have with the nest of rattlesnakes that we can't drag out from under that bluff?"

"It is a very simple matter, sir, if you would permit me to explain," William said more coldly and deliberately than ever. "Mr. Alston is merely making a trade for a boatload of horses, and simply asked me, as his attorney, to meet him at Duff's Fort to draw up the contract with Mason and Sturtevant."

The judge stared blankly for a moment, so overwhelmed by surprise that he forgot his anger. "Mason and Sturtevant," he repeated. "Do you mean to tell me that a man of half Alston's intelligence doesn't know that those men never have a horse that they haven't stolen?"

William Pressley said nothing more; he suspected that his uncle had been drinking a little more heavily than common. Moreover, it scarcely seemed worth while to argue with blind prejudice, drunk or sober.

"Then if you've got nothing more to say, it's with Alston that I will settle this matter. But all the same, I forbid you to go near Duff's Fort. I have a right to forbid you, as a member of my household. I have a right to forbid any one belonging to my family to do anything that touches my own honor, my good name. And this touches both to the quick."

"Very well, sir. I shall tell Mr. Alston what you say. I must, of course, give some reason for breaking a professional engagement," said William.

"I shall tell him a few things myself," stormed the judge. "It's all very well for him to put on his high-and-mighty tolerant air about the state of things hereabouts, and to keep on saying, soothingly, that everything will come right after a while, as it does in all new countries; but neither he nor any honest man can afford to handle pitch. It sticks to the cleanest hands. See that you keep yours out of it. Nobody belonging to me shall be smirched—and just now, too, when we are going to cleanse the whole country of it at last, thank God! We have only been waiting for a chance to carry out the plan which was arranged while General Jackson was here. Joe Daviess has now found the opportunity, and our campaign has already begun. He is determined to put it in motion before he leaves for Tippecanoe—"

"Then he is really going?" broke in William, quickly, with a marked change of tone and manner.

The judge paid no attention to the question. He seldom noticed what his nephew said, and his thoughts were now solely of the undertaking which absorbed him heart and soul. After thinking deeply in silence for a few moments, he spoke of the plan more fully, even freely, as he was in the habit of speaking in the bosom of his own family. There was no one else present; even the servants were gone out of the room. Moreover, he had been drinking, as his nephew suspected, and the stimulant, together with the excitement, carried him beyond all prudence. He did not even lower his tone.

"Yes, we begin the good work this very night. We've got the chance we have been waiting for—the chance to catch those cutthroats red-handed! We had news yesterday that three men were coming over the Wilderness Road, bringing a large sum of money to buy land. The negotiation has been under way for weeks. We have learned that this fact, and the time when these men are expected to pass through here, are both as well known at Duff's Fort as they are to us. We have also had news of the coming of a large flatboat with a rich cargo, which is due to pass down the river by Duff's Fort some time during to-morrow night. Those hungry demons are said to be ready and waiting for the travellers by land and water—and we are ready and waiting for them! Just let them lift a hand to rob or murder, and we will be on hand, too! The attorney-general has sent a large posse of picked men down the river to come up overland on the further side of the fort. Another posse has gone round by the swamp to guard that quarter, and there is a boat in readiness on the other side of the river, well armed and fully manned. Yes, we've got the scoundrels safe enough this time! We've run them to earth at last. There is only one loophole, and the attorney-general himself is to guard that— the path round Anvil Rock. That is the band's highway. The rock is their rallying-point and we couldn't see at first how we were to watch it without putting the scoundrels on their guard. To send any number of men, even two or three, in that direction, would have been to give the alarm at once—as the moon is about full. After consultation, it was decided that the attorney-general alone should attend to this delicate part of the plan. It was his own suggestion that he should go to Anvil Rock immediately after dark to-morrow night, and wait there in the shadow—watching everything that passes—till his men join him, after beating the bushes and going over the country with a drag-net. It's a dangerous task that he has taken on himself, notwithstanding that the posse guarding the swamp should be in hearing of his voice by the time he reaches Anvil Rock. I told him so; but he said that it must be done by some one man, since more than one would defeat our whole undertaking, and that it was the duty of no one but himself. However, he has ordered all his men—the different posses sent out in various directions—to draw in toward Anvil Rock, so that he will not be there long alone, and not at any time beyond the hearing of his men, should he find it necessary to call for help. Anyway, I couldn't dissuade him from going alone. It was no more than General Jackson had done, he declared, when I protested; and he also thought that being alone made it unlikely that he would be observed. The main object was for him to be near by when his men should need him, and that purpose would be best served by his waiting in the shadow of Anvil Rock. I said what I could, and urged him to let me go with him, but he stuck to it that only one man must go." The judge spoke anxiously, wearily now, all anger forgotten. "And he will be there. He never knew what fear was, in doing his duty; he would walk straight into the devil's den and attack him single-handed, without the quiver of a nerve."

"Allow me to congratulate you, sir," William Pressley said distantly, with an air of polite concession to somewhat foolish enthusiasm. "I think you have perhaps been rather more troubled over certain outbreaks of lawlessness than you need have been. They are to be expected, I suppose, in all new countries, and they gradually disappear before the advance of civilization, as Mr. Alston says. All that is in the natural order of human events. However, since you have been so much disturbed, I am truly pleased that you are so soon to be relieved of all uneasiness from this source. May I ask, sir, if you can tell me the precise date of the attorney-general's departure—for the seat of war, I mean—for Tippecanoe?"

The judge shook his head, hardly hearing the inquiry. The agitation which had shaken him was leaving him greatly spent. The old look of abstraction came back, quickly dulling his gaze, and, sinking down in his chair, he very soon began to nod and doze.

"With your permission, sir," William went on with a touch of sarcasm in his cool, slow voice, "I should like to call upon Mr. Alston to-morrow. You have, I presume, no objection to my going to see him in his own house. It is impossible to drop a matter of business without a word of explanation. And if you have no objection, I will mention to him the matters of which you have just been speaking. No one has a deeper interest in the public welfare, and certainly no one could be more eminently discreet. However, I shall, of course, speak in the strictest confidence."

The judge bent his head, but it was in nodding not in assent, for he had not heard a word that his nephew said. And William saw nothing but the nod with a sidewise glance of aversion at the signs of his uncle's weakness.

It was the boy who heard and saw everything, and remembered and weighed it, with a feeling of alarm that he knew no reason for, and could not explain to himself. It was his instinct to dislike anything that William Pressley said or did, and to distrust everything in which Philip Alston was concerned. He looked round at Ruth to see if she shared his feeling, and saw that she was gazing at William Pressley with troubled eyes.

They had scarcely exchanged a word since their quarrel, although she had made many timid advances toward a reconciliation. It was conscience and not love which had moved her in all that she had done, but this fact was not yet clear to her own mind. She was beginning to see it, but she tried to shut her eyes to the truth, being a loyal soul, and firm in her high regard for the man whom she had promised to marry. There had been no opportunity to tell him what she felt; and she was still more distressed to see that he avoided seeing her alone. It was of this cloud between them that she was thinking now, and it was that which shadowed her face. She had not noted very keenly what was going forward about her. She had shrunk from the judge's excitement and agitation, as she always did from all violence; but the meaning of his words had not impressed her deeply or even clearly. Her gentle nature and her tranquil life were too far from strife, cruelty, and crime for her to grasp the full purport of the story. She had heard William Pressley speak of telling Philip Alston, without giving the matter a thought. It was right in her eyes that he should be told everything. The mention of his name caused her to think that it would be well to tell him of her quarrel with William and of her regret and self-reproach. He was wise and kind, and would know what was right and best to do. Perhaps he might even see some way by which the engagement could be broken without wrong or hurt to William's feelings. A measure of peace came with the hope, and she was presently gazing into the fire, dreaming more than thinking, and feeling assured that the doctor would stop when he went by on the next morning.

The boy saw how absorbed she was, and felt that there was no use in waiting to speak to her, to tell her of the vague alarm which had seized him. And then what was there to tell her or any one? He would only be laughed at for fancying things, as he often had been before, and remembering this, he crept off to his own cabin and went to bed. But he could not go to sleep for a long time, and when he awoke at dawn the formless dread was still dark in his mind, like some fearsome shape behind an impenetrable curtain. And there it stayed all the day through, never quite coming out into the light, but growing steadily larger and darker and more terrible as the long heavy hours wore on. When—at last—the dusk began to creep down the river, he grew so restless in his nameless misery that he wandered into the forest, and there met the doctor riding along the path on the way to his lonely cabin.

Paul's face brightened at the sight of the boy; he had always liked him, and had been drawn to him before knowing of Ruth's existence. Still the thought of her was now foremost in his mind as he looked at David. We are all glad to see those who are near the one whom we love; we are even eager to seek those whom we would otherwise avoid when they are near our beloved from whom we are parted. This eagerness was in Paul Colbert's face as he looked at the boy and asked with some hesitation if he was in haste.

"If you are not," he said, "I should like to have a little talk with you. Let's sit down on that fallen tree."

Dismounting, he led his horse along the path, with the boy following in silence. They sat down side by side on the tree-trunk, the doctor holding his horse by the bridle. There were new lines in his face which did not belong to youth, and which had not been graven by his fierce struggle with the Cold Plague. The boy noticed them and knew that they had not been there when he had last seen the doctor's face. Its look of gloom also had come back. That had lifted at the moment of meeting, but it was too deep to go so suddenly, and it had now returned. He turned to the boy uncertainly, for there had been no clear purpose in his speaking to the lad. He had spoken on an irresistible impulse to learn something of Ruth, blindly clutching at a possible bond between her and himself. It seemed years rather than days since he had heard from her. But in a single glance his trained eyes saw that David was in trouble, and by asking a few adroit questions he brought out all that the boy knew. The doctor sat so still for an instant after hearing what had passed between the judge and William Pressley, that David looked up in surprise to see what was the matter. Paul Colbert was very pale, and his eyes were glancing round, searching the deepening shadows of the forest. He made a gesture, warning the boy to speak lower, and his own voice was scarcely above a whisper.

"What time to-day did Pressley leave Cedar House? Had he come back when you came away? Tell me again just what he said about telling Philip Alston. Try to remember every word—a valuable life may hang upon it. Keep as cool as you can—and be careful, don't be alarmed, but be quick. Every word now—once more."

The boy repeated everything as accurately as he could. While he was speaking, the doctor, rising to his feet, gathered up the bridle-reins, and hastily bending down, was tightening the girth. When the last item of information had been gathered, he vaulted into the saddle.

"There isn't any time for our talk. I must gallop home for a fresh horse. This one is too tired for the speed we need." He saw the surprise and, the alarm in the boy's gaze, and leaning over, took his trembling hand. "Don't be troubled. You are in no way to blame, whatever happens. You have done the very best thing possible in telling me this. It may not be too late. I shall try. I am going at once to do all that I can to warn or to guard a great man's life. The delay in getting the fresh horse is the worst; but," hastily grasping his hand again, "if I am too late, if I fail and never come back, tell Ruth that I did my best. Tell her that I have done my best ever since I have known. I have kept away from Cedar House—have only seen her far off, feeding the birds. But that was all I could do. I couldn't help thinking of her, I couldn't help what I felt. You will remember—and tell her?"

He looked down in the boy's frightened face with a strange smile, and then touching his horse with the spur, he flashed out of sight among the trees.

XVIII

THE GENTLEST ARE THE BRAVEST

The boy stood staring after him in dazed alarm. He could not comprehend the cause of his friend's sudden agitation and abrupt departure, but they filled him with vague, helpless terror. He did not know what to do till he suddenly felt the urgency of the message to Ruth, and the thought of her made him turn and start running back to Cedar House.

As he went, he instinctively tried to calm himself; he was fast learning to hide the emotion which was always shaking him. On reaching the door he paused for a moment, and strove hard to control his panting breath. He almost hoped that this might prove to be merely one of the fancies which were constantly swaying him. And then there was an instinctive feeling that it would be best not to tell any one except Ruth what had occurred. The meaning of the message to her was not yet clear to him, but he nevertheless felt it to be something which she might not wish others to hear. He did not remember that the message was not to be given her unless Paul failed to come back. There had not been time for Paul to impress this upon him, and it was natural enough that the boy, startled and frightened, should not have noted all that was said.

His one aim now was to get a word alone with Ruth, and hastily looking round the room, he saw her sitting near the hearth. But there was no chance to approach her, or to speak without being overheard by the whole family. Every member of the household was present, it being the evening hour when all households come closest together around the fireside. The supper-table was laid, and a servant moved about lighting the lamps and candles. William Pressley was sitting near Ruth, but it was she who had last taken a seat and he was silent, save as some timid advance from her compelled him to make a coldly civil reply. His resentment was as implacable as ever; the wound to his self-love had only grown deeper with nursing, as it always does with a nature like his. The breaking of the engagement was with him, now, merely a question of timeliness, of discretion and expediency. In these matters he was not considering Ruth's feelings as she was considering his, despite her own most eager wish to be free. He was thinking first of the light in which he, himself, would be placed. After this he was considering Philip Alston's view of his conduct. Knowing that he wished the marriage to take place, William Pressley felt reasonably sure that Philip Alston would be displeased at any breach, and that he would make his displeasure felt, should the first movement toward the breaking of the engagement come from himself. The displeasure of Philip Alston was not a thing to be lightly incurred at any time. No one knew this better than William Pressley, and he saw it to be particularly undesirable to displease him and possibly incur his enmity, just at the moment when his good-will might be useful in the matter of the appointment. William Pressley did not believe Philip Alston's influence to be at all essential—merit was in his opinion the only essential. Still it seemed best, under the circumstances, to let the engagement stand till a time more auspicious for breaking it. And then his sore self-love found some balm in the girl's self-reproach, which he saw plainly enough, without understanding it in the least. It was like him to consider the effect which the breaking of the engagement might have on his political prospects, and to postpone it on the bare chance of its affecting them adversely. But it was still more like him merely to postpone it with an immovable determination in his mind, utterly unaffected by all the girl's winning gentleness and open regret. And it was most of all like him never for an instant to allow any thought of Philip Alston's fortune to make him waver. All the gold in the world could have done nothing to make William Pressley forget, or forgive, the wound which his self-love had received.

She continued for a while in her shy, gentle efforts to win him back to something like the old friendliness, which had existed between them before they had become engaged to be married. It was this which she longed to have restored, with her craving for affection and her dread of hard feeling. But despairing at last, she arose with a sigh and went to the hearth, and began talking to the two old ladies, who left off quarrelling when she came, as they nearly always did. From the hearth she turned to the supper-table, to give it the delicate finishing touches, and then there was a general movement as the family settled into their places.

It seemed to David that the meal would never end, that he should never be able to tell Ruth. As he sat looking down at his untasted food, and had time to think, he came gradually to understand something of the meaning of the young doctor's sudden agitation, his solemn message, and his hurried departure. The boy could not keep his distress out of his face, and Ruth saw it in her first glance at him across the table. In the shadows of the room she had not seen him distinctly until now, and the sight of his trouble touched her as it never failed to do even when she believed it to be imaginary. As soon as possible she left the table and went to the door, glancing at him over her shoulder. He followed instantly and, passing her swiftly as she stood in the doorway, he beckoned her to come outside.

"What is it?" she asked, running to him.

She grasped his arm and turned white and began to tremble, not knowing what she feared. There was something in his look, and something in her own heart, which told her that this was no boyish whim or fancy, such as she was often called to comfort and beguile for him. She could not see his face distinctly enough to gather anything from looking at him; they were standing beyond the broad band of light streaming from the open door. But there was no need for sight; he poured out the story almost in a breath, ending with Paul's message to her. And she understood more than he had said, far more than he could ever say or understand, before the words had fairly left his lips. The divination of a woman's love—that marvellous white light—flashed the whole truth, and she uttered a smothered cry as she saw it. So crying out, she shrank away from him, and threw off his hand and struck at him fiercely, like some soft little wild thing suddenly hurt.

"How could you? Why did you tell him?" she cried. "I hate you. I'll hate you for this as long as I live. You have sent him to his death—you meddler, you simpleton! And you don't even know what you have done. You have sent him to his death, I tell you! Yes, that's what you have done, and I will never forgive you while I breathe. He has gone to warn the attorney-general, and he will be killed, too. You heard what uncle said about the danger. What are the robbers or the country to me—beside him? What do I care about what happens to the attorney-general? I wouldn't care if every other man in the world was lying dead, this minute, if I could know that he was safe. Oh! Oh! And you knew that he and the attorney-general were friends. You knew he would go to help him. And yet you told him—and he is gone—"

She broke into a helpless passion of weeping so pitiful that the boy could do nothing but go to her and take her in his arms. She did not resist; her anger was instantly melted in grief. Her arms went round his neck, and she sobbingly implored his pardon.

"Forgive me—forgive me. I didn't know—I don't know what I am saying. Oh! my heart is breaking, David! Help me—help me to think! We must do something—we mustn't stand here crying like this. Think! Think! Help me to think what we can do."

She pushed him away and stood pressing her trembling hands hard against her temples, trying desperately to clear her thoughts. The thought of calling on any one in the house did not cross her mind. There was nothing to expect from the judge; he had fallen asleep in his chair at the table. William Pressley would not believe there was any danger. He never believed in any trouble or agitation. It would only annoy him. Indeed, she scarcely thought of him at all. She caught the boy's arm wildly, with her tears suddenly dried.

"Why don't you say something—do something!" she cried bitterly, "You are no better than, a girl yourself."

She turned toward the house and ran a few steps only to come flying back.

"I have thought of something—you must go after him! That's what you must do! He may be wounded. He may need you to help him. Surely you could fight if you tried. I could, myself! And you will try, dear, I know you will, for my sake. Come! Run! Run! Let's go to the stable and get the pony. He goes fast."

Her passionate excitement swept them along, and she and the boy were now running toward the stable, hand in hand, hardly knowing what they did. Her head was bare, her white dress and her delicate slippers were very thin, and the chill of the autumnal night was already coming on. But she thought of none of these things, felt none of them, and did not stop at the door of the stable, although she had never entered it before, and it was now very dark within. But there was nothing for her to fear, she knew all about the horses, as every girl of the country did, since riding was a part of the life of the wilderness. Keeping close to David's side, she followed him to the pony's stall, and when she heard him take down the saddle and bridle that hung overhead, her hands eagerly went out in the darkness to help him buckle the girth.

"There! You will ride as fast as you can—I know you will. And you will help him fight. Make haste. Why didn't we think to get your rifle? Oh, why! You are very slow. There! Isn't it ready?"

But as the boy started to lead the pony from the stable, a sudden thought flashed through her mind, and she acted upon it as quickly as she grasped it.

"Let me have the pony," she gasped. "You can get one of the other horses for yourself. Make haste! I must have the pony because he is all ready. Hurry! Hurry! I have just thought— uncle Philip will help us. He can do anything. He will do anything in the world for me if I can only reach him. He is nearly always coming to Cedar House about this time. I am going to meet him. Everything will be safe and right if I can find him and tell him. Help me up to the saddle, quick! quick!"

They were now out of the stable and could see each other dimly. He exclaimed in affright, grasping her skirt and holding her back when she attempted to mount.

"It's my saddle, too, you couldn't ride that!" he cried.

"What difference does the saddle make? I have ridden it many a time—and many a time without any. If you will not—"

She caught the pommel, and he, seeing how utterly useless it was to contend further, now held out his hand and she set her foot in his palm. With a leap and a swift, lithe turn of one knee under the other she was seated in his saddle as easily and firmly as if it had been her own, and grasped the reins.

"Follow as quickly as you can," she called back over her shoulder. "I am going to meet uncle Philip in the buffalo path beyond Anvil Rock."

And then the pony sprang away and was running into the falling night.

XIX

UNDER THE HUNTER'S MOON

It was not very dark, and all the cleared country rolling widely away from Cedar House could be dimly seen. A gusty wind was driving wild clouds across the stars, and tall cloud mountains rose on the north covering the great comet; but higher in the dark blue dome of the firmament the Hunter's Moon swung full and free, casting its wonderful crystalline light over the darkened earth.

This most marvellous of crystal lamps always appears to be shining by its own living radiance, and never to be beaming by the merely reflected glory that gilds the lifeless Harvest Moon. The Hunter's Moon has indeed no rival among all the lights which heaven lends to the world of night. It is the whitest, the brightest, the most sparkling that ever falls on the darkness, and it was in truth the hunter's very own. By its light he could see how to go on with his hunt hours after the close of the short November days, and far into the long November nights, and still find his way home through the deep heart of the mighty wood.

So that even on this dreary November night, when its clearness was dimmed by the flight of the wind-hunted clouds, it was able to lighten in a measure the furthest and darkest reaches of this wild new world. It touched the mystery of the burial mound; it lifted the misty winding sheet spread by the swamp; it raised the pall laid along the horizon by the sable tops of the cypress trees; it reached almost to the darkness hanging over Duff's Fort—that awful and mysterious blackness—which the noonday sun could never wholly remove.

But the girl's gaze was not following the moonbeams. Looking neither to the one side nor the other, she gave a single glance ahead. This was only to see that she was going straight toward Anvil Rock by the shortest road. And the one look was enough for she knew that the great shadowy mass glooming in the dark distance must be what she sought. And then bending forward and low over the pony's neck, she sent him onward by an unconscious movement of her own body. She had known how to ride almost as long as she had known how to walk—the one was an easy and as natural as the other. Instinctively she now bent still lower, and still farther forward over the pony's neck, as a boy does in riding a race; for she also was riding a great race, and for the greatest of stakes. She did not stop to think how great the stake was; she had not yet realized that it was the life of the man she loved; she had not yet had time to face the truth, and to know that she loved Paul Colbert. She only realized that she must reach Anvil Rock before Philip Alston could pass it on his way to Cedar House, or turn into another path. Raising her head, she flashed another look into the dark distance, where the goal was and grew sick with fear, seeing how far off it was. And then rallying, she began to use her voice as well as the reins, to urge the pony to greater speed.

"That's it! Good boy. But faster—faster!"

Thus crying she silently prayed that Philip Alston might be within hearing of the sound of her voice. She never doubted that he would come at her first cry. It never once crossed her mind that he could hesitate to do what she wished in this. He had never in all her life refused her anything, and she knew of no reason to fear refusal now. The only fear that she felt was the dread of reaching Anvil Rock too late. She tried to still the quivering of her nerves by reminding herself that he nearly always came to Cedar House at this hour, if he had not been there earlier in the day. But she could not help remembering that there were times when he did not come. If he should not be on the way now, if she should fail to meet him, if he should be still at his far-off home, or have gone elsewhere—But she threw the paralyzing thought from her and suddenly began to strike the pony again and again, with her soft little open hands.

"Faster! You must go faster—you must! Surely you can. Please! It isn't very far. We must be almost there!"

It would have been hard to tell whether the short, sharp strokes were blows or caresses, and they ceased almost as abruptly as they had begun. She was now nearly lying across his straining shoulders, and her soft, bare arms were around his rough, shaggy neck. She did not know what she was doing, the boy had taught her to ride so—barebacked in the fields—when she was a child. And she did not know that the pony's mane was wet with her tears. There was no sound of weeping or faltering in the tone with which she urged him on. That rang clear and strong with the invincible courage and strength which love's miracle gives to the most timid and the weakest.

She was not holding to the saddle, but was clinging to it as unconsciously as the mist clung to her skirts. Her long black hair, fallen away from its fastenings, streamed in the wind; but she gave it no heed except to toss it out of her eyes so that she might see the pony's head, and try to look beyond toward Anvil Rock. How far off it still seemed! Would she never reach it? The night seemed to be growing darker, and she could not make out the mass glooming through the darkness as she had seen it at first. But she was not afraid of the growing blackness. This timid, gentle girl, who had hitherto been afraid of her own shadow, was now suddenly lost to all sense of fear. She thought nothing of the wild darkness into which she was thus flying blindly and alone. She had forgotten the terror of the time, and the dangers of the wilderness. She was oblivious of the utter silence, which wrapped the region in awful mystery. She heard nothing but the rush of the pony's running feet, and felt nothing but the leaping of her own heart. Her only thought was to reach the goal in time; her only fear was that she might fail.

Her ceaseless cry was goading the brave little beast like a spur. He still leapt in response to it; but his every sinew was already strained to breaking, and he was nearing the end of his endurance. The night had now become so dark that neither the pony nor the girl could see whither they were speeding. And then suddenly the Hunter's Moon broke the frail bars of its cloud prison, and was again free to cast its full splendor over the blackness. Under this sudden burst of light, Anvil Rock leapt out of the shadows—vague, black, huge, terrible—and she uttered a cry startled and relieved at seeing it so near by, when she had thought it much farther off. But as she looked again to make sure that it was real, and not some delusion of the mist, the first pang of fear struck back her leaping heart. She drew up the panting, staggering pony with a convulsive clutch on the reins—and waited, trembling and scarcely daring to breathe. Some large dark form moved among the shadows around the base of Anvil Rock.

Another swirl of the shrieking wind sent the fugitive clouds flying again across the white face of the moon. But only for an instant, and once more the darkness fled before the light of the crystal lamp. Yet its bright beams could not pierce the thick gloom which hung heaviest at the foot of the dark mass. Something still stood there, large, shadowy, and motionless. Ruth's trembling hand unconsciously went up and threw back the wildly blown hair which obscured her vision. As the white moonlight thus fell full on her face, the dark shape instantly sprang out of the gloom, and she recognized Paul Colbert almost as soon as he saw her.

Neither uttered a cry of surprise or even of relief, for neither felt any strangeness in this most strange meeting. When two hearts and two souls and two spirits have rushed together at the first meeting of the eyes,—as these two had,—no separation of mere flesh and blood can ever again really keep them apart. These two were now only facing outwardly the images which they constantly bore within their breasts. He had been thinking more of her through that wild ride than of the friend whose life he was perilling his own to save. She had felt his presence at her side with every step of the pony's flying feet; it was merely his body which she was striving to find and shield from harm. So that when they thus suddenly came face to face in the moonlight there was no need for a cry or a word. He sprang from his horse and leapt to the pony's side; and she—as silently and as naturally—held out her arms to meet his embrace.

But they started apart before touching one another. The distant sound of horses' beating hoofs came with a gust of wind. It was borne from the direction of Duff's Fort, and out from among the dark trees there now rushed into the misty moonlight a score or more of dim shapes, vague and terrible as phantom horsemen. Nearer and nearer these came rushing through the wavering mists, with scarcely a sound after that first warning roar brought by the wind. Paul sprang to regain his horse, but the animal was startled by the suddenness of the attempt, and frightened by the rapid approach of the other horses, so that he jerked the bridle from his master's grasp and reared beyond the reach of his hand. There was no time to pursue the horse; worse still, there was no chance to seize the rifle which hung from the pommel of the saddle. Paul had only one other weapon, the long hunting-knife carried by all the men of the wilderness. He drew this from his belt and it flashed in the moonlight as he ran back to the pony's head and stood between Ruth and the dimly visible danger which was rapidly approaching.

"They are coming the other way, too," she gasped. "I hear them behind us."

He did not reply and could not turn. She said nothing more and began sending up silent prayers. They could no longer see even dimly, for thick clouds again covered the moon. But she heard a fearful clash in the darkness, and then there followed those awful muffled sounds which are heard when men close silently in mortal combat. There was no sharp sound of firing—only the hideous thud of furious flesh against furious flesh—the one sound that the bravest woman cannot hear in silence. Ruth's cry for help pierced the very heavens. Again and again her anguished appeal rang through the night. In the height of her frenzied fear she heard the galloping of a horse and knew that it was coming nearer. This must be Philip Alston. The flash of the thought brought a gleam of hope and sent her louder cry farther into the darkness.

"Uncle Philip, for God's sake, come to me! Quick! quick! It's Ruth—uncle Philip! Philip Alston!"

Instantly all was still. The invisible conflict which had been waging with such fury so near by, now ceased as suddenly and as completely as if it had been ended by an unseen lightning stroke. The assailants silently drew back and stood motionless; but Ruth could not see what was taking place, and this sudden, strange stillness falling upon utter darkness filled her with greater terror. She thought that Paul had been killed. Alive, he would not leave her alone like this. Not for an instant would he forget her if he had strength to creep to her side. He was dead. He would never let these torturing moments pass without speaking to her if he had breath to speak.

"Uncle Philip! Philip Alston!" she cried again and again. "Don't you know me? It's Ruth."

"Here, I'm coming!" a man's voice shouted out of the distance. "Where are you? Speak again. Let me find you by the sound."

"They have killed him!" she shrieked. "I can't find him in the dark."

She was out of the saddle now, bending down and groping with her shaking, tender little hands on the torn and trampled earth. A wilder gust of wind brought the beat of rapidly retreating hoofs to her strained ears. She sprang up with a new fear and cried it aloud high and far above the shriek of the wind.

"They are taking him away! Will you never come? Is it you—uncle Philip? Oh—why—don't you come to me? It's Ruth."

"It is I—Father Orin," said the priest near by.

She did not reply, nor even glance at him, although the cloud curtain was now suddenly lifted again, and she could see clearly. She did not notice that all the horsemen had vanished. She saw only the motionless form of the man she loved lying some distance away. It was plain that he had pressed the assassins as far from her as he could; that his outstretched arms had fallen in some supreme effort. The hunting-knife glittered in the moonlight at a distance from his hand. He must have fought on with his bare hands after his only weapon had been struck from his grasp. His eyes were closed, and his face was like the face of the dead.

Ruth, dropping to the earth beside him, had taken his head on her lap before the priest could come up and dismount. She did not reply, nor even hear his alarmed questioning.

"See if he is living, Father," she said. "Here, put your hand on his heart—here—where my hand is. Make haste. Why are you so slow?" Then flashing round on him in her impetuous way: "Why don't you say that you feel his heart beat? Of course you do! Of course he is alive. How could he be dead—in a moment—a flash—like this! He is so young. He has only begun to live. And so strong and brave. Oh, so brave, Father! Dear Father Orin—if you could have seen how fearlessly he stood, between them and me—waiting for them to come! Only one, too, against so many. But I wasn't afraid while I could see him. No, not for a moment, even against them all. And then when it was dark, and I couldn't see him, and I could only hear—" she broke down, shuddering and weeping.

While she spoke the priest had been unfastening Paul's collar and was trying to find the wound. The bosom of his shirt was already darkly dyed with blood.

"He is alive; his heart is still beating," said Father Orin, huskily.

This daring, gifted young doctor had come to be like his own son in their work together for the suffering. He turned back his coat and found the deep knife-wound in his shoulder, and set about stanching the flow of blood with the simple knowledge of surgery that the life of the wilderness taught to all. But it was Ruth who thought of Paul's medical case which always hung on his saddle. The horse was gone, but the case was lying not far away, on the ground where it had fallen, and there were bandages and lint in it, as she hoped there would be. But when they had done all that they could, he still lay motionless and barely breathing. She dropped down beside him in fresh alarm, and again took his head on her lap. Father Orin stood up, looking helplessly through the moonlight and murmuring something about getting the doctor back to his cabin.

"We will take him to Cedar House," she said. "There is no one to nurse him in his own cabin. Oh!" with a smothered scream. "They are coming back!"

She could not suppress that one cry of fright which burst from her lips. But there was only one, she stilled the others and tried at once to control the trembling of her knees under his head. The dove will sit still when a cruel hand comes close to her nest; but no living creature has the courage of the gentlest woman when the man she loves is helpless—through no lack of strength or courage in himself—and in danger. The things which timid women have done then, stand among the bravest that have ever been set down to the credit of humanity. Believing that some hideous, unknown peril was sweeping upon them, this mere slip of a girl now bent quietly over the prone head and spoke close to the deaf ear without thinking whether or not it could hear.

"There, dear heart, there! Never mind. All is well. Lie still, or your wound will bleed. We are here, Father Orin and I. We will take care of you. Only lie still."

Two horsemen were now in sight and they were spurring straight toward Anvil Rock. While they were yet a long way off, Ruth felt, rather than saw, that one of them was David. She told the priest who it was, and they both knew that only a friend could be coming with the boy. Her whole form relaxed under the relief. If Paul could but open his eyes, if his breath would but come a little more quickly, and a little less faintly! Her tears were falling on his still, white face, now that there was no further need for self-control, or courage. She steadied her voice, and told the story as clearly as she could, when Father Orin asked again how she came to be in such a place, and what it was that had led to the wounding of Paul Colbert.

While she was speaking the horsemen reached them, and they saw that the man with David was the attorney-general. He hurriedly knelt down by his friend's side. He did not ask what had happened. He had already gathered much of the truth from what the boy had told him. He knew that Paul Colbert lay there, badly wounded, dying perhaps, in his place. He was too much moved at first to speak.

"He knew that I was coming alone over this road to-night. He suspected a plot to waylay me, too late to warn me. When he could not do that he came to share the danger. It was like him," he said when he found voice.

He took the nerveless hand and held it a moment in silence, and then he laid it gently down and stood up, looking about through the moonlight, toward the cypress swamp and Duff's Fort.

"But why did the scoundrels run away before finishing their infamous work? And where is the doctor's horse? Ah! They have stolen that, of course. Which way did they go? Did you see or hear them, Father?"

"No; Toby and I were too far off," the priest replied. "We were coming back from a sick call. It was too dark to see. The first and only sound I heard was Ruth's voice, calling Philip Alston's name."

"Oh!—I begin to understand," said the attorney-general.

He stopped—remembering—and looked down at Ruth. She had not heard what he said. She was bending closer to Paul's white face and listening to his laboring breath.

"We must get him home as quickly as possible," the attorney-general went on. "My duty at Duff's Fort must wait on this. And I am not sacrificing the state to a friend, or to gratitude. It would be worse than useless to go on to-night, now that our plans are betrayed. I am very anxious about my men. They should be here before now. According to our plans, they should have been within hearing of the first sound of trouble and ready to come at once. I am afraid they, too, have fallen into a trap; but I can't do anything now for them, and I must do my best for this poor fellow, and quickly, too. Come, Father,—come, David,—let us consult as to the best way to get him home."

The three men drew a little apart and stood talking together in a low tone, so that Ruth was left for a moment alone with Paul.

"Dear heart!" she breathed, with her cheek against his. "Listen, love. Can you hear what I say? Try. Try hard. For if you can hear, maybe my heart will not break. Listen, then," as softly as if her spirit spoke to his. "Listen. I am yours and you are mine. Can you hear—dear heart? If you live or if you die—it is just the same—always—to me and to you. We belong to one another forever."

XX

BALANCING LIFE AND DEATH

While they consulted, several of the attorney-general's men galloped up. They had been delayed and sent astray by a false message purporting to come from him. But they had met with no harm and were now in time to help in lifting the wounded man's helpless weight into the priest's saddle. This was the best plan that could be devised in haste, and Father Orin hastily mounted behind the unconscious body, to hold it in place. He being much the strongest among the men, the duty naturally fell to him. It was also natural that the double burden should be laid upon Toby, because the heaviest burdens of life are always laid upon those who are readiest to bear them.

And Toby appeared to feel his responsibility, for, setting out at a rapid pace, which seemed to show that he knew the need of haste, he yet moved with so steady a step that Father Orin did not require the aid of the other hands which were held out to help him. Nevertheless, every hand was constantly in readiness, and all kept close together; so that thus moving through the dim light, the shadowy mounted figures looked like some fabulous monster of gigantic size and with many arms, all extended toward a common burden. But the pony kept closest to Toby's side and in the gloom that followed the going down of the Hunter's Moon, a trembling little hand stole out now and then, to touch the still, cold one which swung so pathetically over Father Orin's strong arm.

The stars were paling, and the dark east was growing wan, when Cedar House rose at last out of the gray shadows. At the first glimpse of it Ruth suddenly sent the pony forward and urging him to a run, left the others far behind. Reaching the house, she leapt to the ground and ran to the front door. It was deeply in shadow, but she did not need sight to find the latch string, which she had played with as a child, and in another instant she stood in the great dark room. It was deserted all the household being asleep, and never dreaming that she also was not safely in bed. The fire had been covered as it always was at night, but it blazed when she stirred it, and by the light of the flame she found a candle on the tall mantelpiece. Holding this to the blaze, it seemed to her as if it would never catch the flame. When the wick caught she went running up the stairs with the lighted candle in her hand, arousing the sleeping household by repeated calls. She did not pause to answer the alarmed cries that came in response. She heard a scream from Miss Penelope's room, with, muffled sounds from the widow Broadnax's, and the disapproving tones of William Pressley's voice. But she was utterly heedless of everything, except the necessity of getting the room ready in time, so that there should be no waiting before doing what might be done. She quivered with terror to think how long the delay had been already. The servants were too far away to be summoned quickly, so that there was only herself to do what must be done, and she set about it in desperate haste. Hers was the only chamber that could be given him. Every room in Cedar House was occupied, and it was always her room which was given to a guest, so that she often slept on a couch in Miss Penelope's chamber. But she did not think of that; there was no thought of herself, beyond wishing to give him her own room. Had there been ever so many guest chambers, she would still have wished him to have hers. But to get it ready in time! To make sure that there should be no further waiting before doing all that human power could do. Even now it might be too late. The wood fire had almost burned out, and to kindle a blaze was the first thing to be done, so that she ran straight to the hearth and dropped on her knees beside it. There was a little heap of sticks in the chimney-corner, but her hands trembled so that she could hardly put them on the dying coals. The breath that she coaxed the flame with came in gasps, but a blaze quickly sprang up and leapt among the sticks, and then she flew to prepare the bed. If she might only get it ready before they came! The thought of that helpless head lying against Father Orin's shoulder was like a stab at her heart.

Footsteps were rushing up and down stairs, and excited voices were calling her name all over the house, but she did not pause or turn from her task. It was Miss Penelope who first found her and clamored to know what had happened; but she did not stop to answer, and went on turning back the covers of the bed—the last thing needing to be done—and listening for the sounds of the horses' hoofs. They could now be heard approaching with that sad, slow, solemn rhythm—that subdued beat, beat, beat, of horses' feet—which has fallen on all our bruised hearts as an awful part of the funeral march. She ran out of the room and downstairs, drawing her skirt away from Miss Penelope's frightened grasp, and passing William Pressley, as if his restraining words had been no more than the gusty wind. She was waiting outside when the three horsemen drew up at the door. The burden which they bore was still apparently lifeless, and with a sickening pang of fear she bent over the parted lips as they lowered him from the saddle, thinking for one despairing moment that he no longer breathed. But the faint flutter went on, and she gave way so that he might be borne up the stairs, and running before, she told them where to lay him down.

William Pressley made one or two efforts to direct what was being done, and although the girl's passionate excitement swept him aside, he still did what he could, and offered to furnish a fresh horse for the quicker fetching of the doctor, when the attorney-general said he would go for him at once. It was like William Pressley to do this; it would have been unlike him to neglect any duty that he saw. But the offering of the horse and the full performance of his own duty did not keep him from looking at Ruth in severe displeasure. He did not yet know how this thing had happened, and was far from suspecting that she had been out of the house that night. Yet it disturbed and angered him to see her flying here and there, and running to and fro to get things that were wanted, as though the servants could not be quick enough. With all this in his tone, he coldly and strongly urged her to join the rest of the family, pointing out the fact that there was nothing more to be done by any one till the doctor should come. But she merely shook her head, without speaking, and slid softly into a seat by the bedside, and there William Pressley left her, disdaining to contend. She thought that she was alone—so far as she thought of herself at all—but the boy sat unseen and forgotten in a shadowed corner of the chamber. He was gazing at her, but her gaze never once wandered from the still white face on the pillow.

The rest of the family were gathered around the hearth in the great room downstairs. The judge had been summoned from the cabin in which he slept, and he was now plying Father Orin with questions. There was a cry of alarmed amazement when the priest told of finding Ruth at Anvil Rock. Only William Pressley said nothing, and sat perfectly still, with a sudden stiffening of his bearing. It was not easy for the priest to make the whole story clear, for he did not understand it quite clearly himself. But he told as much as he knew of the night's events. And when he was done, the judge's voice stilled the clamor of the other excited voices.

"How can the child have known what was going on? Where is she? We must find out at once how she came to do so wild and strange a thing. What under heaven could she have been doing there—in such a place, at such a time? Where is she?" But he went on with another thought, without waiting for an answer. "How can those murderous scoundrels have known that the attorney-general would ride to Anvil Rock alone? It is plain enough that they did know. The question is—How? By what means can they possibly have learned anything about the plan? That's the thing! How did they find out enough to enable them to set this villanous trap? All those assassins hidden there in the darkness of the Cypress Swamp, waiting to spring out on one man!" He turned suddenly to the priest. "What is your opinion, Father? Have you the slightest idea how they could have learned anything of our plan?"

Father Orin looked straight at William Pressley.

"Yes, I have an idea," he said quietly, with his gaze still fixed on the young lawyer. "But it is merely unfounded suspicion. I have no real reason for my suspicions."

"Well, what are they?" asked the judge, eagerly. "You can hardly be afraid of doing any injustice to those scoundrels. It would be hard to suspect such murderous villains of any sneaking treachery that they wouldn't be guilty of if they could. How do you think they found out? That's what I want to know."

Father Orin was still looking steadily at William Pressley, who returned the look just as steadily with one that was easier to read than the priest's. William Pressley's gaze expressed a large, patient tolerance for prejudice, slightly touched with calm contempt, and there was no doubting its entire sincerity.

"I think," said Father Orin, slowly, "that these banded robbers and murderers must have learned of the plan through some one's inadvertence. It is my opinion that the plan was betrayed by some one who did not mean to betray it, and who may not have known what he had done."

William Pressley regarded him with an incredulous smile. "It is hardly likely that the plan can have been revealed in any such way as you suggest, sir," he said, with the politeness which is more exasperating than rudeness. "You are certainly over-looking the fact that only a few knew what the attorney-general intended to do, and that those who did know are the ablest and most reliable men in the country. It is therefore utterly out of the question to assume that any one among them, any man of their intelligence and standing, could have made such a blunder. Really, my dear sir, if you will pardon my saying so, the idea is absurd."

The priest made no reply and his eyes were still fixed on the young lawyer's face, but as he gazed, the expression of his own face changed. A half smile lighted it for a moment. The good man's sense of humor was keen. But this passed quickly and in its stead there came the compassion which any purely human weakness, however great or small, always awoke in his truly compassionate breast.

The judge apparently had not heard what his nephew said. He always began to feel impatient as soon as the young man commenced to speak. And he now gave his tousled head the old, unconscious toss, like a horse shaking his mane at the lighting of a persistent fly. And then, paying no more attention to William Pressley and drawing his chair nearer Father Orin's, he went on with the grave talk. It was he, however, who did all the talking now; the priest had suddenly become a passive listener. He had no more ideas to advance.

The three men turned many anxious looks on the open door. It was still a framed space of misty gray, filled only with the melancholy mystery of the wintry dawn. It seemed to the watchers to stay unchanged for a long time, as it always does to those who watch for its brightening in trouble and anxiety. Yet while they longed for the light they dreaded to see it, as the troubled and alarmed always dread, lest it should reveal something terrible which the darkness has concealed. Their words grew fewer, also, under this strain of waiting, and they gradually fell into the tone that night watchers use, when they speak of mysterious things under the gloomy spell of this sad half-light which is neither night nor day. In the silences between their hesitating words, they bent forward and listened. All was still—there was no distant sound of the attorney-general's return or of the old doctor's coming. In the tense stillness they could hear only the sad murmur of the river gliding under the darkness and—now and then—the sudden hurrying of footsteps in the chamber overhead where the wounded man lay.

And so a long, heavy hour dragged by. The leaden gray framed by the doorway began to glimmer with a silvery pallor. The quicker breath of the awakening world sent a heavier shower of leaves from the trees. The birds still lingering among the cold, bare branches were already awake, and calling cheerily to one another, as if the higher world in which they lived was all untouched by the struggle and strife of this lower human world. The heavy-hearted men in the great room of Cedar House listened with the vague wistfulness that the happiness of bird voices always brings to the troubled. They also heard the low trumpeting of the swans as the breath of the morning swayed the rushes and that, too, filled them with a deeper longing for peace. But suddenly the far-off echo of a horse's rapid approach made them forget everything else. The doctor was coming at last! As one man, the three men sprang to open the door, and leapt out into the pallid daylight. The horseman was now near by and in another moment they saw that the rider was not the doctor, nor yet the attorney-general, but Philip Alston.

The priest shrank back with an uncontrollable recoil and then stood still and silent, watching every movement of the tall figure which had reined up and was dismounting with the ease of a boy. The judge and his nephew had made an exclamation at the sight of him; but they were merely surprised at the unusual hour of his appearance and he explained this at once.

"Where is Ruth? What is wrong? Has anything happened?" he asked, turning in visible agitation from one to another. "What was it that those men on horseback brought here? I could barely make out something moving this way. Has anything happened to Ruth? The light was dim, and I was a long way off. I was coming from the river where I had been attending to the loading of a boat, and so happened to see that something was going on. But I wasn't near enough to tell what it was. Of course I came at once to see if there was any trouble, and to do what I could. Is anything wrong with Ruth? My horse fell and lamed himself, or I should have been here much sooner. Tell me instantly! What have you done with the child? What have you allowed to happen to her? By God, if—"

He demanded this accounting in a tone of passionate fierceness such as none of those present had ever heard in him, turning first upon William Pressley and then upon Robert Knox. His face was white, and his eyes were blazing, and they did not at once resume their natural look when he had been assured of Ruth's safety. But he said nothing more, and only Father Orin noted how altered and worn and old he looked, when he entered the room and the brighter light fell upon him.

He came to the fireside and sat down with the light of a swinging lamp falling full on his face. His clear blue eyes, growing quiet, now looked straight into Father Orin's—which were openly searching and suspicious—during the second telling of the story of the night. It was not easy for suspicion to stand against such a gaze. The priest's wavered in spite of its strength. No one could believe evil of Philip Alston while looking in his noble, open face. He did not speak immediately after the story was told. When he did, it was to say, quietly and naturally, precisely what any right-minded man would have said under the circumstances:—

"This young stranger is certainly a man of courage. He has protected the attorney-general at the risk of his own life. In doing this, he has done a great service for all of us—for the whole country. We must now do what we can for him. Is he badly, hurt? Where is he? Who is with him?"

The priest saw that he flinched for the first time when told that the wounded man had been taken to Ruth's room.

"That was wrong," said Philip Alston, with a subtle change in his tone. "Ruth must have nothing further to do with this extraordinary and most unfortunate affair. She has had far too much to do with it already. That mooning, foolish boy must have led her into this romantic folly through some girlish enthusiasm about Joe Daviess, the popular hero of romance. It is plainly the boy's fault that she was induced to do so dangerous and unheard-of a thing. She could never have thought of it herself. I shall see that he keeps his place hereafter. We must look to it, William," turning upon the young man with more severity than his voice often expressed. "Where is she? What is she doing? I wish to see her."

It was the judge who told him that she was in her own room, together with the older ladies, all in attendance upon the injured man. The priest then saw the second swift darkening of Philip Alston's face.

"I will go up to her room," he said quietly. "I wish to be sure that she has not been harmed."

As he rose, there was a sound outside. He turned to the open door and saw two horsemen approaching at a gallop. It was light enough for him to see and recognize the attorney-general and the doctor. The other men hurriedly went out to meet them. Philip Alston stood still in a shadowed corner of the great room, while the rest hastened up the stairway and into the chamber where Paul Colbert lay. And then he followed them with his swift, light step, and pausing upon the threshold, looked into the open room, his gaze first seeking Ruth. She stood on the other side of the chamber, apart from the group around the bed. But she did not see him; her eyes and hands and thoughts were on the bandages which she was hastily preparing. He shrank from what she was doing and turning hastily away fixed his eyes on the attorney-general. Thus, silently looking and listening, he presently heard him say how deeply he regretted being compelled to leave the country before knowing the result of his friend's wound, adding that he was leaving on the next day for Tippecanoe. Philip Alston barely glanced at the white face lying against the pillow. He was disturbed and even shocked to see it there. He felt this stranger's presence in her chamber to be a desecration. And then the sight of suffering always made him uncomfortable. He wondered how she could endure it. The repulsion which the average man feels for any affliction of mind, body, or estate was so intensified in him that he could not, with all his intelligence, understand that the very sight of great suffering nobly borne, does much to win a woman's heart.

Nancy Huston Banks

XXI

THE EAGLE IN THE DOVE'S NEST

The worst hurt that Paul Colbert had received was from a blow on the head, which had stunned and nearly killed him. But there had been no lasting injury, even from this, and the knife-wound in his shoulder had healed rapidly; he was young, and strong, and healthy.

On the morning of the seventh day he awoke and looked at Ruth. He was feeling almost well, but had no inclination to stir. It was pleasant enough just to lie there and look at her, and let his gaze wander around her chamber. This white shrine of maidenhood! He had felt its influence before he was able to understand, and the reverential awe had grown with his returning strength. How dainty it was, for all its rough board floor and rude log walls! Even those were as white as the driven snow. The bed was like the warm, soft breast of a snow-white swan, and its drawn curtains like folded wings. There were spotless muslin curtains over the windows, and the little toilet table also was draped in white and strewn with bits of carved ivory. The whole room showed the same mingling of luxury and simplicity that was to be seen in the great room below.

These fine ivory carvings, the rare prints and a painting or two on the rude walls, the alabaster vase on the rude stand,—filled with fresh, late-blooming flowers,—the costly white fur rug on the floor, the delicate work basket with its coquettish bows of riband, contrasted oddly with the other simple things which had evidently been made in the wilderness by unskilled hands. Yet even those were tasteful and all painted white, so that the whole was purity, beauty, and exquisiteness.

Yet his gaze quickly turned from the room to her. He knew that she believed him to be asleep; but it was so pleasant to watch her that he did not hasten to let her know that he was awake. She was very busy at the window, with her back to him, and deeply absorbed in something that she was doing. Moving lightly and swiftly to and fro across the light, she was working hard, with no more noise than the sunbeams made in glancing about her slender form. He lay watching her for some time in dreamy delight, before he saw what it was that she was doing. But presently he knew that she was making an aeolian harp. The two fragile bits of vibrant wood to hold the strings were already in place on either side of the window, just where the upper and lower sash came together. She was now engaged in carrying the threads of fine silk floss, which were to form the strings of this simple wind-harp, from one piece of wood to the other. Back and forth she wove them across the current of air, moving with swift, noiseless motions of exquisite grace. As the last fine fibre thus fell into place and was firmly drawn, a soft, musical sigh breathed through the shadowed room, the very shadow of music's sweet self.

"Thank you," Paul Colbert said. "What beautiful things you think of, what lovely things you do!"

She turned quickly with a smile and a blush, and came to the bedside.

"Why—you were not to wake up yet! It's much too early for a sick man to open his eyes."

"But I am not a sick man any longer. I am almost well. I could get up now, if I wished," jestingly, "I am getting well as fast as I can, just to convict the other doctor of a mistaken diagnosis. What a fine old fellow he is!" with a quick change to earnestness. "How kind he has been, how untiring in his attention and goodness to me. And so skilful, too. I am ashamed of my presumption. A mere beginner like myself, to question his methods in dealing with the Cold Plague! I don't believe he made the mistakes they said he did. He couldn't!"

It was an unlucky recollection. The thought of this mysterious epidemic which had grown worse, till it was now devastating the whole country, made him suddenly restless. His patients were needing him sorely while he lay here, still bound hand and foot by weakness. He turned his head miserably on the pillow. It was not the first time that this thought had troubled him, and she knew the signs. Laying a gentle, soothing hand on his tossing head, she spoke in the quieting tone that a woman always uses to soothe and comfort a child or a man whom she loves.

"It will not be long now. You can soon go back to them," she said.

The tone was none the less soothing because a bitter pang went through her own heart with the words. What should she do when he was gone? And he was almost strong enough to return to the work which was calling him. But the aching of a true woman's own heart has nothing to do with the peace that she gives to those whom she loves. And then it may have been only the sweet sadness of the spirit harp's sighing that made Ruth's lips quiver under their bright smile.

"But they need me now," he groaned. "They are dying untended while I lie helpless here. The old doctor cannot take care of them. He has too many patients of his own. He is riding day and night. He tries to hide the truth, but I know it. The Cold Plague grows in violence every day."

He suddenly raised himself on his elbow with a great effort.

"Maybe I can sit up if I try very hard," he gasped. "The will has much to do with the strength. I am determined—"

"No! no!" cried Ruth in alarm.

But he had already sunk back exhausted. His lids drooped heavily for a moment through weakness. And then he looked up in her frightened face with a reassuring smile as she gently pressed his head down upon the pillow.

"What strict little mother," he murmured.

She shook her head and drew the counterpane closer about his neck, carefully lightening the weight over his wounded shoulder. With soft light touches she smoothed out the smallest wrinkle marring the comfort of the narrow, bed. When this was done and he lay quiet again, she began to talk quietly but brightly of other things, hoping to divert his thoughts. She told him all the innocent gossip of the neighborhood. Most of this had come to her from the Sisters, for she seldom saw any one else. There was much to tell of their little charges, and particularly of the three babies whom he and Father Orin had taken from the deserted, plague-stricken cabin in the wilderness. She did not say that these little ones had become her own special care, but caused his smile to grow brighter by telling how like children the gentle Sisters themselves were. She repeated what they had said of Tommy Dye's last visit. Their serious, perplexed account of it was now unconsciously colored by her own gentle, fine sense of humor which also came so close to pathos that a lump rose in Paul Colbert's throat as he listened. He could see just how poor Tommy Dye had looked, but his eyes grew dim while his lips smiled. And now another and deeper shadow swiftly swept over his face.

"So even poor old Tommy Dye has gone to Tippecanoe. Everybody but me is gone or going. I alone am left behind. And yet—even if this hadn't happened—I must still have stood at my post," he said sadly.

Her hand fluttered down upon his like a startled dove. There was a sudden radiance in her dark blue eyes. She barely breathed the next words that she spoke:—

"Yes; you must have stayed, anyway. The doctor of the wilderness—the healer everywhere—can never march with other soldiers. He can never go shoulder to shoulder with cheering comrades at the roll of drums and the blare of trumpets under waving banners—to seek glory on the battle-field while all the world looks on and applauds. No—no—the doctor of the wilderness—the healer everywhere—is a solitary soldier, who must always go alone and silently to meet Death single-handed, and struggle with him, day after day, and night after night, so long as he may live, fighting ceaselessly for his own life as well as the lives of others."

There was a quivering silence, filled only with the sighing of the wind-harp. The young doctor's hand had closed over hers. She went on in a lower tone:—

"And surely the man who risks his life to save is braver than he who risks it to slay."

Startled at her own boldness, she drew away when he tried, with the slight strength that he had, to draw her to him. They had not spoken to each other of love. He knew little of what had taken place that night at Anvil Rock when she had believed that his soul and her heart were parting with all earthly things. He had not heard what she had said then, and they had not been left alone together since his hurt until this morning. There had been many constantly coming and going about the sick bed during the first days, and to him those days were mere blanks of suffering and blurs of pain. It was only to-day that he had begun to regain in a measure the power of his mind and will. If he could but have had for one instant the old power of his body! He did not know whether this beautiful, tender young creature beside him was still under promise to marry another man. There had been no opportunity for any confidential talk. The name of William Pressley had never been mentioned between them. The thought of him was like a touch of fire to Paul Colbert, so burning was the contempt which he felt for this conceited dullard whose blundering had nearly been his own death. But he could not say anything of this to her—the fact that she had once been engaged to be married to the man held him silent. It might be that she was still bound, and yet there was something in her soft eyes that led him to hope that she was free—something, at least, which seemed to give him leave to wrest freedom for her from the strongest that might try to hold her against her sweet will. If only he were not stretched here, a mere burden, a clog.

The look in his sunken eyes,—glowing like coals,—the burning words which she read on his silent lips, made her slip her hands from his and move hastily away. She went confusedly over to the window and hailed the sight of the birds on the sill with sudden relief.

"My little feathered family are all here," she said without looking round. "Can you see the blue jay? He is on the window-sill trying his best to peep over it at you."

"I hope he is jealous of me," trying to speak lightly.

"He's a great tyrant. He has driven away all the other birds. He will not allow them to have one of the crumbs that I put out. Most of them are sitting in a forlorn little row on the nearest tree. I wonder what he is saying to them in that rough voice, yet maybe it is better not to know. It must be something very rude, the redbird's bearing makes me think so. He is standing very straight and holding his head very high, but he isn't saying a word—of course. He is too much of a gentleman to quarrel with a rowdy like the blue jay. Just hear how he is domineering! These little song sparrows must surely be ladybirds—they are talking back in such a saucy twitter. Can you hear them? I wish you could see them. They are turning their pretty heads from side to side as much as to say, that he can't keep them from speaking their minds if he does keep them from getting the crumbs. Can you hear the silvery ripple of their plaints? Nothing could be sweeter. There! I will raise the window just a hair's breadth. Listen! Isn't it like a chime of fairy bells, heard in a dream? But I hope you haven't felt any draught. It is much colder than yesterday."

Dropping the sash she went to the fireplace and laid several sticks on the blaze. She stood still for a moment, gazing down at the fire and then she took a low chair beside the hearth. She knew that Paul Colbert was looking at her, but she did not turn her head to meet his gaze. For she also knew that he was merely biding his time, merely gathering strength to speak, merely waiting till he had found words strong and tender enough. If her eyes were to meet his, she must go to him—she could not resist—and yet she felt that she must not go while her plighted word was given to another man. It did not matter that the promise had been made under persuasion and in ignorance of what love meant. It made no difference that she was sure that William, too, longed to be free. The promise had been made, and she was bound by it, until she could tell William Pressley the truth and ask him to set her free. Soft and feminine as her nature was, she had nevertheless a singularly clear, firm sense of honor as most men understand that term— and as few women do. She had already tried more than once to tell him, but he had been almost constantly away from home of late. It was to her mind simply a question of honor. The dread of giving him pain which she had shrunk from at first, had now wholly passed away. It was so plain that he also recognized the mistake of this engagement and would be glad to be free, that the last weight was lifted from her heart. She had been truly attached to him as she was to almost every one with whom she came in daily contact, and this affection was not altered. Hers was such a loving nature that it was as natural for her to love those about her as for a young vine to cling to everything that it touches. Every instinct of her heart was a tender, sensitive tendril of affection, and all these soft and growing tendrils reaching out in the loneliness of her life had clung even to William Pressley, as a fine young vine will twine round a hard cold rock when it can reach nothing softer or warmer or higher. Her own rich, warm, loving nature had indeed so wreathed his coldness and hardness that she could not see him as he really was. And now—without any change in either the vine or the rock—everything was wholly different. It was as if a tropical storm had suddenly lifted all these clinging tendrils away from the unresponsive rock and had borne them heavenward into the eager arms of a living oak.

She knew now the difference between the love that a loving nature gives to all, and the love which a strong nature gives to only one. Her heart was beating so under this new, deep knowledge of life, that she feared lest the man whom she loved might hear. Yet she sat still with her little hands tightly clasped on her lap, as if to hold herself firm, and she held herself from looking round, though the silence continued unbroken. William must be told before she might listen to the words which she so longed to hear from Paul's lips. It was noble of him to hold them back. Every moment that she had been sitting by the hearth she had been expecting to hear them. So that she sat now in tense, quivering suspense, waiting, fearing, longing, dreading, through this strange, long silence; filled only by the sighing of the wind-harp and the crackling of the fire. And then, being a true woman, she could endure it no longer, and turning slightly she gave him a shy, timid glance. As she looked she cried out in terror.

His head, which had been so eagerly raised a moment before, had fallen; his eyes, which had been aglow but an instant since, were closed. The effort, the agitation, had been too great for his slight strength. The strong spirit, impatient of the weak flesh, was again slipping away from it.

She thought he was dying, and forgetting everything but her love for him, she flew to him and fell on her knees by his side. Raising his heavy head in her arms she held it against her bosom. She did not know that her lips touched his, she was seeking only to learn if he breathed. When his eyes opened blankly, she kissed them till they closed again, because she could not bear to see the dreadful blankness that was in them. When he moaned she fell to rocking gently back and forth, holding his head closer against her breast, and presently began to croon softly. She never once thought of calling for help; it was to her as if there had been no one but themselves in the whole world. And presently his faintness passed away, and when his arms, so weakly raised, went round her, she did not try to escape. After a little he found strength to speak a part of all that was in his heart, and she told him what she could of all that was in hers. And both spoke as a great love speaks when it first turns slowly back from facing death.

XXII

"A COMET'S GLARE FORETOLD THIS SAD EVENT"

When the barriers had thus been broken down, she had spoken of the breach between William and herself. There had not been a bitter word or a harsh thought in all that she said. It had been merely a mutual mistake; they had both mistaken the affection which grows out of familiar association, for the love that instantly draws a man and a woman together, though they may never before have seen one another, and holds them forever, away from all the rest of the world.

"I know the difference now," she said several days later, with a deeper tint in her cheeks and a brighter light in her blue eyes. "And I am sure that William does, too. It's plain enough that he will be glad to be free, but he cannot say so, because he is a gentleman. Don't you see?

For that very reason, just because he is so high-minded, I am all the more bound to do what is right. You do see, don't you?"

He was sitting up for the first time that day, his chair was by the window and she was sewing beside him.

"I see what you think is right," Paul said smilingly. "And he certainly should be told at once. But perhaps I might—"

"Oh, no! I must tell him myself. That would only be treating him with due respect. And William thinks a great deal of respect—much more than he does of love. But I can't get a chance to speak to him. He is always coming and going of late, and all the family are present when I do see him. You must wait; you must not say a word to uncle Robert till I have told William; it wouldn't be honorable on my part."

"But you are forgetting, little girl, that there may be scruples on my side, too. If my strength should come back as fast in the next two or three days, I shall be able to leave Cedar House before the end of the week. I cannot go away in silence; there must be no sort of secrecy. You perceive there is a question of honor there, too. I must speak to the judge—"

"It isn't any question of secrecy. There is nothing to keep secret," she protested and coaxed. "I am thinking only of William's feelings, and trying to spare his pride. I know him best and I am fond of him. Don't forget that. There has not been the least change in my affection for him," holding her beautiful head very straight. "Don't think for a moment that my regard for William has been lessened," suddenly dimpling, softening, and beaming, "by my falling in love with you. That is an entirely different thing."

"I should hope so, indeed!" suddenly bending forward and catching her in his arms with a happy laugh. "You see how strong I am. Well, then, you needn't expect to have your own way all the time much longer. I yield only so far as to give you three days—exactly three days from the moment that I leave this house, and not one moment more. At the end of that time I shall come to see the judge."

"And uncle Philip. I couldn't be happy without his approval. I have been longing to tell him. I would have told him at once if I hadn't felt bound to speak to William first. Dear uncle Philip! He is always happy over anything that makes me happy. Next to you, dear heart, there is no one in all the world that I love so much—not half so much. And there is no one whom he loves as he does me; he thinks only of my happiness."

Her eyes sought his with a wistful look. She felt that he did not like Philip Alston, and there was distress in the thought that these two, whom she loved most out of all on earth, should not be the warmest of friends.

"You mustn't think him indifferent because he hasn't been to see you," she pleaded. "Please don't think that, for it isn't true. He hasn't come because he never can bear the sight of suffering. He says it's purely a physical peculiarity which he cannot control. Anything that makes him think of violence or cruelty shocks and repulses him. He shrinks from it as he would from a harsh sound or an evil odor. He says it's because his refinement is greater than his humanity. But it is really his tender heart. Some day when you know him better you will find his heart as tender as I have always found it."

He, knowing what was in her loving heart, could not meet her gaze, and hastily looked away gazing across the river. His thoughts swiftly followed his eyes, for he would not have been the man that he was, could even this great new love which was now filling his heart, and was to fill all his future life, have made him forget his old love for this great new state, and the awful crises through which it was passing.

For that was a time of great stress, of deep anxiety, and of almost intolerable suspense. Those early days and nights of November in the year eighteen hundred and eleven, were indeed among the most stressful in the whole stormy history of Kentucky. And through her—since her fate was to be the fate of the Empire of the West—they were as portentous as any that the nation has ever known. On that very day in truth, and not very far off, there had already been enacted one of the mightiest events that went to the shaping of the national destiny. Over the river on the banks of its tributary, the Wabash, the battle of Tippecanoe had been fought and won between the darkness and daylight of that gloomy seventh of November. The young doctor, like all the people of the country, knew that the long-dreaded hour had struck, that this last decisive struggle between the white race and the red must be close at hand; but neither he nor any one in that region knew that it was already ended. There had not been a single sign or sound to tell when the conflict was actually going on. It was said that the roar of the cannon was heard much farther away, as far even as Monk's Mound, where the Trappists— those most ill-fated of Kentucky pioneers—had found temporary refuge. But if this be true, it must have been by reason of the fact that sound carries very far over vast level prairies, when it cannot cross a much shorter distance which rises in hills covered with forests, such as shut out every echo of the battle from Cedar House.

Paul Colbert got up suddenly and began to walk the room, though he staggered from weakness. He could not sit still under the torture of such suspense, when he thought of all that was at stake on the outcome of the conflict which might even then be waging beyond those spectral trees. The safety of the people living along the river, their homes, their lives—all these were hanging upon the strength of the soldier's arm. He knew how small the white army was. If it should be conquered, the opposite shore might at any instant be red with victorious savages rushing to the great Shawnee Crossing. And then—he looked at Ruth, feeling his helplessness as he had not felt the keenest pain of his wound. She saw the look, and felt its distress, although she did not understand all that it meant. She gently urged him back to his chair, frightened to see how weak he was.

"Sit still till I come back. I will run downstairs and see if there is any news," she coaxed in a soothing tone.

The household was gathered in the great room waiting and watching. The old ladies by the hearth scarcely noticed one another. The judge sitting apart half started up at the faint rustle of Ruth's approach, but finding that it was no messenger bringing news, he sat down again with a weary sigh, and his gaze went back to the other side of the river. His appearance told how great his anxiety was. His rugged, homely face was haggard and unshorn, and his rough dress was even more careless than common. William Pressley arose and came forward to give Ruth a chair. There was no visible change in him, his dress was as immaculate as it always was. His manner was just as coldly implacable as it had been ever since the quarrel; but then his temper never had anything to do with his looks or his manners. No degree of uneasiness could ever make him forget appearances or the smallest form of courtesy; and he would have thought it a pitiable sort of man who could be moved by emotion to any kind of irregularity. His way of placing the chair proclaimed that he never failed to do all that became a gentleman, no matter how neglectful emotional people might sometimes become.

Philip Alston, coming in just at that moment, saw something of this with mingled amusement and satisfaction. The candor of William Pressley's self-consciousness, the sincerity of his self-conceit, the firmness of his belief in his own infallibility, claimed a measure of real respect, and Philip Alston gave it in full. He thought none the less of him because he could not help smiling a little at the solemn progress which the young lawyer was then making across the great room. To be able to smile at anything on that day of strain was a boon. And then it was always pleasing and cheering to see any fresh sign that he had read the young lawyer's character aright, and he was glad to see again what a good-looking, well-mannered, right-minded young fellow he was. Nothing could be said against him. Everything—or almost everything—was to be said in his praise. The open fact that he thought all this himself would be nothing against him with Ruth. A man's faith in himself is indeed often the chief cause of a woman's faith in him. No one knew this better than Philip Alston. As he looked at William that day, a new feeling of peace came into his perturbed breast. He was beginning to be disheartened by unexpected opposition to his plan to have the young lawyer appointed to the office of attorney-general. Had he been closer in touch with the governor, he would have known that all his efforts were useless, for the office was held by appointment in those days, and not by election as it is now. But it was a long way to the state capital on horseback, and he had seen no newspapers, so that he knew nothing positively, and was only beginning to fear. And thinking about the uncertainty, he was encouraged to feel that even failure in this would not alter his belief that the marriage was the best Ruth could make. There was something purely unselfish in the content that he felt. With clouds lowering around his own head, it comforted him to feel that her future would be safe whatever came. He smiled at her, shaking his head when she asked if he had heard any news, and drew her down by his side. At the first opportunity he must ask about Sister Angela's progress with the wedding clothes. It was not long now till Christmas Eve, and he wanted to hear more about the preparations for the marriage. These had seemed to lag of late.

* * * * *

The blood-red sun went down behind threatening clouds on that terrible day, and the second morning came in with a wintry storm of icy winds and swirling snow. Then followed two more gloomy, gray days and two more wild, black nights. The fifth day dawned still wilder and darker, but Paul Colbert found strength to go away. On the sixth it seemed to Ruth that her heart would break with its aching for his absence; and with the sadness that came from listening to a sobbing wind which sighed despairingly through the naked forest; and with watching a melancholy rain which hung a dark curtain between Cedar House and the other side of the river. And thus the dreadful time dragged on into the seventh endless day, and still there was no news from Tippecanoe. A courier could have brought it in a few hours by riding fast through the wide, trackless wilderness, and swimming broad, unbridged rivers. But no couriers came toward Cedar House. There was no reason for sending a special messenger to a corner of one state when the whole nation was clamoring to hear. So that the couriers were speeding with all possible haste toward the National Capital, and the people of Cedar House could only wait and watch like those who were much farther off.

And thus it was that after a whole week had passed, they still did not know that the battle of Tippecanoe had been fought, and that a precious victory had been bought at a fearful price. And even now, who knows whether or not that fearful price need have been paid? It is hard to see the truth clearly, looking back through the mists of nearly a hundred years. In the strange story of that famous battle, only one fact stands out clear beyond all dispute, and that is so incredible as to stagger belief. It appears at first utterly past belief that the white army, marching against the red army with the open purpose of attacking it on the next day, should have lain down almost at the feet of the desperate foe, and have gone quietly to sleep. Only the recorded word of the general in command makes this fact credible. He also says, to be sure, that the soldiers "would have been called in two minutes more;" but he admits that they had not been called when the red army made the attack, without waiting till the white army woke of its own accord to begin fighting at leisure by daylight, without even waiting those two minutes for the general's convenience. What happened to the helpless sleepers then, when the waking warriors thus fell upon the sleeping soldiers, may be most eloquently told in the general's own words. "Such of them as were awake or easily awakened, seized their arms and took their stations, others, more tardy, had to contend with the enemy at the doors of their tents." Turning the yellowed pages of this most amazing report, the reader can only wonder that the furious tide of battle which set so overwhelmingly against the soldiers in the beginning, ever could have been turned by all the brave blood poured out before its turning.

On the eighth anguished day of suspense Ruth went to the door to welcome Philip Alston, and looking toward the forest path, saw Father Orin and Toby approaching. There was something in the way they moved that told they had news, and when they reached Cedar House, the whole household was breathlessly waiting for them. The white family was gathered inside the front door, and the black people, running up from the quarters, crowded round the door on the outside, with ashen faces, for their fear of the savages was, if possible, greater than the white people's. All pressed around Toby, and Father

Orin told the good news as quickly as he could, without taking time to dismount; but his voice trembled so that he could hardly speak, and his eyes were so full of tears that he could not see. He was not yet able to rejoice over a victory which had cost the life of a dear friend.

"And Joe Daviess?" asked Philip Alston.

Father Orin silently turned his face toward the river and made the sign of the cross; but he turned back and patted Ruth's head when she pressed it against Toby's mane and burst into sobbing.

"It was he who saved the day," the priest said huskily. "He led the desperate charge that won the battle, when everything seemed lost. He received his death wound in the charge, but he lived long enough to know that the victory was ours."

"He was a great man; his name will never be forgotten. His sword has now carved it imperishably on the key-stone of the new state's triumphal arch," said Philip Alston.

"And Tommy Dye?" asked Ruth, lifting her wet eyes. "The Sisters are so anxious."

"And poor Tommy Dye, also," answered Father Orin.

These two brave men who lived their lives so far apart, had fallen almost side by side. Joe Daviess, the noble, the fearless, the highly gifted, the honored, the famous; and Tommy Dye, the kindly, the reckless, the poorly endowed, the misguided, the obscure,—both had done all that the noblest could do. The mould and the dead leaves of the wilderness would cover both their graves. Only the initials of his name roughly cut on a tree would mark the glorious resting-place of the one. Only an humble heap of unmarked earth would tell where a noble death had closed the ignoble life of the other.

XXIII

LOVE CLAIMS HIS OWN

The tears had been heavy on Ruth's dark lashes when she had fallen asleep, but she awoke with a smile, radiant and expectant. She could not remember at first what made her so happy, and a pang touched her heart at the sudden recollection of the night's sadness. And then suddenly she began to glow again at the thought of her lover's coming. The week of his exile was ended on that day, and he would come. She knew just how he would look when he came with his head held high, and his clear eyes, so kind, and yet so fearless, looking straight in every face. She could tell the very moment when he would come, for she had the happiness—which every woman prizes and few ever know—of loving a man who kept his word in the letter as well as the spirit. If men could but know the difference there is to a woman! But they hardly ever do know, because this is a little thing, and they can never understand that it is the little things and not the large ones that make the happiness or the wretchedness of most women.

She exulted in the thought that he would come at the very instant he had named, no sooner and no later, and this would be precisely at four o'clock. She looked round with a smile, trying to tell by the mark on the window-sill what the time was then. But the day was gloomy, and there was no sunlight to mark the hour. Solitary snowflakes were drifting irresolutely across the window, as if uncertain whether to go on earthward or return whence they came. The birds sat on the bare branches near the window waiting for their breakfast in ruffled impatience, the blue jay having done his best to call her to the window earlier. And he said so, in his own way, as she scattered the crumbs with a cheery good morning.

When she went down to breakfast, the family received her much as the birds had done. Her coming cheered them also, as if a sunbeam had entered the dark room. Miss Penelope left off what she was saying about the calamities that must be expected in consequence of the comet's tail coming loose from its head. The widow Broadnax relaxed her watch for a moment, as the fair young figure came toward the hearth and stood by her chair, resting a hand on her shoulder. The judge brightened, without knowing what it was that suddenly heartened him, and David came out of his corner under the stairs, as he never did, unless she was in the room. Only William held aloof after a formal bow. At the sight of her, smiling and radiant, the sullen anger within him glowed like a covered fire under a sudden breeze. She had not been punished enough; her face was far too bright, her manner far too frank. When she approached him and tried to speak to him in a tone that no one else could hear, he arose, and murmuring a stiff apology moved away, just as he had done every time she had made the attempt. She flushed and lifted her head, for there was no lack of pride or spirit in her softness. Yet by and by she could not help looking at him across the table with another soft appeal in her sweet eyes which plead dumbly for old times' sake. And after breakfast was over she tried again, knowing that this would be the last opportunity, and yearning with all her loving heart to win back some of the old friendliness that she still prized as a precious thing, which she could not give up for a mere touch of pride. Such soft persistence is even harder to evade than to resist, and she followed William to the door as he was going away later in the day, and was bravely gathering courage while he looked at her in implacable coldness.

He was not softened by the fact that his hopes were high that morning over what appeared to be the certainty of his receiving the appointment. There was, he thought, not the slightest doubt if he could manage to secure the influence of one or two other leading citizens. As it was, there seemed to be little danger of failure, and when he now saw Philip Alston coming, he paused and waited for him to come up, so that he might tell him what he had been doing. He did not know that he was merely telling Philip Alston how his own orders had been carried out, and there was nothing in that gentleman's manner to remind him.

William Pressley, accordingly, went on talking with the modest consciousness of having done all that was possible for any man to do, and he said, as they were entering the great room, that he considered his success a mere question of time.

"A mere question of time, and a very short time, too," repeated Philip Alston, heartily. "I congratulate you. I am proud of you. We are all proud of him—hey, judge?"

"I hope he knows what he is trying to undertake," the judge said abruptly, turning a glum look on his nephew. "I trust, William, that you are realizing the responsibility of this office. Most men would hesitate to assume it. I should tremble at the thought."

"I think, sir, that I shall be able to do my duty." William Pressley spoke stiffly, with a touch of condescension and a shade of resentment, such as he always evinced at any sign that the censer might cease to swing.

"It isn't a simple matter of duty. It's a much more complicated matter of ability," the judge said sternly.

"Pardon me, sir, but it really does not seem to me such a difficult place to fill," said William, loftily. "In this, as in any other position of life, the man who is influenced solely by the profoundest and most conscientious conviction, and who is firm in following his convictions, can hardly go far astray."

The judge looked at him over his big spectacles in perplexed, troubled silence for a moment. So gazing, he gave the old impatient toss of his tousled head, and the old quizzical look came under his suddenly uplifted eyebrow.

"All *right*, William!" he said at last, almost immediately lapsing into silence, and presently beginning to nod.

Philip Alston scarcely glanced at the judge and his nephew. He was looking at Ruth, and noting with adoring eyes that her beauty had blossomed like some rare flower of late. It seemed to him that the roses on her fair cheeks were of a more exquisite, yet brighter tint, that her eyes were bluer and brighter and softer than ever. There also appeared to be a new maturity in the delicate curves of her graceful figure. But there was no change in the childlike affection of her bearing toward him. She clung round him just as she had always done, and when she turned to leave his side to take a chair, he called her back, unconsciously falling into the tone of fond playfulness that he had used in her childhood.

"If a little girl about your size were to come and look in her uncle's pockets, she might find something that she would like—"

Ruth did not wait for him to finish what he was saying, but ran to him as if she had been the little toddler of other days, needing only the sight of his dear face, or the sound of his kind voice, to fly into his outstretched arms. In a moment more her eager hands were swiftly searching his pockets, and making believe to have great difficulty in finding the hidden treasure. She knew all the while where it was, but she also knew that he liked her to be a long time in getting it out. His worshipping eyes looked down on her hands fluttering like white doves about his heart,—for it was hard to keep away from that inner breast pocket—and at last, when she could not wait any longer, she went deep down in it, and drew out a flat packet. This looked as if it had travelled a long distance. There were many wrappings around it, and many seals and foreign marks were stamped upon it. She laid it on his knee, and pretended to shake him, when he made out that he meant to take time to untie the cords which bound the wrappings, instead of cutting them. And when he had cut the cords with his pen-knife, the wrappings fell off, disclosing a jewel case of white satin richly wrought in gold. At the quick touch of her fingers the lid of the case flew up, revealing a long string of large pearls,—great frozen drops of the rainbow, wrapped in silvery white mist,— treasures that a queen might have coveted.

The girl did not know how wonderful the pearls were and had not the faintest conception of their value. But she saw their beauty and felt their charm, for a beautiful woman loves and longs for the jewels that belong to her beauty, as naturally as the rose loves and longs to gather and keep the dewdrops in its heart.

"Oh! Oh!" was all that she could say, and she could think of nothing to do, except stand on tiptoe and touch Philip Alston's cheek with a butterfly kiss. And then when he had put the string of pearls around her neck, so that it swung far down over her rounded young bosom, she danced across the room to the largest mirror. But the corner in which it hung was always full of shadows and so dark on this gloomy day that she could not see, and with pretty imperiousness she called for candles to be lighted and brought to her. William Pressley mechanically got up to obey, but Philip Alston moved more quickly. Going to the hearth he took two candles from the mantelpiece, lit them at the fire, and carried them to her. He expected to have the pleasure of holding them so that she might see the lovely vision, which he was already looking upon. But she took them from his hands and raising them high above her head, danced back to the mirror, and stood gazing at her own image, as artlessly as a lily bends over its shadow in a crystal pool. And as she thus gazed in the mirror, it suddenly reflected something which moved her more than her own likeness. It showed her the opening of the front door, and gave her a glimpse of her lover standing in the room. She whirled round, blushing, and with her eyes shining like stars, and cried out:—"See, Paul! See—was there ever anything so lovely?"

She went swiftly toward him, holding the candles still higher, so that the pearls caught a rosy lustre from the light that fell on her radiant face. She was laughing with pure delight at the sight of him, forgetting the pearls. She did not know that she had called him by his Christian name but she would have called him so, had she taken time to think. She had called him so ever since they had known that they loved each other, and she did not stop to realize that this was the first time they had met in the presence of others since becoming plighted lovers. She realized nothing except his presence—that alone filled her whole world with joy and content. He came straight to meet her, holding out his hands; but before he could cross the great room, or even had time to speak, Philip Alston stepped forward and spoke suddenly in clear tones:—

"Yes, see the wedding gift! The bridal pearls are here at last; all ready for Christmas Eve."

Paul Colbert paused. He was an ardent and bold lover, but the words were like a breath of frost on love's flowering. No ardor, no confidence, can keep a sensitive man from feeling a chill when he sees the woman he loves decked in the beautiful things which are beauty's birthright, and realizes for the first time that he cannot give them to her. With the painful shock which this feeling brought to the young doctor there was a greater shock in the sudden thought of the possible source of the riches which the pearls represented. A feeling of horror rushed over him, as if he had seen that soft, white throat encircled by a serpent, and he sprang forward to tear it off.

Ruth had turned her head to look at Philip Alston, with a start of surprise and a little disquietude, but without fear or distrust. She could not believe that he would wish her to marry William after he knew that she loved Paul; such a thought never crossed her mind. Yet, as she looked, a strange feeling of alarm which she did not comprehend swept over her, filling her with formless terror. Some instinct made her shrink, as if this wonderful string of pearls, which she had thought so beautiful a moment before, had turned into a cruel chain and was binding her fast. She did not know that many a weaker man has thus bound many a stronger woman with chains of gold and ropes of pearls. But she felt it, and her instinct was quicker than her lover's thought. Had her hands been free she would have thrown the fetters from her, and finding herself helpless, she turned to Paul Colbert for help.

"Take them off! Quick—quick! They are too heavy," she gasped.

It was Philip Alston who reached her first, and took the pearls from her neck and the candles from her hands; but she did not look at him, and went to her lover as if he had called her. Paul's arm going out to meet her drew her to his side, and then, as the young couple thus stood close together, the truth was plain enough to every one whose eyes rested upon them. Philip Alston's face turned very white, and he made a movement as if he would spring between them and part them by force. But he checked the impulse, after that uncontrollable start, and stood still, bearing in enforced silence, and as best he could, as hard a trial as love ever put before pride. William Pressley also stood still and silent, suffering bitterer pangs through his wounded self-love than love itself ever could have inflicted upon him. Judge Knox straightened up from his doze in bewildered astonishment, and made a displeased exclamation, but it passed unheard. The old ladies by the hearth were dumb with amazement. The boy stood unnoticed in his dark corner under the stairs.

The young doctor now began to speak deliberately, calmly, and clearly, being fully prepared with every word that he wished to utter. He told the whole story with the simple directness that was natural to him. He explained why he had not spoken sooner, and dwelt upon Ruth's scruples because he wished her position to be fully understood, not because he felt it necessary to excuse anything upon his own account. When he had said everything that he thought should be said, and when he had spoken modestly and proudly of their love for each other, he went on to make frank mention of his affairs, his family, and his place in life. And then he turned to the judge:—

"There is, as you see, sir, no reason why I should not ask you to give her to me," he said with a boyish blush dyeing his handsome young face, "since I have been so honored, so happy, and so fortunate as to win her consent. I am ready and eager to tell you anything else that you may wish to know, sir."

The judge lurched heavily out of his chair and rose unsteadily to his feet in the sudden, angry excitement that flames out of drink.

"By—! 'Pon my soul, young sir, you are taking a high hand in my house. Keep your place, sir, keep your place! Who are you that come here putting your hand on my niece, and ordering the family about? Come to me, Ruth! Come to me instantly!"

Philip Alston laid a restraining hand on his arm, and even William Pressley uttered a warning word. In the presence of the girl there must not be a violent word, much less a violent deed, no matter what the feelings of the men might be, and no matter what might come after. That was the first article in the code of chivalry toward women which ruled these first Kentuckians, as it rules most brave, strong men living simple, strenuous lives in the open. It ruled the judge also, as soon as he had time to think, and controlled him through all the fog that clouded his faculties.

"My dear," he appealed humbly, piteously, bending his rough gray head before the girl, "I beg your pardon."

She flew to him and ran her arm through his, thus ranging herself on his side with a fiery air of loyalty, and she turned on her lover with her soft eyes flashing:—

"How can you, Paul! I am surprised. I wouldn't have believed it of you. What do you mean by speaking so to my uncle Robert? Don't you see he isn't well? You must know that when he is well everybody respects and looks up to him—that the whole county depends on him," she said.

The old judge and the young doctor looked at each other over her head as men look at one another when women do things as true to their nature as this was to hers. And then, in spite of themselves, the judge's left eyebrow went up very high, and a sunny smile brightened the doctor's grave face. Even Philip Alston smiled and felt a sudden relief. With such a child as Ruth had just shown herself to be, there must be some hope of leading her by gentleness and persuasion. There was, at least, a chance to gain time, and he moved eagerly to seize it. He looked at William Pressley with an expression of undisguised contempt, seeing him stand utterly unmoved. He could not help giving a glance of scorn, which measured him against Paul Colbert. Who could blame the girl? Nevertheless Philip Alston went to her and took her hand from the judge's arm, and placed it within his own. Holding it fast against his side, he turned to the doctor.

"It might be best for all concerned if you would allow us to talk this matter over quietly among ourselves. We hardly know what to say, having it sprung in this totally unexpected way. If you would be so kind as to leave us for the present—"

The doctor had drawn himself up to his full height. He was about to say that he recognized no right on the part of Philip Alston to interfere, and to declare that he held himself accountable to no one but the judge. Yet as this purpose formed, his gaze instinctively sought Ruth's, and he saw that she was looking up at Philip Alston with love—unmistakable love—in her face. The sight brought back all the helplessness that he always felt when forced to realize her fondness for the man. He felt as he might have done had he seen some deadly thing coiled about her so closely that he could not strike it without wounding her tender breast. The trouble had been like that from the first and it was like that now—perhaps it always would be. He did not know what to do or say, with her blue eyes appealing from him to Philip Alston. He was glad when

William Pressley broke the silence. The young lawyer had been thinking hard; he never did anything on mere impulse. He always stopped to consider how a thing would look, no matter how angry he might be. His vanity had been slowly swallowing a bitter morsel, and it was now quite clear to him that he must act promptly in order to escape a still bitterer humiliation. Moreover, the chief consideration which had kept him from allowing Ruth to break the engagement sooner, was now removed. Philip Alston could hardly blame him in view of what had happened; no one could think ill of him now.

"Just a moment, if you please," he said coldly and bitterly, addressing all who were present. "There is no cause for delay or hesitation so far as I can see—certainly there need be none on my account. The engagement between Ruth and myself was tacitly broken some weeks ago. She has been over-scrupulous in thinking that anything was due me. She was quite free from any promise to me. You owe me nothing," turning to her with a bow. "You have my best wishes."

She went to him, holding out her hand. "William, it hurts me to hear you speak like that. I did my best to tell you—alone— and earlier. We were both mistaken—neither was to blame. There surely is no reason for hard feeling. My affection for you is just the same. William, dear—just for old time's sake."

He took her hand, not because her loving gentleness won his forgiveness, but because he thought that no gentleman could refuse a lady's hand. And when she turned away with a long sigh and quivering lips, he stood firm and invincible, supported by the conviction that he alone of all those present had been right in everything. And such a conviction of one's own infallibility must be a very great support under life's trials and disappointments. There can hardly be any other armor so nearly impenetrable to all those barbed doubts and fears which perpetually assail and wound the unarmored. Think of what it must mean!—never to feel that you might have been kinder or more just, or more generous or more merciful than you were; never to have doubts and fears come knocking, knocking,

knocking at your heart till you are compelled to see your mistakes when it is too late to do what was left undone, and—saddest and bitterest of all—too late to undo what was done. But no one except Ruth looked at William Pressley or thought of him. Philip Alston calmly and courteously repeated his request, and with Ruth's gaze urging it, Paul Colbert could not refuse to grant it. He took up his hat and went toward the door with Ruth walking by his side. And then, with his hand on the latch, he paused and turned, and looking over her head, gazed steadily and meaningly into the eyes of the three men. He looked first and longest at Philip Alston; then at William Pressley, and finally at the judge, with a slight change of expression. To each one of the three men his look said as plainly as if it had been put into words, that he held himself ready for anything and everything that any or all of them might have to say to him—out of her sight and hearing and knowledge. And they, in turn, understood, for that was the way of their country, of their time, and their kind; and having done this he went quietly away.

XXIV

OLD LOVE'S STRIVING WITH YOUNG LOVE

That night Philip Alston stayed later than usual at Cedar House. He was waiting for the others to go to bed, so that he might have a quiet talk with Ruth. On one or two rare occasions they had been left alone together before the wide hearth, and they both looked back on these times as among the pleasantest they had ever known. But the opportunities for privacy are very few where there is only one living room for an entire family, and the size and publicity of this great room of Cedar House made them fewer than they could have been in almost any other household. And Ruth, seeing what he wished, was looking forward now with even greater delight than she had felt heretofore; the delight that young love feels at the thought of giving its first confidence to a loving, sympathetic heart. She looked at him often through the waiting, with shining eyes, so happy, so eager to ask him to share her happiness that she could hardly wait till the others were gone. William Pressley did not tax her patience long and the judge, too, soon went away to his cabin with David to see that he reached it safely. The old ladies were slower in going; Miss Penelope had many domestic duties to perform, and the movements of the widow Broadnax were always governed entirely by hers. But they, also, went at last with Ruth to assist the stouter lady in getting up the stairs.

The girl came flying down again, with her eyes dancing and her heart playing a tune. Philip Alston rose as she approached, and stood awaiting her with a look on his face that she had never seen before.

"You are tired, dear uncle Philip," she said, taking his hand and holding it against her cheek as she raised her radiant eyes to his face. "Come to the fire and take this big chair. I will sit on the footstool at your knee. There, now! You can rest and be happy. Isn't it sweet to be alone—just you and I—together like this! I love you so dearly, dear uncle Philip. It seems as if I had never before really known just how much I do love you. It seems as if my heart couldn't hold quite all the happiness that fills it to-night. And the tenderness filling it to the brim brings a new feeling of your goodness to me."

She had taken the low seat by his side, and now laid her head down on his knee. He stroked her hair with an unsteady hand; sorely troubled and not knowing what to say. He suddenly looked very old, and felt more helpless than ever before in his life. Looking down on this beautiful head he realized in every sensitive fibre of his soul and body that this lovely young creature, clinging to his knee, was the one thing in the whole world that he had ever loved—deeply, truly, purely, and unselfishly; that her gentle heart was the only heart out of all the hearts beating on the earth that had ever loved him as the innocent love the good. Thinking of this he shrank and trembled, feeling that he held in his grasp a fragile treasure precious beyond all price, which a rude touch might destroy forever. He knew the evil reputation which rumor had given him, and he had seen that Paul Colbert believed the worst. There had been no disguise in the expression of the young doctor's eyes. His gaze bold and keen as an unhooded falcon's, had frankly proclaimed his dislike and mistrust, making it only too plain that he asked no favor by pretending ignorance or on the score of any friendliness that he did not feel. His look and attitude had indeed been so unmistakable that Philip Alston now wondered in sudden terror if she had not already observed them, and he—who had feared nothing in all his life—quailed and quivered before this sudden fear with abject cowardice. In another moment he knew that her trust in him had not been

Nancy Huston Banks

shaken; the resting of her head on his knee told him so much. But how long would it or could it stand against the doubts of the man she loved? That was the question which went through Philip Alston's breast like the thrust of a sword. Her husband's influence would be supreme. A tender, gentle creature, she would be easily influenced through her affections. The young doctor might keep silence, seeing her love for himself and respecting her regard for her foster-father; but he was not the man to hide what he really thought and felt, and she must divine the truth before long. Philip Alston had no hope of changing Paul Colbert's opinion of himself; he knew the world and mankind too well to think for a moment that any man might hope to live down such charges as those which had been brought against himself. Ruth must know sooner or later, and, knowing, would she still love him? There came now a sort of piteous appeal in the touch of his unsteady hand on her hair. The slightest suspicion must blast the exquisite flower of her tender love. With his quick, full appreciation of everything truly noble he had often noted the firm principles, which lay under her sweet gentleness like fine white marble under soft green moss. He did not know that this very trait for which he had loved her, and which now made him afraid, had already been tested again and again; and that her love for him and trust in him, had stood against every attack as firmly as great rocks stand against shallow waves. No, he knew nothing of all this, and he was now in such desperate fear that he dared not speak or move or do anything but stroke her hair with a shaking hand, and stare over her head at the fire trying to clear his mind. She had been silent also, but presently she spoke, putting up her hand to pat the one that was stroking her hair.

"I am waiting, dear heart," she said softly, "waiting to hear what you think of my Paul. I have been wanting so long to tell you; it was on account of William that I waited. But you know now, and I am so glad—so glad! Tell me what you think of him. There is no one but you who can see all that he is. And there is no one but him who can see all that you are. But you two, my dearest, are capable of appreciating each other. And I am a happy, happy girl."

He was feeling faint and sick under the hopelessness of any struggle between old love and young love. With every look of her radiant eyes, with every gentle word that fell from her sweet lips, he was feeling more and more how utterly useless would be any attempt to come between her and her lover. And looking at her he could not think of making any such attempt. When an all-absorbing love has taken complete possession of an empty and worldly heart, that heart becomes more powerless before that love, than a fuller and softer heart ever does. He could not speak, but he murmured something and she went on:—

"How sweet it is to be here alone with you, like this, in the dear, dark, big, old room. Why, uncle, dear, it seems only yesterday that you were rocking me in my cradle, over there in the chimney-corner; when you were already petting and spoiling me, just as you have always done. And to think that I am talking to you to-night about my Paul! Can you realize that it's true? Well, it is—the very truest thing in all the world."

She paused for a moment, but she did not observe that he made no response, and she began again:—

"You see, dear uncle, I didn't mean to love him. I meant to love William and I did in a way as I do now. He is such a good man, but I have found out that goodness, just by itself, is not enough. It may make love last, but it can't make it begin. Why, I never even thought whether my Paul was good or not. I must have loved him just the same."

"But you couldn't love a man if you found out that he was bad, after believing him to be good. It wouldn't be possible for you to do that, would it?" in strange, agitated haste.

She lifted her head and looked at him wonderingly. "I don't know what you mean. My Paul is good! Why, he is here in the wilderness solely for love of humanity, giving his strength, his skill, his time, and all that he has to the service of his country and his kind, just because he is good, and for no other reason.

There is no better man living, not even Father Orin, not even you, sir," throwing her arms around his knee and giving it a loving squeeze. "And you know it, too, you are only laughing at me. I don't mind at all. I am too happy to care for teasing."

She laid her head back on his knees and fell happily silent, gazing dreamily into the flames. The wind was rising, and went roaring through the trees around the house; but she heard it with the peaceful feeling of shelter and safety that only happiness feels in wild weather. Presently she asked him if he thought that souls could speak to one another.

"It was at Anvil Rock," she said as simply as if she had been thinking aloud. "I had never thought about loving him. He had never told me that he loved me, but I knew then that he did. Something told me while he was lying on the ground like a dead man. What do you think it could have been? What was it?"

Looking up she saw the shrinking in his face, and she thought it came from his dislike of any mention of painful subjects; but her whole heart was in this question so that she could not let it go without pressing it a little further.

"But tell me, dearest, can souls communicate without speech or sign—if they only love enough?" she urged.

"You are a fanciful, romantic child," he said, trying to smile and to speak lightly. "Why—the man was an utter stranger then—you didn't know him at all."

He had taken her chin in his hand, and his eyes were now looking steadily into hers; but the courage of the moment fled when she involuntarily drew away. He was alarmed at the effect of this one slight effort.

"Such things are too subtle for an old man, my child, too subtle, perhaps, for any man either young or old," he said hurriedly and confusedly. "You women see and feel many things that fly high above our heads. And then I am duller than usual to-night. I am anxious about business matters. The river is rising rapidly, there is danger of a disastrous flood. My boats are not in safe places, and worst of all the Cold Plague broke out to-day on one of them. The boat is tied up to the island. I sent it over there immediately so that you, and the rest of the family, might be in no danger from the spread of the epidemic. But it worries me, and one of the boatmen is said to be dying."

"Send for my Paul. He can cure him. The plague-stricken hardly ever die if he can get to them in time."

She said this with a pretty air of pride in her lover, and a gentle lift of her head. He made no reply, and she turned her eyes from the fire to his face to see why he was silent so long. He was pale with a strange gray pallor, and he met her gaze with a startled, alarmed look. It was the look of a man who blanches and shrinks before some sudden great temptation. She misread the look, taking it for unwillingness to send for her lover.

"You mustn't think of sending for Doctor Colbert if you prefer the other doctor," with swift, fiery jealousy. "But I warn you that if you do, the man will certainly die."

"Do you know where he is to be found in case I should want to send for him?" he said after a moment's silence, and with constraint and hesitation.

"He is riding so much that it is hard to tell; but, uncle, dear," melting and putting her arms about him, "I should not be really offended, of course, if you were to send for the other doctor. You can, dear, if you want to. I like him ever so much better myself, since he took such good care of my Paul."

He laughed uneasily and got up, saying that he was going to see about the trouble on the boat. He saw that he must have a cleared mind and steadied nerves with time to think. And he could not think in her presence, he could only feel her blue eyes on his face and her little hands clasped around his knee or about his arm. He tried not to look at her, and hurriedly began buttoning his coat before starting on his cold way home. In drawing his coat closer, his hand came in contact with the pearls which he had forgotten. He drew them out and hung them again around her neck. She thanked him with a smile, but he saw that she scarcely looked at them, that she was thinking only of her love and her lover, though she held his hand and walked beside him to the front door. From it they could see dimly and were able to make out the black bulk of the boat lying far out in the river beside the island. As he looked at it a feeling of the worthlessness of all that he owned swept over him, overwhelming him with despair. All the gold that he had gathered, or ever could gather, would be worthless yellow dust if he might not use it to give her comfort or pleasure or happiness. He realized suddenly that this was everything that his riches had meant to him ever since she had wound herself around his heart. Money could do little for him; he was weary and old and sad and had come to feel—as every rich man must come to feel sooner or later—that for himself his riches meant, after all, only food and clothes. And now he found himself facing the end of the sole interest and happiness that he could ever hope to find in life. Henceforth it would be with the utmost that he could do, as it had been just now with these pearls. He fully recognized the hopelessness of trying to win her away from her lover. That had grown plainer with every gentle word that she had said while they had sat before the fire. And he knew that this proud young fellow, whose glance had met his like the crossing of swords, would never allow her to touch a penny of his money, or anything that it could buy, if he could help it. The thought was like tearing the heart out of his breast, and another thought sprang up again in defence of all that he held dear. He began to breathe quickly and heavily, like a man who has been running. He feared that she must feel the plunging of his heart, for she was leaning against him, looking out at the wild, windy night. But she heard only the mournful wail of the wind through the great trees, and the roar of the river rushing under the misty darkness. There was no moon, but the stars were shining in the dark dome of the universe.

"I wonder why the stars look so old, while the world looks so new," she murmured, with her head on his shoulder and her face upturned. "I wonder why there is such a look of change-lessness about the heavens, while the earth seems changing so fast!"

Her eyes were wandering over the infinite starry spaces with wondering awe, but he was looking down at her and he started when she cried out in amazement, touched with alarm. She lifted her hand and pointed, and following its direction, he saw that the comet had disappeared.

The celestial visitor was gone almost as suddenly and mysteriously as it had come.

XXV

THE PASSING OF PHILIP ALSTON

The cold wind died down with the coming of dawn. Going to the window to call the birds, she found the air grown unseasonably warm and saw that it was filled with a dull mist. Leaning from the window, she looked up the forest path, wondering if Paul had ridden along it during the night on his way to the boat. The low, broad craft was still lying in the same place beside the island, with no movement about it. She thought of the sick man with pity, wishing that she could do something for him; but if Paul had been called in time, all must be well—she had not a doubt of that; and an unconscious smile of pride touched her anxious face. She hardly knew why she felt vaguely anxious and uneasy, but thought that it might be on account of the gloom of the dreary morning, and the strange look of the swollen river. How gray and dark it was, and how heavily it ran, almost like molten lead.

As her wandering gaze followed the stream, she saw something which was still grayer and darker than the troubled waters. She could not tell at first what it was, for it was a long way off, and far up the river. With her hands over her eyes, she strained her sight, but the distance was too great, and the yellow haze too thick. She could make out only a wide, dark line, wavering down from the woods to the water—a strange, moving thing without beginning or end—which seemed to be going faster than the river. The strangeness of the night alarmed her and as she gazed at it, fascinated, she saw David running toward the house and waving his arms to call her attention.

"Look! Look up the river!" he shouted as soon as he had come within hearing. "I was afraid you wouldn't see it. It's an army of squirrels marching steadily, just like soldiers, millions and millions of them! It has been like that for hours. I have been watching it since daylight. The squirrels are trying to cross the river, and thousands and thousands are already drowned. The water is brown with their bodies."

"The poor little things! What in the world can it mean, David? And look at the birds! They don't come at all when I call them. What is the matter with them? I don't see anything to disturb them, yet see how they look! And hear the waterfowl screaming! And the trees, too. Why do the leaves droop like that? How can it be so hot in December? It was never like this before. There isn't a breath of air."

"I have noticed how strange everything seems. The forest is stiller than I ever saw it, but the wild things that live in it are strangely restless. I have been watching them all the morning, and I heard them in the night."

"But what does it mean, dear? Surely some dreadful thing must be going to happen! I wish Paul would come. Have you seen him? He is always riding, and the woods are dangerous in a storm, and it can't be anything else. Why don't you answer? I asked if you had seen him."

The boy turned from gazing at the strange, dark line which was still wavering ceaselessly from the woods to the water.

"Yes, I saw him and Father Orin going home an hour or so ago. They had been out all night." He said this absently, with his eyes turning back to the wonderful spectacle.

"My Paul is wanted in many places at once," she said, forgetting her uneasiness in a woman's pride in the power of the man she loves. "But I hope he found time to visit the sick man on uncle Philip's boat," mindful even then of a woman's wish to draw together the men she loves. "Can you see any clouds, David? I can't—and yet this strange yellow vapor that thickens the air is certainly growing heavier every moment. What can it be? It isn't at all like a fog. I am frightened. Come indoors. I am coming downstairs. Maybe uncle Robert or William can tell us what all this means."

But there was nothing to be learned in the great room below. The men of the family were as helpless as the women. All were waiting and watching for some nameless calamity, weighed down by that overwhelming, paralyzing dread of the unknown which unnerves the bravest and makes the most powerful utterly powerless. The old ladies, trembling and silent, clung close to the chimney-corner, scarcely looking at one another. The judge and his nephew were sitting in silence near the front door which had been opened on account of the sudden heat. They got up hurriedly, and turned nervously, startled even by the faint rustle of Ruth's skirts on the stairs. And before they could speak, the strained stillness was violently torn by a sudden loud, shrill sound, such as none of the terrified listeners had ever heard before—a long, unearthly shriek, which seemed to come from neither brute nor human. For a moment not a cry was uttered, not a word was spoken, and terrified eyes stared unseeingly into whitening faces. And then the judge, suddenly realizing what the sound was, broke into shaken, painful laughter.

"It is the whistle of the steamboat—the first steamboat on the Ohio. How could we have forgotten?" he said. "It is the *Orleans* passing down the river. Come to the door. We must see it go by. It doesn't stop here and none of us should miss seeing it, for the sight of the first steamer on western waters is something to be stored in memory. Never mind the signs of the storm. There will be many other storms, but never another first steamboat down the Ohio. Come out and see it."

"We can get a better view from the river bank," cried Ruth.

"Come along, David!"

Holding hands, the girl and the boy ran to the shore, leaving the others to watch the great spectacle from the doorstep. And thus all stood, marvelling like every living creature whose eyes followed it down that long river. But only the judge could partly grasp the greatness of the event; only he could partly realize what it meant to the West and the world. Yet every one waited and watched as if spellbound, till the last of those first victorious banners of blue smoke thus unfurled over the conquered wilderness, had waved slowly out of sight around the great river's majestic bend.

This had brought a momentary forgetfulness of the strange look of the heavens and the earth; but the consciousness of it now rushed back with increased alarm. There were still no clouds to be seen anywhere, no visible signs of an approaching storm; but the thick veil of yellowish vapor was fast drawing an unnatural twilight over the noonday. Through this awful dimness the sun was shining faintly, like a great globe of heated copper, thus shedding a strange light, even more alarming than the sinister darkness.

Every soul in the wilderness must now have shrunk, shuddering and appalled, before this unmistakable approach of some frightful convulsion of nature. The people of Cedar House, like all the rest, could do nothing but wait in agony for the unknown blow to fall. It seemed an endless time in falling; under the breathless, torturing suspense the moments became hours, with no change except a darkening of the unnatural twilight, an increase of the unnatural sultriness, and a deepening of the unnatural stillness. The little group in the great room of Cedar House sat still and silent, save as they unconsciously drew closer together, moved by the instinct of humanity in common danger.

The girl alone kept her post by the open door and her watch over the forest path, looking for the coming of her lover. She knew that but one thing could keep him from her side, and with all her longing for his presence, a thrill of happiness came from his absence. Through all its distress her heart exulted in the thought that he was faithful in his service to suffering humanity, even when love itself beckoned him away. A great tide of religious gratitude rose in her heart sweeping all fear before it. The love of a man who was both strong and good— the greatest gift that life could give to any woman—was safely hers. Holding this assurance to her heart, she grew wonderfully calm. There could be nothing to fear. In this world or the next, all was well. A wonderful spiritual exaltation bore her upward on its strong, swift wings, high above all the surrounding gloom and terror, till she rested on a white height of perfect peace. There was a rapt look on her quiet, pale face as she sat thus with it turned toward the forest path. She arose quietly and stood in the door, gazing at a shadowy form which came suddenly from under the dark trees. The thick yellow mist wrapped it darkly, but she presently knew by intuition rather than by sight that Paul was really coming at last, and she flew toward him like a homing bird. He was urging his horse, but the animal held back with an unwillingness such as he had never shown before; so that when the young man saw the girl flying toward him he leapt from the saddle, leaving the horse to follow or not as he would, and ran to meet her. As soon as she could speak, she told him that she was not afraid now that he had come, saying it over and over; yet she nevertheless clung to him as if she would never let him go.

"And you will take care of the others, too," she said. "Uncle Robert doesn't know what to do, nor William. Oh! Look! The poor black people! There they come running up from the quarters. See how they are crowding round the door, wild with terror! But you will know what to say to them as well as the others. I am not afraid, with you," quietly looking up in his grave face. "Is it the end of the world, dear heart?"

He said that he knew no more than herself what it could be, unless some terrific tempest might be near. They moved hurriedly on toward the house, and as they went he told her that he was going to the boat where he had been called to see a man ill of the plague. The call had come during the night, but he could not leave another patient to answer it more quickly. And now he would not leave her, for all the rest of the world, till they knew what this awful thing was which seemed about to happen. The white people had come out of the house and stood speechless and motionless, looking up at the heavens and down at the earth, seeing both but dimly through that ghastly twilight so awfully lit by that lurid ball of fire.

"Here comes Father Orin!" cried the doctor. "Look at Toby and my horse; see how they are walking!"

The horses could be indistinctly seen advancing slowly and reluctantly through the yellowish gloom with a curious, sliding motion, as if stepping on ice. Paul started toward them, but paused, struck motionless, and held by a sight still more strange. The same breathless stillness brooded over everything; the windless air now weighed like lead, and yet at this moment the greatest trees and smallest bushes suddenly began to quiver from bottom to top. As far as the horror-struck eyes could reach through that unnatural twilight, the mightiest cotton-woods were now bending and nodding like the frailest reeds. And then there arose in the far northeast a faint rumbling which rushed swiftly onward toward the southeast, growing, louder as it came, and breaking over Cedar House in a thunderous roar. At the deafening crash Paul turned and ran back to Ruth, catching her in his arms. The ground was now sliding beneath their feet. The solid earth was waving and rising and falling like a stormy sea.

"It's an earthquake," he whispered, with his lips against her cheek. "Don't fear, it will pass."

A second shock followed the first, and there was no lightening of the dreadful gloom which was one of the greatest horrors of that horrible time. But the men were rallying now that they knew what they had to meet, and they quickly and firmly drew the terror-stricken, helpless old women further away from the house, fearing that the massive logs of its walls might be shaken down.

"That isn't far enough," said Father Orin. "Come still farther,"glancing round for the safest refuge. "Merciful God! Look at the river!"

The Ohio, beaten back by the lashed and maddened Mississippi, was leaping in great furious waves, high and wild, as the ocean's in a tempest. These monstrous, foaming billows were springing far up the shores on both sides of the river, and devouring vast stretches of land covered with gigantic trees. The giants of the forest fell, groaning, into the boiling, swirling flood which leapt to catch them and swallowed them up with a hideous, hissing noise. Sunken trees which had lain for ages on the bottom of the river rose above the water like ghosts rising to meet the newly slain.

"The boat," moaned Ruth. "Uncle Philip's boat, and the sick man!"

Every eye turned in the direction of the island. No one spoke after that first look. None marvelled to see that the boat was missing; nothing afloat could live in that seething maelstrom, thickened with melted earth and tangled with fallen trees. The overwhelming thing which their faculties could not grasp was the fact that the island itself was gone. They could only stand staring, expecting to see it between the mountainous waves, utterly unable to believe the truth, that it had sunk out of sight and was resting on the bottom of the river. And as they were thus still searching the wild, dark flood with incredulous eyes, they suddenly saw a small row-boat in the middle of the stream. It darted down a towering wave and flew up the next, and came flying on like some wild, winged thing, toward the Kentucky shore. Another and a wilder wave caught it, lifted it aloft, and tossed it still nearer the land. It was not far away now, and there came a sudden lightening of the gloom, so that they could see two men in the little boat.

"They can never live to reach the shore!" cried the doctor.

"As God wills," said the priest.

Instinctively every eye but the girl's was scanning the shore, trying to find something that would float, something that might help to save the men in the boat. But there was nothing in sight; the fierce waves had swallowed everything, and the helpless people on the bank could only turn again to watch the little boat. Ruth's gaze had never wandered from it, and she still watched it flying from one wave to another, gazing as intently as she could through the tears that rained over her pale cheeks. She saw it go up a gigantic wave with a flying leap and dart down again, and then it was lost to sight so long that they thought it was gone. But at last it came up near the shore, overturned, and with only one man clinging to it. He was on the far side of the frail shell, so that they could not see him distinctly, although he was not far from the shore and there was more light. And then a swirl of the wild waters brought him to the nearer side, and raised him higher.

"It's an old man!" sobbed Ruth. "His head is white. Oh! Oh! It's uncle Philip! It's uncle Philip! He has been to the island. Save him, Paul!"

The doctor had already thrown off his coat, and was throwing aside his boots. He had not waited for her last words; he was not sure that it was Philip Alston; but he knew that some fellow-creature was perishing almost within reach of his arm. He was now running down the trembling bank, and in another instant had plunged into the boiling, roaring, furious flood, and was swimming toward that wildly rising and falling silver head, which shone like a beacon, through the lurid light. It was hard to keep anything in sight. He was a strong swimmer, but his full strength had not come back, and the fury of the waves was swirling trees like straws.

After that one involuntary appeal, Ruth was silent. Her heart almost stopped beating as she realized what her cry had done. A woman's mind acts with marvellous quickness when all she loves is at stake. As in a lightning flash she knew that she had sent her lover to risk his life for her foster-father, without knowing what she did. What she would have done had there been time to hesitate she could not tell, dared not think. It must have been a bitter choice, this risking of her lover's life against the certainty of her father's death. But now she realized nothing, felt nothing, except that the desperate die was cast. She did not notice that the others followed as she flew after Paul to the river's very brink. The earth had ceased quivering, but the shores were still crumbling under the crushing blows of the maddened waves. The thick, dark water coiled unheeded about her feet, as she stood silent, straining her eyes after her lover as he swam toward that silver head which still rose and fell with the waves. She did not move when she saw a gigantic cottonwood lean, uprooted and tottering. She did not utter a cry when it fell behind him, cutting him off and hiding him, so that neither he nor the silver head could be seen from the land. She stood as if turned to stone, waiting—only waiting—hardly hoping that it had not carried them both down. She began to weep softly, and her hands were suddenly and unconsciously clasped in silent prayer, when she saw him once more swimming—still swimming—but coming back around the top of the tree.

It had struck the little boat in its fall, sending it down to come up in fragments, but the man was left hanging to a bough, and it was toward him that Paul Colbert was struggling against the fury of the flood. The tree hung to the bank by its loosened roots, but its trunk and branches were swaying wildly, fiercely tossed by the waves. The man was sinking lower in the water, his strength almost was gone, and his hold was giving way, when Paul reached him. The white head, turning, revealed Philip Alston's face and Paul Colbert thought that he shrank under his touch. Neither spoke for a moment; both needed all their breath to reach a higher bough.

"Let me help you," gasped Paul Colbert. "Try to climb to the next limb. It is stronger and steadier."

"Thank you," panted Philip Alston.

They reached it together and could now see the shore, and both looked at Ruth through the swaying boughs and flying spray. The young man's heart leapt and his courage rose at the sight of the slender, girlish form. He saw her stretch out her arms, and remembering that she loved this old man, panting and struggling at his side, he shouted with all the power that he had, telling her that he would do his best to bring him to land. Philip Alston gave him a strange look, and then turned his gaze again toward the little figure on the shore. In a tone that was even more strange than his look, he murmured something about being on his way back from the island. He also said something about going to the boat early in the morning to countermand an order that he had given on the night before.

"I changed my mind—I found I couldn't do—"

Paul Colbert did not understand, and scarcely heard the confused, gasping, hurried words. He was looking at Ruth, and longing to loose his hold on the bough, long enough to wave the assurance that his voice could not carry across the roaring waters. And this was the instant that Nature chose to mock the pitting of his puny powers against her resistless forces. A fierce wave tore away the roots that the tree bound to the bank, and hurled it into the flood. It swung round and turned partly over, burying the bough that they clung to, deep under the water. Both went down with it and Paul Colbert thought, with the quickness and clearness of mind that comes to the drowning, that they could never come up again. When he found his own head once more above water, with his hand grasping a bough of a smaller tree, which had been driven close to the shore, he looked round for Philip Alston. There was no silver head anywhere to be seen now above the thick, dark river. Half stunned, he gazed again blankly, feeling vaguely that his own head must go down very soon; his strength was wholly gone; he could not even see the shore, though it was very near, because he was not strong enough to lift himself above the trunk of the tree which hid it from his sight. And then at last he heard Father Orin's voice:—

Nancy Huston Banks

"Hold fast, my boy. Hold fast just a moment longer. We are coming, Toby and I. Try to hold on. We are almost there."

They reached him as his hand let go and his head sunk, and they bore him to the shore and laid him down at Ruth's feet, unconscious, but alive.

*　*　*　*　*

When Nature has thus rent the trembling earth and thus smitten appalled humanity by some stupendous convulsion, the outburst of passion nearly always passes quickly, and she hastens to console by concealing its traces. These fatal throes were hardly over before she was quelling the frenzied river by her sudden coldness, and only a few days had passed before she was covering its subdued waters with a heavy white sheet of glittering ice. And then, as if to make the torn land lovely again at once, she wrapped it in a dazzling robe of spotless snow. Above this she hurriedly hung the broken boughs of the wrecked cottonwoods with countless flashing prisms, encrusting the smallest twigs to the very top in sparkling crystal; and coming down she stilled the murmur of the reeds under icy helmets—binding all together with crystalline cables of frost. So that under the rainbow light of the brilliant winter sun the world was once more radiant with peace and joy and beauty unspeakable.

And Cedar House, too, was now just as it had been before. From its open door nothing could be seen of the marks left by Nature's passionate fury; marks which must remain forever unless some more furious passion should come to erase them. It was hard to tell just how and wherein the whole face of the country had been so greatly changed. The people of Cedar House knew that a great lake nearly seventy miles in length and deeper in places than the height of the tallest trees whose tops barely showed above the water, had taken the place of a range of high hills covered with primeval forest. But this was too far away to be seen from Cedar House, and no one there had the heart to approach it. One sad pilgrimage had been made, and that was to the ruins of Philip Alston's house. It was now a mere heap of fallen logs, and although these were lifted and laid in orderly rows, and the ground searched over inch by inch, there was nothing but his fine clothes and some simple furniture to show that it had ever been occupied.

"To think that he lived like this—that he gave me everything and kept nothing for himself," Ruth said softly through her tears, looking up in Paul Colbert's troubled face. "Such a desolate, lonely life. It breaks my heart to think of it. But I would have lived in his house if I could. I wanted to live in it—I wouldn't have cared how plain and rough it was. I wanted to live with him and cheer him and make him happy, as if he had been my own father. I couldn't have loved him more dearly if he had been. And you would have loved him, too, if you had known him better. I am sure that you would. You couldn't have helped loving him—if only for his goodness to me. And he was kind to every one. I never heard him speak a harsh word of any living thing. It was in being kind that he lost his life; he must have gone to see the man who was ill on the boat."

The young doctor looked away and fixed his eyes on the men who were going over the ground around the cabin.

"Who are those men, Paul? And what are they doing here?" she asked suddenly, observing that they seemed to be looking for something. "It hurts me to have strangers handling these things that belonged to him. What are they looking for? Who are they?"

"Dearest, when a thing like this happens the law has to take certain—"

"What has the law to do with my uncle Philip's clothes? No one shall touch them but me or you!" bending over the garments and gathering them up in her arms. "What are they digging for? Make them stop. Oh, stop them; this spot is like his grave, the only grave he can ever have."

*　*　*　*　*

Paul could not tell her then, nor for months afterward, that it was impossible to stop the search for the gold which was believed to be buried in the earth of the forest near the ruined cabin. He waited till the forest was once more quivering with tender young leaves and the river was gentle and warm again— and she had become his wife. When he gently told her at last, she looked at him wonderingly like a child, and was silent for some time. She knew so little about money or the eagerness for riches. And then she smiled and said that she herself would certainly claim any gold belonging to Philip Alston that ever might be found, and that David and the Sisters and Father Orin and Toby should have the spending of it.

"For that is what he would like and we have no need of more, now that you are becoming famous. We have all and more than we want. Uncle Robert has plenty for himself and his sisters. William will soon be going to Congress, if you and uncle Robert work hard for him. Yes, David and the Sisters and Father Orin and Toby shall have dear uncle Philip's gold. He would wish them to have it. Think how generous he always was to them and every one, and how kind to all. If you only could have known him just a little longer, dear heart! Knowing him better, you would have known, as I do, how truly he loved everything fine and noble and great."

He did not reply but silently laid his hand on hers. Sighing and smiling, she nestled closer to his side. And then as they sat thus with their eyes on the glorious afterglow, the Angelus began to peal softly through the shadows, and the Beautiful River seemed in the softened light to curve its majestic arm more closely around this wonderful new country, from which a blighting shadow was lifted forever.

Choose from Thousands of 1stWorldLibrary Classics By

A. M. Barnard
Ada Leverson
Adolphus William Ward
Aesop
Agatha Christie
Alexander Aaronsohn
Alexander Kielland
Alexandre Dumas
Alfred Gatty
Alfred Ollivant
Alice Duer Miller
Alice Turner Curtis
Alice Dunbar
Allen Chapman
Alleyne Ireland
Ambrose Bierce
Amelia E. Barr
Amory H. Bradford
Andrew Lang
Andrew McFarland Davis
Andy Adams
Angela Brazil
Anna Alice Chapin
Anna Sewell
Annie Besant
Annie Hamilton Donnell
Annie Payson Call
Annie Roe Carr
Annonaymous
Anton Chekhov
Archibald Lee Fletcher
Arnold Bennett
Arthur C. Benson
Arthur Conan Doyle
Arthur M. Winfield
Arthur Ransome
Arthur Schnitzler
Arthur Train
Atticus
B.H. Baden-Powell
B. M. Bower
B. C. Chatterjee
Baroness Emmuska Orczy
Baroness Orczy
Basil King
Bayard Taylor
Ben Macomber
Bertha Muzzy Bower
Bjornstjerne Bjornson

Booth Tarkington
Boyd Cable
Bram Stoker
C. Collodi
C. E. Orr
C. M. Ingleby
Carolyn Wells
Catherine Parr Traill
Charles A. Eastman
Charles Amory Beach
Charles Dickens
Charles Dudley Warner
Charles Farrar Browne
Charles Ives
Charles Kingsley
Charles Klein
Charles Hanson Towne
Charles Lathrop Pack
Charles Romyn Dake
Charles Whibley
Charles Willing Beale
Charlotte M. Braeme
Charlotte M. Yonge
Charlotte Perkins Stetson
Clair W. Hayes
Clarence Day Jr.
Clarence E. Mulford
Clemence Housman
Confucius
Coningsby Dawson
Cornelis DeWitt Wilcox
Cyril Burleigh
D. H. Lawrence
Daniel Defoe
David Garnett
Dinah Craik
Don Carlos Janes
Donald Keyhoe
Dorothy Kilner
Dougan Clark
Douglas Fairbanks
E. Nesbit
E. P. Roe
E. Phillips Oppenheim
E. S. Brooks
Earl Barnes
Edgar Rice Burroughs
Edith Van Dyne
Edith Wharton

Edward Everett Hale
Edward J. O'Biren
Edward S. Ellis
Edwin L. Arnold
Eleanor Atkins
Eleanor Hallowell Abbott
Eliot Gregory
Elizabeth Gaskell
Elizabeth McCracken
Elizabeth Von Arnim
Ellem Key
Emerson Hough
Emilie F. Carlen
Emily Bronte
Emily Dickinson
Enid Bagnold
Enilor Macartney Lane
Erasmus W. Jones
Ernie Howard Pie
Ethel May Dell
Ethel Turner
Ethel Watts Mumford
Eugene Sue
Eugenie Foa
Eugene Wood
Eustace Hale Ball
Evelyn Everett-green
Everard Cotes
F. H. Cheley
F. J. Cross
F. Marion Crawford
Fannie E. Newberry
Federick Austin Ogg
Ferdinand Ossendowski
Fergus Hume
Florence A. Kilpatrick
Fremont B. Deering
Francis Bacon
Francis Darwin
Frances Hodgson Burnett
Frances Parkinson Keyes
Frank Gee Patchin
Frank Harris
Frank Jewett Mather
Frank L. Packard
Frank V. Webster
Frederic Stewart Isham
Frederick Trevor Hill
Frederick Winslow Taylor

Friedrich Kerst
Friedrich Nietzsche
Fyodor Dostoyevsky
G.A. Henty
G.K. Chesterton
Gabrielle E. Jackson
Garrett P. Serviss
Gaston Leroux
George A. Warren
George Ade
Geroge Bernard Shaw
George Cary Eggleston
George Durston
George Ebers
George Eliot
George Gissing
George MacDonald
George Meredith
George Orwell
George Sylvester Viereck
George Tucker
George W. Cable
George Wharton James
Gertrude Atherton
Gordon Casserly
Grace E. King
Grace Gallatin
Grace Greenwood
Grant Allen
Guillermo A. Sherwell
Gulielma Zollinger
Gustav Flaubert
H. A. Cody
H. B. Irving
H.C. Bailey
H. G. Wells
H. H. Munro
H. Irving Hancock
H. R. Naylor
H. Rider Haggard
H. W. C. Davis
Haldeman Julius
Hall Caine
Hamilton Wright Mabie
Hans Christian Andersen
Harold Avery
Harold McGrath
Harriet Beecher Stowe
Harry Castlemon
Harry Coghill
Harry Houidini

Hayden Carruth
Helent Hunt Jackson
Helen Nicolay
Hendrik Conscience
Hendy David Thoreau
Henri Barbusse
Henrik Ibsen
Henry Adams
Henry Ford
Henry Frost
Henry James
Henry Jones Ford
Henry Seton Merriman
Henry W Longfellow
Herbert A. Giles
Herbert Carter
Herbert N. Casson
Herman Hesse
Hildegard G. Frey
Homer
Honore De Balzac
Horace B. Day
Horace Walpole
Horatio Alger Jr.
Howard Pyle
Howard R. Garis
Hugh Lofting
Hugh Walpole
Humphry Ward
Ian Maclaren
Inez Haynes Gillmore
Irving Bacheller
Isabel Cecilia Williams
Isabel Hornibrook
Israel Abrahams
Ivan Turgenev
J.G.Austin
J. Henri Fabre
J. M. Barrie
J. M. Walsh
J. Macdonald Oxley
J. R. Miller
J. S. Fletcher
J. S. Knowles
J. Storer Clouston
J. W. Duffield
Jack London
Jacob Abbott
James Allen
James Andrews
James Baldwin

James Branch Cabell
James DeMille
James Joyce
James Lane Allen
James Lane Allen
James Oliver Curwood
James Oppenheim
James Otis
James R. Driscoll
Jane Abbott
Jane Austen
Jane L. Stewart
Janet Aldridge
Jens Peter Jacobsen
Jerome K. Jerome
Jessie Graham Flower
John Buchan
John Burroughs
John Cournos
John F. Kennedy
John Gay
John Glasworthy
John Habberton
John Joy Bell
John Kendrick Bangs
John Milton
John Philip Sousa
John Taintor Foote
Jonas Lauritz Idemil Lie
Jonathan Swift
Joseph A. Altsheler
Joseph Carey
Joseph Conrad
Joseph E. Badger Jr
Joseph Hergesheimer
Joseph Jacobs
Jules Vernes
Julian Hawthrone
Julie A Lippmann
Justin Huntly McCarthy
Kakuzo Okakura
Karle Wilson Baker
Kate Chopin
Kenneth Grahame
Kenneth McGaffey
Kate Langley Bosher
Kate Langley Bosher
Katherine Cecil Thurston
Katherine Stokes
L. A. Abbot
L. T. Meade

L. Frank Baum
Latta Griswold
Laura Dent Crane
Laura Lee Hope
Laurence Housman
Lawrence Beasley
Leo Tolstoy
Leonid Andreyev
Lewis Carroll
Lewis Sperry Chafer
Lilian Bell
Lloyd Osbourne
Louis Hughes
Louis Joseph Vance
Louis Tracy
Louisa May Alcott
Lucy Fitch Perkins
Lucy Maud Montgomery
Luther Benson
Lydia Miller Middleton
Lyndon Orr
M. Corvus
M. H. Adams
Margaret E. Sangster
Margret Howth
Margaret Vandercook
Margaret W. Hungerford
Margret Penrose
Maria Edgeworth
Maria Thompson Daviess
Mariano Azuela
Marion Polk Angellotti
Mark Overton
Mark Twain
Mary Austin
Mary Catherine Crowley
Mary Cole
Mary Hastings Bradley
Mary Roberts Rinehart
Mary Rowlandson
M. Wollstonecraft Shelley
Maud Lindsay
Max Beerbohm
Myra Kelly
Nathaniel Hawthrone
Nicolo Machiavelli
O. F. Walton
Oscar Wilde
Owen Johnson
P.G. Wodehouse
Paul and Mabel Thorne

Paul G. Tomlinson
Paul Severing
Percy Brebner
Percy Keese Fitzhugh
Peter B. Kyne
Plato
Quincy Allen
R. Derby Holmes
R. L. Stevenson
R. S. Ball
Rabindranath Tagore
Rahul Alvares
Ralph Bonehill
Ralph Henry Barbour
Ralph Victor
Ralph Waldo Emmerson
Rene Descartes
Ray Cummings
Rex Beach
Rex E. Beach
Richard Harding Davis
Richard Jefferies
Richard Le Gallienne
Robert Barr
Robert Frost
Robert Gordon Anderson
Robert L. Drake
Robert Lansing
Robert Lynd
Robert Michael Ballantyne
Robert W. Chambers
Rosa Nouchette Carey
Rudyard Kipling
Saint Augustine
Samuel B. Allison
Samuel Hopkins Adams
Sarah Bernhardt
Sarah C. Hallowell
Selma Lagerlof
Sherwood Anderson
Sigmund Freud
Standish O'Grady
Stanley Weyman
Stella Benson
Stella M. Francis
Stephen Crane
Stewart Edward White
Stijn Streuvels
Swami Abhedananda
Swami Parmananda
T. S. Ackland

T. S. Arthur
The Princess Der Ling
Thomas A. Janvier
Thomas A Kempis
Thomas Anderton
Thomas Bailey Aldrich
Thomas Bulfinch
Thomas De Quincey
Thomas Dixon
Thomas H. Huxley
Thomas Hardy
Thomas More
Thornton W. Burgess
U. S. Grant
Upton Sinclair
Valentine Williams
Various Authors
Vaughan Kester
Victor Appleton
Victor G. Durham
Victoria Cross
Virginia Woolf
Wadsworth Camp
Walter Camp
Walter Scott
Washington Irving
Wilbur Lawton
Wilkie Collins
Willa Cather
Willard F. Baker
William Dean Howells
William le Queux
W. Makepeace Thackeray
William W. Walter
William Shakespeare
Winston Churchill
Yei Theodora Ozaki
Yogi Ramacharaka
Young E. Allison
Zane Grey

www.ingramcontent.com/pod-product-compliance
Lightning Source LLC
Chambersburg PA
CBHW030124180626
46812CB00002B/550

* 9 7 8 1 4 2 1 8 3 9 9 1 2 *